S0-ARC-524

SARATOGA HEADHUNTER

Stephen Dobyns

PENGUIN BOOKS

PENGUIN BOOKS
Published by the Penguin Group
Viking Penguin, a division of Penguin Books USA Inc.,
375 Hudson Street, New York, New York 10014, U.S.A.
Penguin Books Ltd, 27 Wrights Lane, London W8 5TZ, England
Penguin Books Australia Ltd, Ringwood, Victoria, Australia
Penguin Books Canada Ltd, 2801 John Street,
Markham, Ontario, Canada L3R 1B4
Penguin Books (N.Z.) Ltd, 182–190 Wairau Road, Auckland 10, New Zealand

Penguin Books Ltd, Registered Offices:
Harmondsworth, Middlesex, England

First published in the United States of America by
Viking Penguin Inc. 1985
Published in Select Penguin 1986
Published in Penguin Books 1991

1 3 5 7 9 10 8 6 4 2

LIBRARY OF CONGRESS CATALOGING-IN-PUBLICATION DATA
Dobyns, Stephen, 1941–
Saratoga headhunter
(Penguin crime fiction)
I. Title.
[PS3554.O2S26   1986]   813'.54   86-4954
ISBN 0 14 01.5606 2

Printed in the United States of America
Set in Times Roman

For Leonard and Diana Witt

Gambling is in the atmosphere. Formerly men of wealth and social position, statesmen and philosophers, students and artists gathered here to drink the waters that nature forces through a hundred fissures and enjoy the crisp, invigorating air and picturesque scenery which have united in making Saratoga America's most famous summer resort. They came to ride, to drive, to dress and to secure that freedom from business and domestic care that gives perfect rest and brings back bodily health and vigor.

Now the great summer population of Saratoga is largely composed of those gathered here to gamble or to live off those who do gamble. From one of the most reputable and most exclusive of American watering places, it has been transformed into the wickedest and wildest.

Nellie Bly
New York *World*
August, 1894

SARATOGA HEADHUNTER

Chapter One

*B*lack Jack Ketchum, the member of the Wild Bunch who turned train robber out of unrequited love, used to hammer himself on the head with a gun butt whenever he made a serious mistake. When Black Jack attempted to stop the train near Folsom, New Mexico, and had his arm shot up by the express agent, what he seemed to regret most was that the subsequent amputation robbed him of the power to punish himself for getting caught.

All through one October, Charlie Bradshaw felt he had Black Jack Ketchum's example of self-abuse ever before his eyes. "I could have kicked myself," he would tell his friend Victor Plotz, "or worse."

Charlie's problems began on a rainy Sunday evening at the beginning of the month. It was the sort of autumn rain that makes the leaves turn color, and even tastes of winter though the days remain warm. So far, the leaves around Saratoga Springs had only begun to turn, but Charlie knew that in the morning bright scarlet patches would show in the maples around his small house on the lake.

Charlie had spent the early part of the evening attempting to fix the stopper on the toilet, with the result that he now had to wiggle the handle for five minutes instead of one in order to make the water stop running. He had just decided to give up and go to

bed when there was a knock at the door. This too was an irritation.
He had to be up at four thirty and it was already approaching ten.
On the other hand, he had heard no car and so was curious.

The man at the door was several inches shorter than Charlie,
about five feet five or six, and at first Charlie didn't recognize
him because he was fat.

"Hey, Bradshaw," said the man, "how you been?"

Charlie stood back to let him enter. He was wearing a tan
raincoat and rain hat and when he took off the hat, Charlie realized
that the man was the suspended jockey Jimmy McClatchy In his
left hand was a blue canvas suitcase.

McClatchy was so much the last person that Charlie expected
to see that he looked at him dumbly as if the jockey were some
creature just sprung from a rock.

McClatchy seemed to enjoy Charlie's surprise. "Long time no
see," he said, grinning.

"I thought you were hiding out," said Charlie.

McClatchy tossed his wet hat and coat onto a chair. "I am.
You got anything to drink?" McClatchy had short mahogany-
colored hair, a flabby, moon-shaped face and lips as thin as a
pair of fifty-cent pieces. He wore a blue blazer and a blue-and-
white polka-dot bow tie. The blazer had shiny gold buttons em-
bossed with good-luck horseshoes.

"A few bottles of beer," said Charlie.

"Beer's fine. And bring some crackers if you have any."

Charlie went into the kitchen to look. He hadn't seen McClatchy
since he had last raced in Saratoga over a year ago. During that
time, McClatchy had gained about forty pounds. He was tall for
a jockey and was known as a puker—that is, a jockey who ate
a lot, then threw it up afterward. But since he had stopped racing,
he clearly had been keeping his food in his stomach.

Charlie got a bottle of Pabst from the refrigerator, then located
a chunk of cheddar cheese. From the cupboard over the sink he
took down a box of Ritz crackers.

All he knew about McClatchy during the past year had come
from newspapers. But this was quite a lot. McClatchy was some-

thing of a celebrity, if that was the right word for a man who had become famous by testifying against old friends and associates.

McClatchy's notoriety had begun a year ago September when he had been subpoenaed by a New Jersey grand jury and later indicted for race fixing in Atlantic City. The indictment was subsequently dropped and during the trial McClatchy had appeared as an unindicted co-conspirator testifying for the prosecution. His testimony helped send a dozen men to jail.

The race-fixing charges had concerned themselves with about fifteen races over a two-year period—all were exacta and trifecta races, where people wager on the first two or three horses to cross the finish line. By slowing certain horses it was possible to greatly increase the odds as to which two or three horses would finish first, while the money to be won in such a fix could be in the hundreds of thousands.

But the more people who got involved, the greater was the chance of discovery. The New Jersey investigation had begun in response to a drunken groom's accusations in a bar. McClatchy, to his credit or discredit, had been able to exchange his prison cell for a secret address and salary paid for by the Federal Witness Program. Nor did his testimony stop with Atlantic City. The grand jury in New Jersey led to a grand jury in Delaware, and again McClatchy was the star witness. This time ten people had gone to jail. Now there was talk of additional grand juries in Massachusetts and Pennsylvania, while a New York grand jury was just beginning to hear testimony in Brooklyn. Only that afternoon Charlie had read that McClatchy was scheduled to appear before the Brooklyn grand jury, again as an unindicted co-conspirator.

Charlie returned to the living room with the beer, crackers and cheese and set them on the coffee table. "Aren't you supposed to be testifying in Brooklyn?" he asked.

McClatchy lay stretched out on the couch in front of the fireplace where a couple of birch logs were burning. "Yeah," he said, "I gotta be there in a week or so."

"Then what are you doing here?" Charlie sat down on the rocker next to the couch.

"To tell you the truth, I didn't feel safe."

McClatchy sat up, drank several mouthfuls of beer, then methodically began cutting small squares of cheese and putting them on crackers. Charlie thought that McClatchy's fingers looked like little cocktail sausages.

"The Feds were keeping me hidden in Allentown. All day I was cooped up in a tiny apartment with nothin' to do except watch the TV or play gin rummy with a coupla assholes. Anyway, there's lots of guys who'd like to make sure I don't show up in Brooklyn and I couldn't trust some cop not to talk, so I lit out."

McClatchy's mouth was full and as he spoke he spat tiny bits of crackers onto the rug. He sat forward with his elbows on his knees, drank some more beer and belched.

"You got any salami or anything like that?"

"No," said Charlie. "How'd you get up here anyway? I didn't hear a car."

"First I took a bus, then I hitched rides. How about another beer?"

Charlie went back to the kitchen. He had no doubt there were people who wanted McClatchy dead. He had told the papers that he had helped fix races in more than a dozen states and all those states had begun to investigate his charges. In many cases, McClatchy had been the moneyman, paying off jockeys to slow their horses. The payoffs had ranged from five hundred to a thousand dollars. Charlie had been surprised that jockeys would risk their careers for so little.

Charlie returned from the kitchen, handed McClatchy the beer and sat down. It was still raining and he could hear the drops hitting the roof. "But what I don't understand," said Charlie, "is what you are doing in Saratoga."

McClatchy drank some more beer, then wiped his mouth on the back of his hand. "I needed a place to hole up for a week. Saratoga seemed the best bet. I mean, I can shoot right down to New York with no trouble."

"Where are you staying?" asked Charlie. He thought it would be difficult for McClatchy to find a place. The jockey had always been a loner and now that he had been testifying to various grand juries, it would be hard to find people to help him. In fact, Charlie doubted there was anyone who would stick out his neck for someone as questionable as Jimmy McClatchy.

"That's what I wanted to talk to you about," said McClatchy.

Charlie experienced a substantial attack of dismay. "You mean you want to stay here, with me?"

"That's about it," said McClatchy.

"But there isn't room."

McClatchy glanced around the cottage, which consisted of three rooms, including the kitchen. "It's pretty small but what choice do I have? Maybe you could sleep on the couch and I could have the bedroom."

"Why can't you go to a motel?"

"Think about it, Charlie. Think about what would happen if I showed my face in Saratoga. If you kick me outta here, I'll be a dead man for sure."

"But why me?"

"You always treated me right. Anyway, who else could I ask? Some trainer or jock? The way things are going I wouldn't trust my own mother. Some guys would pay a lotta money to know where I am. Okay, so we were never what you'd call pals but I figured I could trust you and besides, this is the last place anyone would look."

"So you picked me as your sucker." Charlie began to feel angry.

"Not sucker, Charlie, don't say that. I needed a place to stay and you were the only person I could think of. All right, I took a chance, but right now it's either you or nothing."

Charlie got up and put another birch log on the fire. The loose white bark caught right away, sending a rush of flame up the chimney.

For several years, Charlie had been head of security for Lew Ackerman's Lorelei Stables just outside Saratoga. Then, fifteen months ago, Ackerman had been shot dead in the swimming pool of the Saratoga YMCA. Not long afterward his partner had sold the stable. McClatchy had ridden for him perhaps twenty times, but Ackerman had often accused McClatchy of laziness and stopped using him about two months before the murder.

Charlie himself had never liked McClatchy, primarily because he once heard the jockey making fun of Ackerman for being too scrupulous. Charlie, however, was one of those unfortunate human beings who try to be particularly nice to people they dislike, and so, besides being friendly with McClatchy, he had occasionally lent him cab fare from the stables into Saratoga—money that McClatchy had never returned.

McClatchy finished his beer and set the bottle back on the table. "I'll tell you what," he said, "I'll give you fifty bucks a night to let me stay here."

For some reason it seemed worse to have McClatchy pay. Although it was October and the racing season was long past, Charlie guessed there were hundreds of people who would recognize the jockey, even with all that extra weight. And Charlie felt certain that if it became known that McClatchy was in Saratoga, then someone would try to make sure that this particular federal witness kept his lip buttoned forever. Presumably, McClatchy found this distressing, for despite his apparent calm he appeared wary and seemed to be listening for far-off noises. Charlie knew that if he were in McClatchy's shoes, he would have already moved to Zanzibar or Nepal.

"That's all right," said Charlie, "maybe you can help with the food. You think it will be for a week?"

"That's okay. The grand jury begins tomorrow and I'm supposed to show up on Monday."

Charlie stood in front of the fireplace. He had been poking the fire with a pair of metal tongs and now he put them back in the rack. It had just occurred to him that while McClatchy was using his house as a hideout, he couldn't let anyone else pay a visit. Unfortunately, Charlie had the sort of friends who never called before they came over. Apart from his friends, however, he was also half-expecting a visit from his mother. At the moment she was in Atlantic City gambling with money she had made from the sale of her half of a racehorse. Possibly she could stay with one of his cousins, but that would mean disappointment and harsh words.

But the worst thing about McClatchy's visit was that it meant he would have to break a date with Doris Bailes, whom he had invited to dinner for tomorrow night. Mentally, he kicked himself even as he thought about it. Charlie had planned an elaborate meal. He knew that Doris sometimes went out with other men and he had hoped to show her the seriousness of his intentions. In his random imaginings, he had even seen himself proposing. Now he would have to give her some excuse and he wasn't sure how to do it since his face always turned dull pink when he lied.

"You got any more beer?" asked McClatchy.

Charlie started to move toward the kitchen. "I think so."

McClatchy waved him back and got to his feet. "I can get it all right." The jockey walked with a sort of rolling waddle. He paused at the bedroom door and looked in. "That bed pretty comfortable? The couch feels hard."

"Forget it," said Charlie, "if you're going to stay here, you'll sleep on the couch. Not only that but you'll wash your own dishes and keep your muddy feet off the furniture. How'd you manage to hitch a ride right to my front door?"

McClatchy returned to the living room with a beer and a piece of cold chicken. "Guess I was lucky," he said. "You still working for Lorelei Stables?" When McClatchy asked a question, he tended to leave his mouth open as if waiting for the answer to fill it.

"No, Lew's partner sold it. The land was bought by developers. They were planning a subdivision called Lorelei Acres but ran out of money."

Actually, a model home had been completed and ten other houses begun before the company went bankrupt. Charlie often drove by it. Where there were once wineglass elms and neat green and white shed rows, there was now an expanse of mud, the skeletons of houses and one ugly yellow bungalow.

"So how d'you make your money?"

"I do this and that." The idea of putting up with McClatchy for a week was hardly tolerable. "As a matter of fact, I've got a small private detective agency." Charlie wondered if it was too late to tell McClatchy to leave. Yet he knew that to order him out would be almost like putting a bullet in his head.

"You're pulling my leg," said McClatchy.

"No, I started it almost a year ago." It occurred to Charlie that perhaps he could check into a motel and let McClatchy have the cottage to himself.

"You do a lotta divorce work?"

"I stay away from that if I can. It gets a little shady."

"Isn't that where the money is?" McClatchy had unclipped his bow tie and it lay among the remnants of cheese, crackers and chicken bones like a polka-dot butterfly.

"Sure, I'd probably make more that way." Charlie started to continue, then stopped. Why tell McClatchy that the agency hardly paid the rent for the downtown office? Now and then he'd look for someone's missing husband or wife, maybe a runaway teenager. Occasionally, he would get a shoplifting job. "To tell the truth," he said, "I've applied for a job with the Pinkertons."

McClatchy laughed. "I can just see you out there directing traffic at the track. Why bother? I mean, if I needed the money I'd line up some cute girls and make them work for me. Just bust some college girl for coke, do something to give you a little leverage, then you got it made."

Charlie thought again about checking into a motel. "I'm not too keen on the Pinkertons, but I need a job."

The real reason Charlie didn't like the Pinkertons was that they had been responsible for the infamous Night of Blood when their operators had attempted to trap Frank and Jesse James in the Jameses' house in Clay County, Missouri. An explosion had killed Frank and Jesse's eight-year-old half-brother, Archie, and their mother had had her right arm blown off. Frank and Jesse had been miles away at the time.

"Why don't you become a cop again?" asked McClatchy.

"Because I don't want to be a cop."

"How long you do it, twenty-five years? You should have hung in there for your retirement."

"I worked for twenty years, that was all I wanted." Charlie glanced at his watch. It was past eleven. "This is enough talk for tonight. I've got to be up at four-thirty."

"You goin' fishing?"

Charlie had not wanted to explain. "I've got to be over in Schuylerville at five thirty to deliver milk."

McClatchy gave Charlie an uncomprehending stare. "You're a milkman?"

"No, no, nothing like that. You remember John Wanamaker? He was one of my guards out at Lorelei. Well, he's the milkman. But his mother's sick. She lives in Santa Fe and he flew out to be with her. I guess she's dying. He asked me to take over his milk route until he got back."

McClatchy had begun to grin. Far back in his mouth Charlie could see gold teeth. "Why'n't you just tell him to shove it?"

"John's got a pretty long record. If he lost his job, it'd be hard to get another." Listening to himself, Charlie thought how reasonable it sounded. As a matter of fact, he was furious with Wanamaker.

"So how long you been peddling milk?"

"Three weeks."

McClatchy laughed. It seemed to Charlie that he never laughed at anything funny. "Hey, Charlie," said McClatchy, "that's a pretty long time."

Charlie poked the fire, sending up a shower of sparks. "He was supposed to be back in a week, but then his mother got worse. I don't mind telling you I don't like it much. It's six hours a day, six days a week. That's why I want to get to bed. Wanamaker says his mother could die anytime, that the doctors are amazed she's lived so long. I mean, I'd be perfectly happy if she recovered. What can I say, 'Die, die, so I don't have to get up at four thirty anymore?' That's pretty hard."

McClatchy yawned, then bent over and began to untie his shoes. "Tell him to get lost," he said. "So what if he can't get a job?"

"That's all right. I talked to Wanamaker this morning. He figures he'll be back in a couple of days one way or the other."

"Least delivering milk is pretty safe," said McClatchy.

Charlie stretched, then rubbed the back of his neck. He could hear nothing from outside and guessed it had stopped raining. "Not as safe as you might think. One day I was bit by a dog."

"So who's running the detective agency while you're driving the milk truck?"

"An old friend of mine, Victor Plotz."

Chapter Two

When Charlie was a kid in Saratoga before the war, there used to be a dairy that delivered milk by horse-drawn wagon. Charlie remembered many Saturday mornings when he would hitch a ride on the back, sitting on a shelf where metal racks were stored. Sometimes he'd get a wedge of clear ice from inside and, as the wagon clip-clopped its way through Saratoga, Charlie would suck on the ice and look at the houses and wonder who lived in them. At that time, Saratoga was full of huge elms and the hotels were still turning a profit.

As he drove John Wanamaker's milk truck through Schuylerville that Monday morning, Charlie tried to recapture the sense of peacefulness he had experienced forty years before. But even though he liked riding on milk trucks, he had never wanted to be a milkman. The idea would have struck him as preposterous. His plan was to be a major-league third baseman.

Charlie had left McClatchy snoring on the couch at five o'clock that morning. McClatchy had snored all night. Charlie knew this for certain because he had spent most of the night telling himself: You *must* go to sleep. When he left, Charlie had been surprised by how peaceful McClatchy looked, as if his dreaming mind was completely untroubled by the prospect of testifying against his former friends.

Charlie drew up in front of a two-story house with green asbestos siding, and hurried up the walk with four quarts of skim milk and a container of low-fat cottage cheese. He wore khaki pants and a khaki shirt, a dark blue tie and a rather military-looking khaki hat with a black plastic visor. Embroidered in red on the front of the hat and on his left breast pocket were the words WHOLESOME DAIRY.

Charlie picked up four empties and returned to the truck, which was also khaki colored with the name WHOLESOME DAIRY written in red lettering on the side. It was what Charlie thought of as a typical milk truck, an old Ford that rattled even when empty.

It seemed to Charlie, as he turned left at the corner and headed back to the barn, that his life had reached a new low. The arrival of McClatchy only gave further proof of this. It was nearly eleven o'clock and he imagined McClatchy rummaging through his cabinets and refrigerator for a light snack. Charlie had forgotten to tell him about the broken toilet and he had no doubt that it was running at that very moment. Very likely it would overflow.

Even if Charlie survived this week and was able to send McClatchy off to his grand jury in Brooklyn, he was still faced with the imminent arrival of his mother. For two years she had been traveling the country, following the fortunes of her race-horse. Indisputably, her return would make Charlie's life more difficult. If she had money and was able to open the motel that she had dreamed about for thirty years, she would expect Charlie to help her. If she was broke and had to return to waitressing, she would also expect Charlie to help her. As it was, she called him every week to make sure he was doing nothing to embarrass his wealthy and thoroughly respectable cousins: three men who had been the bane of Charlie's life since the age of two, when Charlie had realized that his various clumsinesses were being compared to their successes.

At the moment, his cousins seemed to think there was a smidgen of hope for Charlie after all. This, however, was because they mistakenly assumed that his job as a milkman was permanent. Several times during the past week Charlie had received calls from his cousin Jack, congratulating him and even threatening to drop in on the Wholesome Dairy to "see how he was adjusting." Charlie knew he ought to tell his cousins that his career as a milkman would be as brief as possible, but he was so unaccustomed to their praise that he had remained silent.

As it happened, Jack was the cousin Charlie liked best, even though he felt bullied by his many successes. Jack was a year older than Charlie and, as they grew up, it had seemed that Jack had no faults, was surrounded by friends and had never experienced an unhappy day in his life. Now he owned a successful hardware store in downtown Saratoga, was happily married to a beautiful wife and had three sons, all doing well in college.

Long ago Charlie had decided that Jack passed through life in much the same way that Moses had passed through the Red Sea, while his own method he likened to the Egyptians'. Certainly, this would seem no reason to love his cousin, but Jack's easy passage was done with such innocence and good humor that Charlie hardly minded his triumphs. Even so, he did not gladly anticipate a visit from his cousin to the Wholesome Dairy. Consequently, when he drove the milk truck into the yard and saw Jack standing by the barn idly tossing pebbles against a circle drawn onto the wall with white chalk, Charlie felt a vague displeasure.

Jack was five inches taller than Charlie, had wavy brown hair and a chin as ruddy and square as the end of a brick. Although he never seemed to exercise, he was in tremendous shape. When Charlie climbed from the truck, Jack grabbed his hand and squeezed it so hard that Charlie had a mental image of the bones being transformed into a sort of protoplasmic mush.

"Charlie," Jack said, "you can't imagine how glad it makes us to know that you've gone and gotten yourself a decent job. I wish my father were alive to see it."

Charlie extricated his hand and started removing the racks of empties from the back of the truck. Jack grabbed half a dozen racks and began to help, somehow giving the impression that he had done this all his life. Charlie considered telling his cousin that being a milkman was only temporary, that Wanamaker would soon return from Santa Fe and free him from this ordeal. Instead he said, "Your father was a great man, Jack."

Jack made a sad, clucking noise in the back of his throat. The sun twinkled on the gold Masonic pin in his lapel. "You know, Charlie," he said, "it pained us to see you floundering. I think when it becomes known that you're working again, you'll see a big difference in people's attitudes."

It was clear that Jack didn't consider the detective agency to be work. They finished stacking the empty milk crates and Charlie began leading Jack in the direction of his car. "That's great, Jack. I'm glad you're happy. How'd you find out I was delivering milk?"

"Chief Peterson told me. You know, Charlie, he really has your best interests at heart. I wouldn't be surprised that if you give a good showing as a milkman, he might someday find a place for you again in the department."

Charlie's car was a 1974 red Renault station wagon that often wouldn't start. As he opened the door, he hoped this wouldn't be one of those days. Of all the people who disliked Charlie in Saratoga, Chief Peterson disliked him most.

"I appreciate that, Jack," he said, "but as you know I left the department by my own choice and I can't imagine going back. As for Peterson having my best interests at heart, that's"—Charlie again thought of his mother—"perhaps an exaggeration."

Charlie got into the Renault and turned the key. There was a fateful silence, then the engine turned over. He glanced up at his cousin beaming down at him. Soon Jack would learn that Charlie's life as a milkman was short-lived and Charlie would have to deal with his cousin's disappointment.

"Well, Jack, I'm glad for the chance of this little talk but I've got to rush now."

"Still swimming, Charlie?" There seemed just of hint of mockery in Jack's voice.

"That's right, still swimming." Charlie gave a wave of his hand and drove out of the yard. If he hurried, he could reach the YMCA in Saratoga at noon. For several years, Charlie had been coping with his expanding waistline by swimming laps. Now he swam a mile a day, four days a week. Although thinner than he had been as a policeman, Charlie was more or less resolved to the fact that he was someone who would always be about twenty pounds overweight.

Quickly, Charlie drove the twelve miles into Saratoga. The morning was warm and cloudless. Patches of orange and red showed in the trees on either side of the road. Reaching the Y at noon, Charlie spent the next forty minutes laboriously collecting the seventy-two lengths that made up a mile, concentrating on keeping his legs straight and trying to ignore the faster swimmers. One Skidmore girl seemed to zoom by every other lap, her black tank suit passing within inches of his nose. If he bit her, it would only mean trouble. Deep down, Charlie hated to be passed. As he hopelessly tried to increase his speed, he thought his cousin might have been right to mock him.

By one o'clock Charlie was drying himself off with his big blue towel in front of his locker. His arms ached and despite his shower he was sweating slightly. As Charlie began pulling on his shirt, George Marotta came out of the shower and nodded to him.

"Say, Charlie, wait for me outside, will you? I want to talk to you."

"Sure. What's it about?"

"Just wait."

Marotta turned away and began dialing the combination of his lock. He was a thin man of about Charlie's height, with curly gray hair, which at the moment was dripping with water. His face was narrow and bony with a long thin nose that had once been broken and badly set. The swelling in its center looked like a fat knuckle. Charlie guessed that Marotta was in his mid-fifties. He had never liked swimming next to him because although Marotta was nearly ten years older, he passed Charlie constantly.

Charlie finished tying his shoes, then walked to the mirror to comb his hair. About a dozen other men were in the locker room: Saratoga businessmen, students, some officers from the naval base. A few Charlie knew only from swimming, others he had known all his life. Some puddles dotted the blue and gray tiles near the row of sinks, and a small boy, late for tadpole swim, was stamping in them. Several men nodded to Charlie or smiled. Although they weren't exactly friends, they were close acquaintances and Charlie knew enough about them to follow their lives with affection and concern.

Charlie combed his hair straight back over his scalp. There seemed less of it each day, while the bald spot was definitely growing. Once the color had been what he called dog-brown, but since he had started swimming, it had been bleached by the chlorine and was turning gray besides. It was strange to think he could no longer clearly remember what his hair color had been for over forty years: that what had been a commonplace was now a mystery.

Charlie had a round, pink face with few wrinkles, and large blue eyes. His nose, he thought, was too short and puggy: more like a big toe than a nose. At least his teeth were good. He thought of his face as serviceable, like a plain suitcase, and he prided himself that it never showed any expression. This was perhaps not as true as he hoped. He had changed from his milkman's uniform and wore a light blue shirt and dark blue pants. It occurred to Charlie that even after three years of not being a policeman, he continued to dress like one.

As Charlie walked outside to wait for Marotta, he began to wonder what the other man wanted. Marotta owned a large restaurant out in the country, west of Saratoga. Some people swore that his bills were paid by New York racketeers who used the restaurant to launder money. Charlie had no knowledge of that one way or the other, but he knew that outside of August the restaurant was nearly empty and there was no indication of how it stayed in business.

Marotta appeared a few minutes later dressed in an immaculate light gray suit. "Let's get a sandwich at the Executive," he said.

They turned right down Broadway, then crossed Congress Park. A cool wind sent a few fallen leaves chasing one another over the grass, and riffled the surface of the duck pond.

"Your stroke's looking better," said Marotta.

Charlie shrugged. Since Marotta had lapped him a dozen times, he wasn't feeling like any Johnny Weissmuller. They walked by the three-story, red brick Canfield Casino, which was currently a museum. It had once been the center of Saratoga gambling and as they passed the game room, Charlie liked to think he could hear the click of roulette wheels.

The Executive was a bar and delicatessen a block away on Phila Street. The front of the building was covered with dark-stained pine boards interrupted by large windows. Behind the bar were two very heavy young men standing side by side with their elbows on the counter. They had black curly hair and wore T-shirts that said, "I ate it all at the Executive."

Marotta led the way to a booth toward the back of the bar. Charlie followed, nodding to several people he knew. The room smelled of fried food. Marotta sat down, then seemed disinclined to speak. He appeared embarrassed. For a moment, Charlie worried he might know something about Jimmy McClatchy, but that seemed impossible. When the waitress arrived, Marotta ordered a sandwich and a beer, then contented himself with shredding his red paper napkin. From the back room came the click of pool balls.

Charlie waited. The girl brought their sandwiches. Marotta took several bites of his hot pastrami, then pushed away his plate and sat back.

"You know, Charlie," he said, "we've never talked much, but over the years I've heard a number of good things about you, mostly from Lew Ackerman. He said you were pretty smart. I guess that's why I decided to talk to you."

Marotta paused. Two patrolmen came in to pick up a take-out order. One waved to Charlie, the other pretended not to see him.

Marotta put his hands on the edge of the table and leaned forward, wrinkling his brow and looking suddenly angry. "What I want to know, Charlie, is if you're having me followed."

"Are you serious?"

"Never been more. I know you're working as a detective and that you gotta take jobs where you find them, but some things I don't like and taking advantage of a foolish woman is one of them."

Charlie liked to think he was difficult to surprise, yet this was the last thing he expected to hear. Marotta continued to look furious. The swelling in the center of his nose was like a small knot and all his anger seemed to radiate out from it.

"Maybe you should tell me what you're talking about," said Charlie. He spoke quietly, half-afraid of making Marotta even angrier.

Marotta picked up his sandwich, then set it down again and shook his head. On the wall to Charlie's left were photographs of folk singers who had appeared at Caffe-Lena up the street.

"My wife likes to imagine things," explained Marotta, "and one of the things she likes to imagine is that I fool around with a lot of women. I'm not saying that I'm the world's most moral guy, but in that particular department I been pretty good. I tell her that but she won't listen and every now and then she gets the bright idea to hire some private detective and have me followed That's what's happening right now and there are a lot of reasons why I don't like it."

Charlie began to feel relieved. "I don't do that kind of work," he said, "and even if I did, I wouldn't accept business from your wife. The town's too small to have you as an enemy."

Marotta leaned forward again, staring at Charlie, then his face relaxed. It had been dark red, as if he were attempting to lift something heavy, now it grew lighter. He started to look embarrassed.

"You sure it's not you, Charlie? I guess it could be someone up from Albany. It's a big guy, maybe a few years older'n me with gray hair that sticks out in all directions. Leastways, he started it. Now there's some punky kid watching me, a lot of black, greasy hair and a leather jacket. I mean, all he does is sit out in the parking lot outside the restaurant and read skin magazines."

As Marotta spoke, Charlie felt his skin begin to prickle. The description of the older man matched his friend Victor Plotz, while the kid could easily be Eddie Gillespie, an ex-car thief who had worked for Charlie as a guard at Lorelei Stables.

"To tell you the truth," said Charlie, somewhat uncertainly, "I've been doing some other work for the past three weeks and have a friend running the office. Possibly, he took the job. You say he had gray hair?"

Marotta started to look angry again. "Yeah, and sort of a fat face and big nose. He was wearing a gray sweat shirt."

Charlie had no doubt it was Victor. He wondered if lots of people had close friends who constantly embarrassed them. "Well, I don't think it's anyone I know," he said, "but I'll check with my partner and if he took the job, then I'll make him quit."

Marotta narrowed his eyes and looked suspiciously at Charlie. "If you can remove this guy, I'd appreciate it. If you can't, then I'll remove him myself. I don't like people talking about me and something like this makes talk. If there's any problem about money, I'll make it up to you."

"Forget it," said Charlie, although he guessed the money from Marotta's wife was all that was paying the rent on the office.

Marotta wiped his mouth and tossed a ten-dollar bill on the table. "At least let me pay for lunch." He stood up, then leaned over the table. "And Charlie," he said, "I'd appreciate it if you didn't tell anybody about our conversation. I like my wife and wouldn't want this to get around."

Five minutes later, Charlie was trotting up Phila Street toward his office, which was on the third floor of a brick building between Broadway and Putnam. As he hurried along, he alternately swore at Victor and felt guilty for upsetting Marotta. The door to the stairs was next to a used-book store. Charlie pulled it open and began to climb. When he reached the top, he paused to catch his breath. Before him was a narrow hall with faded blue walls, while at the far end was a door with Charlie's name painted in large black letters: Charles F. Bradshaw. "Simple, but classy," Victor had said. The door was locked and Charlie unlocked it. Beyond was a small anteroom separated from the main office by a wall of frosted glass. Victor wasn't there. The office was furnished with an old wooden desk, several straight chairs, a file cabinet and a safe. Two windows with green shades looked out on Phila. Tacked to the wall behind the desk was a nude Playboy calendar that had not been there the previous day. Charlie considered removing it, then figured it didn't matter. Why should he worry about offending clients when he didn't have any? He turned and left the office.

He still had to break his date that evening with Doris Bailes. It was terrible to think of trading her for McClatchy. As Charlie walked toward his car, he imagined McClatchy's dirty feet on his couch and his refrigerator ransacked. He was also certain that his toilet was running and that McClatchy was spitefully letting it run. The thought sprang into his mind that if he had told Marotta that the jockey was hiding out in his house, then McClatchy would be gone in a couple of hours. Marotta would call his friends in New York and in no time a big black car would arrive at Charlie's house and take McClatchy away. Guiltily, Charlie started his Renault and drove toward the Backstretch, the bar on the west side of Saratoga where Doris worked.

The Backstretch occupied a one-story, yellowish building on a residential street. Although its name suggested a bar dedicated to horse racing, its walls were covered with the photographs of prizefighters. Each picture bore an inscription to the owner of the Backstretch, Berney McQuilkin. Charlie had once studied these inscriptions only to discover that the handwriting on each was the same. The bar was a long, narrow room; a larger room in the back served as a Chinese restaurant by day, and at night was the province of a topless dancer.

Entering, Charlie waved to several men that he knew, then reached across the bar to shake hands with Berney McQuilkin. A retired policeman bought Charlie a beer, and before he could make his way to Doris he had to discuss the merits of a trotter named Whiskey Breath that had been going great guns at the harness track. Doris was sitting at a table near the jukebox reading a paperback. She had short, dark hair and a smooth, oval face. The book lay open on the table and she leaned over it, wrinkling her forehead. Although about forty, Doris had an eager quality that made her seem younger. She was wearing a white Mexican blouse and an ornate tin necklace. When she heard Charlie approach, she looked up and smiled.

"I thought I wasn't going to see you until this evening," she said.

Charlie felt himself starting to blush. He sat down and put his beer mug on the table. "That's why I stopped by," he said. "I've got to cancel our date. An old acquaintance has blown into town and will be staying at my place for a while."

"Who is it?"

"I'll tell you some other time."

Doris raised her eyebrows. "Is this person male or female?"

"Male."

"How long is this secret male supposed to stay?"

"About a week."

Charlie said this so sadly that Doris looked sympathetic. "We could have dinner at a restaurant instead, or even at my house."

"That'd be great but I don't trust this guy and I'd like to keep an eye on him, at least for a couple of nights."

"You've got nice friends."

"He's not really a friend. It's just that he had no place else to go."

Doris put a napkin on the page to mark her place, then closed the book. Charlie saw that it was a travel book about Spain. "And you promise to tell me about it sometime?"

"Sure."

"What about your mother? Isn't she coming soon?"

"Yes, but I'm hoping I can keep her away from my house for a bit. Maybe she can stay with one of my cousins or maybe I can sic her on Victor. In fact, I've got to find Victor right now. Then I've got to buy groceries. My guest turns out to be a big eater."

"Did you talk to John Wanamaker? Is he coming back?"

"Not yet. His mother's still hanging by a thread."

Doris had continued to look sympathetic. "Have dinner with me anyway," she said.

"I can't," said Charlie, getting to his feet, "my life has suddenly gotten too complicated for normal pleasures."

It was as Charlie was driving back to his office that he first began to think about Black Jack Ketchum. He found it oddly soothing. Perhaps it was hammering himself on the head with a gun butt that taught Black Jack to face life with a certain humor. Black Jack was the only member of the Wild Bunch to die on the gallows. On the day of his hanging, he seemed cheerful and joked with the sheriff, saying he was glad to be hanged early in the afternoon so he could "get to hell in time for dinner." Maybe self-abuse could accustom a person to the abuse of the world, thought Charlie. Maybe that was the secret.

Parking the red Renault on Phila, Charlie again climbed the stairs to the third floor. This time the door was open. As he passed through the anteroom, Charlie heard a prolonged belch followed by a fit of coughing. Victor was sitting with his feet up on the desk, cleaning his nails with a paper knife. He wore a gray sweat shirt that exactly matched the color of his hair.

"Hey, hey, hey," he said, "if it's not Mr. Wholesome Dairy himself."

Charlie slowly lowered himself into the straight chair next to the desk. "Are you following George Marotta?" he asked.

"Darn right. That's the best money we've made all month."

"I want you to stop. He's a friend of mine."

"I thought he was a Mafia contact. You travel in bad company." Victor reached under his sweat shirt and scratched his chest. Outside, a motorcycle accelerated down the street.

"We swim together. He asked me if we were following him and I said no. Then he described you. Let's just drop the case."

"Charlie, his old lady popped in here with a thousand smackers. So maybe she's a little irrational. Who am I to judge the clientele? That's a thousand smackers just to trail this guy around. One hundred bucks a day just to sit on your fanny. For chrissake, he don't do anything except hang out at that restaurant or go to the

Y. So I got Eddie Gillespie dogging him for forty. That other sixty a day—hey, Charlie, that's pure gravy."

Charlie glanced up at the Playboy calendar, which showed an attractive platinum blond rubbing her naked belly against a fur rug. "I told you, Victor..."

"Vic."

"I told you I don't want to do divorce work. You have anything else like this?"

"Nothing you'd disapprove of. Look, Charlie, you can't start thinking I don't have scruples. Just the other day a woman came by to see if I'd arrest her neighbor for beaming cancer waves at her with a broken TV. Then the ex-wife of my veterinarian tried to hire me to dig up some dirt on him. Did I take these jobs? No way. A good vet is hard to come by and I got my principles like anybody else."

"Just do me a favor and pull Gillespie off the case." Charlie had an impulse to tell Victor about Jimmy McClatchy but knew he couldn't say anything until the jockey had left Saratoga. It made him feel lonely.

Victor pressed a finger to his temple and made an exploding noise with his tongue. "Okay, you're the great white hunter. I'll chase down Gillespie this afternoon."

"What are you doing tonight?" asked Charlie.

"Got a hot date, but I'll drop it if you need me."

"No, no," said Charlie, "I was just wondering." He had been trying to think of a way to tell Victor not to stop by, but could think of nothing that wouldn't make him suspicious. At last he decided to keep silent.

By five thirty, Charlie was on his way home with fifty dollars' worth of groceries in the back of the Renault. Presumably McClatchy would reimburse him. He also had a new tank ball, lift wires and ball-cock assembly for his toilet, and what he hoped was a clear idea how to install them. The sun was low in the sky and the trees along Saratoga Lake seemed to blaze in the sun's last light.

Charlie pulled the Renault into his driveway and parked. His cottage was dark blue with yellow trim around the windows and doors. Although most cottages along the lake were bunched together, Charlie had been able to buy one that was set off by itself and away from the road. Maples and evergreens bordered it on either side. Clumsily, he lifted two bags of groceries from the rear seat, then made his way to the door.

Through the glass, he could see McClatchy sitting with his back to him at the dining-room table. He was leaning forward as if sleeping. The windows on the lake side of the cottage faced west and the setting sun shone on Charlie's face, making it difficult to see into the room. Charlie kicked at the door, hoping to rouse McClatchy so he wouldn't have to set down the groceries. McClatchy didn't move. Through the windows the sun almost seemed to balance on McClatchy's shoulders. Charlie kicked the door several more times, then angrily set the groceries down on the grass.

He opened the door and picked up one of the bags. If McClatchy was going to stay, he'd have to do his share of the work. "Why didn't you get the door?" said Charlie.

McClatchy remained motionless. From the bathroom Charlie heard the gurgling of the running toilet. Staring at McClatchy's back, Charlie knew something was wrong even before he saw the blood: a great pool of it on the floor surrounding the table.

"McClatchy?" said Charlie. Then he saw what had happened. It wasn't that McClatchy was leaning forward with his head on the table. The head was gone completely. It had been sliced off, while the light from the setting sun glistened on the bloody stump of neck. As for the head itself, it appeared to be missing.

Chapter Three

C*hief Peterson* raised the thick, pink index finger of his right hand, looked at it with fatherly affection, then leaned over and used it to poke Charlie in the chest.

"What I'm saying, Charlie," he said, "is that the Feds were chasing their tails all over the country looking for this gumball and here he was getting his head sliced off in your house in Saratoga. I mean, they're going to be none too pleased and I can't say I blame them."

"I didn't invite McClatchy here," said Charlie. "I didn't want him here and I'm sorry he got killed here."

"That doesn't change the fact that it got done here," said Peterson.

Charlie and Peterson were standing in Charlie's driveway next to the red Renault. It was seven o'clock and nearly dark. The small house had been taken over by a mob of Saratoga policemen, state troopers and sheriff's deputies. At least a dozen cruisers with flashing lights were parked along the road and a crowd had gathered at the edge of Charlie's driveway. It was a scene Charlie had witnessed a hundred times as a policeman but the fact that it was his own house made it all new.

Inside, men from the state police lab were measuring, photographing, dusting for fingerprints and gathering up smidgens of dirt and lint, which they carefully tucked away in little plastic bags. McClatchy's head had been sliced off clean and when the body was removed there turned out to be a deep cut in the wood of the table.

"Like a samurai sword," said Peterson. "I used to have one that I brought back from the service. I was always cutting myself with the damn thing. Or maybe a meat cleaver. Or those French things—what do you call them?—guillotines." Peterson rose up on his toes, put a hand on the roof of the Renault to steady himself and looked around the driveway. He was a big man, several inches over six feet, with thick black hair and a gravelly voice that Charlie thought he exaggerated on purpose. He wore a three-piece blue suit with a thin chain across his stomach from which dangled a tiny silver revolver.

"What I don't understand," said Peterson, "is why he came to your house in the first place."

"He said he felt safe here."

Peterson cleared his throat and spat into the dirt. "Guess you fooled him," he said. "Wasn't he supposed to testify in New York pretty soon?"

"Next Monday. How do you think anyone knew he was here?"

"Maybe they followed him. You tell anyone?"

"No one."

"Was the door forced?"

"No. Whoever did it, I guess McClatchy let him in."

"Jesus, Charlie, that's the one thing I hate about this horse racing—it attracts a lot of low people." Peterson tugged one of his ears. They were large and soft looking and resembled the sort of toys a child plays with in his tub.

Charlie had called Peterson immediately after finding the body. Then he had stood back as his house was invaded by the police. That, however, was a minor invasion compared with the death itself. Although Charlie was sorry that McClatchy had been murdered, he was mostly sorry that McClatchy had died in his house, on his table, that McClatchy's blood was all over his floor and rug, had seeped between the floorboards to the dirt below, where, Charlie told himself, it would stay forever.

This was a permanent invasion and Charlie wondered how long it would take to get used to it. He had never liked McClatchy and so he had no great grief for the man, but now McClatchy's murder was part of his home, and the indifference Charlie had felt for his life would be replaced with a kind of intimacy with his death.

For Peterson the most disturbing detail was the missing head. It made him indignant and at first it seemed that the actual murder hardly mattered, that if only the head were found, then these other problems of mortality would quickly clear themselves up.

"Maybe the head was tossed in the lake," said Peterson.

Charlie thought that was unlikely but saw no reason to disagree.

"They sure did a pretty neat job," said Peterson. "Why would anyone want to cut off a head?"

"Maybe to frighten someone."

"You know, Charlie, these guys from New York, these hoods, they're like animals. I wouldn't be surprised if whoever did this had a whole collection of heads. Some shelf in the basement, maybe two shelves, just full of heads."

"What makes you think the murderer was from the City?" asked Charlie.

"Just a guess," said Peterson. "If you want to know the truth, I bet his head got cut off because of that grand jury. You know, to make people keep their mouths shut. Anyway, the FBI should be here soon. McClatchy was their baby and with any luck they'll take over the whole business. I've got enough on my mind with these car thieves."

In the past two months about twenty cars had been stolen in Saratoga; nearly all were expensive foreign cars owned by Skidmore students. Only one had been recovered. A state trooper in Georgia had pulled over a speeding Porsche belonging to a Skidmore freshman. The driver had been hired in New York City and claimed never to have set foot in Saratoga. All he knew was that he had been paid to leave the car in a parking garage in Miami. It was Peterson's theory that the cars were being shipped to and resold in South America.

"I'm already spending eighty hours a week telling these Skiddies to lock up their cars," said Peterson. "If the Feds don't take McClatchy, I might as well quit sleeping for good. By any rights, they should assign a man to this car snatching. After all, crossing state lines, that's their bailiwick."

Around eight o'clock, Peterson let Charlie go back to Saratoga to get something to eat. Not that he had much of an appetite. Mostly he wanted to find Victor and see about sleeping on his couch. The only trouble was with Victor's one-eyed cat, Moshe. Charlie was allergic to cats. Even if Moshe spent the time locked up in the bathroom, the presence of little bits of fur would keep Charlie sneezing all night.

Charlie had called Victor earlier and Victor grudgingly agreed to cancel his hot date and meet Charlie at Lillian's, a bar and restaurant on Broadway that offered bowls of free peanuts. Victor liked stuffing his pockets with them.

When Charlie reached the bar, he found Victor sitting at a table almost completely covered with peanut shells. Charlie sat down and ordered a beer and a cheeseburger, then he told Victor about the murder. Although Victor was surprised about the murder, what surprised him most was that Charlie hadn't told him about McClatchy's arrival.

"No joke, Charlie, I feel pretty hurt. Like I thought I was your best friend. If I'd known he was there, maybe I could have gone out and kept my eyes peeled."

"How'd I know he'd get killed? Anyway, I thought it best not to talk about it." The waitress brought Charlie's cheeseburger. He took a small bite and put it back on the plate. He thought it tasted funny but guessed it was just him.

"You didn't mention it to Marotta?"

"Of course not."

Victor helped himself to some of Charlie's steak fries. He was drinking Jack Daniel's straight up, and was leaning forward with his elbows on the table and his chin resting thoughtfully on the rim of his glass. "Marotta is supposed to be pretty tight with some bad boys in the City," said Victor. "I bet he'd of been real pleased to know where McClatchy was staying."

Charlie shifted uncomfortably in his chair. "That may be so, but he didn't learn anything from me."

"Okay, so they killed him. Why'd they cut off his head?"

"Peterson thinks it was done as a warning. McClatchy's testimony was making a lot of trouble. Killing him like that, well, Peterson says it would keep other people from talking."

"What do you think about all that happening in your house? I betcha feel pretty lousy."

Charlie speared a chunk of cheeseburger with his fork and looked at it. "Sure," he said, "I feel pretty lousy."

"Was McClatchy a friend of yours?"

"No, I never liked him but I certainly didn't wish him harm. It's terrible he was killed but it's also terrible he was killed on my dining-room table."

Victor sat up, yawned and began scratching a place under his arm. His sweat shirt was several sizes too big for him and flecked with white paint. "So Peterson thinks he was killed by those same people who fixed the races?"

"I guess so. McClatchy's sent about thirty people to jail."

"Anyone see you talking to Marotta?"

"Sure, all sorts of people. We had lunch at the Executive. Why?"

Victor tilted back in his chair and looked around the bar. "Marotta's supposedly pretty good friends with these guys that are in trouble at Belmont. I figure that if Peterson doesn't book someone *muy pronto,* as the Ricans say, then you're going to get some funny looks."

Charlie didn't answer. He was thinking of the wreckage of his house, that his toilet needed fixing and that despite McClatchy's death he still had to deliver milk the next morning. After that he wondered what would have happened if he had been out Sunday night or said no to McClatchy. And after that he found himself thinking once again of Black Jack Ketchum.

When Black Jack was led out to the gallows, he had been upset to discover that a high fence had been built to keep away the crowd. "Why don't you rip down that stockade," he had said, "so the folks can see a man swing who never hurt anybody."

It seemed to Charlie that Black Jack Ketchum was a man who had been forced to endure too much. He was just about to tell Victor about Black Jack when Victor glanced toward the door, then ducked his head. "Oh, oh, here comes trouble."

Turning in his chair, Charlie saw Emmett Van Brunt bearing down upon them. Van Brunt was a plainclothesman whom Charlie had originally hired and worked with for years in the Community and Youth Relations Bureau. But ever since Charlie had left the department, Van Brunt seemed to think him responsible for most of the crime in Saratoga. Van Brunt was a youngish man with curly red hair, black horn-rimmed glasses and the thick, rectangular body of a wrestler.

"Peterson wants to see you, Charlie," said Van Brunt. He was sweating slightly and gave off a smell like burning tires.

"Okay, I'll be over in about twenty minutes."

"He said he wanted you right away." Van Brunt stood next to his chair so that Charlie had to twist his neck to look up at him.

Charlie poked at the cold cheeseburger on his plate. He imagined telling Emmett that he was eating and Emmett saying it didn't matter and he beginning to protest. Charlie pushed back his chair and stood up. "Take care of the bill, will you, Victor?"

"Shonuff."

As they walked toward police headquarters, Charlie asked, partly joking, "Has Peterson solved the case?"

"You could say that," answered Van Brunt. He didn't look at Charlie or even walk next to him but stayed about six feet away.

Peterson was waiting in the police lounge. It was a dank basement room and its walls were covered with posters warning about the dangers of smoking, accidents, stress and high blood pressure, detailing the five danger signals of cancer and explaining what to do if someone choked on his food. Glancing at his watch,

Charlie saw that it was nearly ten. He reminded himself that he had to be up at four thirty.

Peterson had been sitting on a tattered couch looking through some papers. When Charlie entered, he got to his feet, raised himself up on tiptoe and looked disgusted.

"So how much did Marotta pay you?"

"What are you talking about?"

"You had lunch with Marotta. He's pals with these guys who are under suspicion for race fixing. I mean, you figure it out—first you talk to Marotta, then McClatchy winds up dead. Seems pretty simple, doesn't it?"

On the right side of the room was a Ping-Pong table and on the table were five smashed Ping-Pong balls. Charlie started to wonder who had smashed them, then stopped himself. Peterson depressed him. "I swear to you," said Charlie, "I never told anyone about McClatchy."

"Then what were you talking to Marotta about?"

"Business."

"You mean you won't tell me?"

What irritated Charlie was Peterson's certainty that he had at last got something on him that made him look small. "If you want to know so much, why don't you ask him."

"Jesus, Charlie, you must think I'm a dope. The Feds will be here in about two minutes and if they don't slap your ass in jail, I'll really be surprised."

Charlie stuck his hands in his pockets and stared down at the floor. "I didn't tell anyone about McClatchy," he repeated.

"Then why were you talking to Marotta?"

For the next half hour, Peterson kept asking about Marotta and Charlie kept repeating that he had said nothing to anybody. He kept looking at the smashed Ping-Pong balls and at last decided that Peterson had probably smashed them himself. They were interrupted around a quarter to eleven by the arrival of an FBI man from New York City.

The door opened and there was a man in a dark gray suit, calmly surveying the room. His eyes settled on Peterson. "You're the police chief, right?" he asked. "I talked to you on the phone. I'm Hank Caldwell."

He entered, leaving the door open, then looked at Charlie. "And you must be Bradshaw, the guy with the mouth." He turned back to Peterson. "You going to lock him up?"

"He says he never said anything to Marotta."

"And you believe him?" Not waiting for an answer, Caldwell walked over to Charlie. He was about thirty-five and had a narrow face and short brown hair. His nose ended in a sharp point and he seemed to use it like a knife to cut through the air in front of him. He stopped so close to Charlie that their shoes bumped. "So what's your little story?" he said.

"I told nobody about McClatchy. He showed up Sunday night needing a place to stay and I gave him one. I didn't want him there, but I didn't sell the information to get him out. Now, if you don't mind, I'd like to go home. I have to be up at four thirty and it's been a long day."

Caldwell reached out and put a hand on Charlie's shoulder, then he squeezed, digging his thumb into the nerve. His breath smelled of mint. Charlie pulled away.

"This is my case," said Caldwell, "and I don't want you fucking with it. As far as I'm concerned, you're an accessory before the fact and the moment I get the tiniest shred of evidence against you, you're going straight to the slammer."

The dog that had once bitten Charlie and had several times come pretty close was a fat yellow Labrador with a lot of gray around the muzzle. Now when Charlie delivered the two quarts of homogenized and a half-pint of cream to the dog's owners, he took along an empty wire milk crate just for swinging. To Charlie it seemed the height of folly to be fighting off dogs at six in the morning.

But Tuesday morning, after successfully dodging the yellow Labrador and clipping it with the milk crate besides, Charlie realized that the height of folly had been to let Jimmy McClatchy ever see the inside of his house. And briefly he considered allowing the dog to bite him just to punish himself.

The sun was barely cresting the Green Mountains and Charlie could tell it would be another clear day. This morning, however, he could see his breath and there was the sense that winter was waiting someplace nearby. Even though he loved the pyrotechnics of the trees, Charlie hated the approach of cold weather. When he was younger, fall had been his favorite season, but now that he was forty-six, he found he preferred spring.

He had slept badly on Victor's couch and spent much of the night sneezing and blowing his nose. But apart from his allergy to cats, there was the question of McClatchy's head. Who had taken it and why? Although Charlie knew he had said nothing to Marotta, it still seemed possible that the restaurant owner was involved. Perhaps he had asked Charlie to lunch simply to keep him away from his house while the murder was being committed. Consequently, as he was leaving Victor's apartment at four thirty that morning, he had roused Victor to tell him to put Eddie Gillespie back on the job.

"That's what I like to hear," Victor said sleepily.

Charlie's other worry was that his mother might arrive and go out to his cottage. McClatchy's blood was still on the floor and at some point Charlie would have to clean it up. He imagined his mother letting herself in with her key and finding the dried pools of blood. Certainly she would call his cousins in hysterics. Charlie felt guilty that he hadn't posted a warning note and even wondered if he wasn't trying to upset his mother on purpose as she often accused him of doing.

Charlie had almost finished his deliveries and was making his way back to the barn when a white Chevrolet drew alongside him and honked its horn. Assuming it was a friend, Charlie waved and kept going, at which point the Chevrolet abruptly swerved in front of the truck and stopped. Charlie had to slam on the brakes. Milk crates slid to the front and he heard the unpleasant sound of breaking glass.

Turning back to the Chevrolet, Charlie saw the FBI man, Hank Caldwell, walking toward him.

"For chrissakes, Bradshaw, when Peterson told me you were a milkman, I thought he was joking."

Charlie got down out of the truck, pushed his hat farther back on his head and decided that Caldwell's remark didn't need an answer. He was struck by how happy Caldwell looked.

"You know, Bradshaw, I been having trouble with the guy who delivers my yogurt. Maybe you could help out."

"You want anything in particular or you just want to make jokes?"

"I want to know if you're ready to tell me about Marotta." Caldwell wore a brown sport coat and tan slacks. His short brown hair seemed the color and texture of a new doormat.

"I've already told you."

"What did you say to him about McClatchy?"

"Nothing," said Charlie. Caldwell had stopped him on a residential street in front of a white house with black shutters. In the driveway, three teenage boys had been looking under the hood of an old Chevrolet. Now they stood watching Caldwell.

"You should be more cooperative," said Caldwell. "I figure we can also get you on a conspiracy charge. And those race-fixing charges against McClatchy? This could make you an accessory after the fact."

"Is this what you nearly wrecked my milk truck to tell me?"

Caldwell was exactly Charlie's height. He stood with his hands in his back pockets and his head tilted to one side. "I don't want you to leave the area. If I have any trouble finding you, I'll lock you up for sure."

Charlie climbed back into the truck, then turned. "Can I clean up my house or d'you still need it?"

"It's all yours."

"Have you found McClatchy's head?"

"Forget the questions, Bradshaw. It's none of your business."

When Charlie arrived at the YMCA at noon to go swimming, he noticed that although people looked at him with some curiosity, no one would speak to him. Marotta wasn't there and Charlie couldn't remember when he had last missed a day. In his hurry to put on his suit and get in the water, he didn't pay much attention to Marotta's absence or link it to the collective cold shoulder of his fellow swimmers. Once in the pool, however, he realized that the cold shoulder was due to McClatchy's death.

Afterward, as Charlie showered, the only other person in the locker room was a friend of his cousin Jack's: a local realtor whom he had known since high school. Charlie made some comment about the weather but the man didn't reply. Perhaps he hadn't heard. Sure he heard, thought Charlie.

Leaving the Y, Charlie considered going home and cleaning up the blood but decided to go to the Backstretch for lunch. There seemed to be something he didn't know and the Backstretch was a place where he might to find out what it was. McClatchy's blood could wait.

The bar was nearly empty. Usually, the owner, Berney McQuilkin, would stroll over and say a few words, but this afternoon he only glanced at Charlie and looked away.

Charlie sat down at the bar where Doris was washing glasses. "You want a beer?" she asked. She wore a full red skirt and a dark blue leotard that accentuated the curve of her breasts.

"No, thanks. Give me a cup of coffee and a ham and cheese. No mustard." Charlie looked into her face and even with her he thought he saw a change. It wasn't as if she were cold or suspicious; rather, she seemed to be watching him in a slightly altered manner, as if waiting for him to show himself to be the old Charlie or somebody new.

"McClatchy?" he asked.

She stopped washing the glasses and dried her hands on a blue towel. "It's been on the radio and television. I guess the paper will have something this afternoon. A reporter was in here asking about you."

"About me?" Charlie was amazed.

"Wasn't McClatchy staying with you?"

"What have they been saying?"

"Just that McClatchy was hiding out at your place and that

someone found him there. Peterson told reporters there was a chance you told someone. There's also a lot of talk about how you had lunch yesterday with George Marotta."

"Do you think I would have told Marotta?"

Doris was silent a moment. Her brown hair was parted in the center of her scalp and fell across her forehead in two symmetrical curves like drapery. Occasionally, one of the curves would half-cover one of her eyes and she would shake her head, flicking it aside. She had dark brown eyes with gold flecks, and looking into them it sometimes seemed to Charlie that he was looking into deep water or night sky.

Doris took the blue towel and wiped off the bar in front of Charlie. "No," she said, "I don't believe you would have said anything."

"I didn't tell anyone about McClatchy," said Charlie, "not Marotta or anyone."

Doris nodded as if the matter were settled. "I'll get your sandwich," she said.

As Charlie waited, he thought about the fact that people seemed so quick to accuse him of selling the information about McClatchy to George Marotta. Then he remembered that he also had thought of telling Marotta, not for money, of course, but just to get McClatchy out of his hair. Didn't that make him as guilty as people thought he was?

Charlie was just trying to determine what sort of punishment would suit him best when he noticed someone in the parking lot approach the door and peer through the glass, linking his hands as a kind of visor over his eyes. The man wore a tattered gray hat with wisps of white hair sticking out from under the brim. He had to bend down to see through the glass, and he looked so peculiar with his hands shielding his eyes and his scrunched-up face that it was with a slight shock that Charlie realized it was someone he had known all his life. At the same instant, the man saw Charlie, waved and gave a nervous smile. It was clear that Charlie was who he was looking for. He opened the door and approached with a sort of sideways gait, constantly glancing around the empty bar as if suspicious that the furniture might leap at him.

The man's name was Rodger Pease and he was a big, bulky fellow who resembled a sack of potatoes. He had a pale, soft-looking face and a small white mustache, which was precisely rectangular and seemed the only element of exactness and precision in the otherwise rumpled landscape of his body. Charlie thought he must be at least seventy-five.

Rodger Pease had been a good friend of Charlie's father, and when Charlie was younger he had often sought out Pease to ask what his father was like. Charlie's father had committed suicide when Charlie was four. He had locked himself in an upstairs bedroom with a bottle of whiskey and a Colt .45 automatic; then, with the whiskey gone and the police hammering at the door, he had blown out his brains. People said he shot himself because he was into the bookmakers for $25,000, but Rodger Pease claimed that Charlie's father had shot himself because he no longer believed in winners.

Pease stopped in front of Charlie and stood uncomfortably shifting his weight from one foot to the other. "I wanted to talk to you, Charlie," he said. "Your friend Victor said you might be here."

"What's on your mind?"

"First of all, I want to say I don't want you to take offense."

"We've known each other a long time, Rodger." It occurred to Charlie that Pease looked frightened.

"I heard about McClatchy," Pease said. He plucked at his white mustache, then looked down at the floor. "I also heard the radio and what people've been saying about you. Charlie, I've got to know for certain if you said anything to Marotta."

"Why do you care?"

"Because I need to know."

"I swear I never told anyone about McClatchy."

Pease winced and shook his head. "That fixes it, then," he said.

"You think I should have told what I knew?" With anyone else Charlie would have been angry, but Pease was so obviously upset that Charlie's curiosity outweighed his indignation.

"No, no, it would have made things easier, that's all."

"What things?"

Pease looked up at Charlie. His lower eyelids were red and droopy like a hound's. "I can't tell you yet. I got some thinking to do."

"Maybe I can help," suggested Charlie.

Pease backed up a few steps. Then he took off his hat, stared into it and hit it several times against his leg. He was mostly bald and his scalp had a pinkness that was almost delicate. "I got to learn some stuff first," said Pease, "then maybe I'll talk to you again."

"Tell me now," said Charlie.

But Pease just shook his head and kept backing toward the door. After he had gone about ten feet, he made a kind of joking salute and hurried out.

As Charlie ate his sandwich, he considered Pease's behavior. Pease had always been eccentric. As long as Charlie had known him, he had barely earned his living by doing odd jobs at the track. Charlie had no idea what he did now. At last Charlie stopped thinking about it. If it was anything important, Pease would contact him again.

When he finished eating, Charlie drove home to clean up his house. He dreaded this but felt it was his obligation, that he couldn't just hire a stranger. As he passed through the doorway, he heard the running of the toilet. He hurried into the bathroom and rattled the flush handle until the tank ball settled into the valve seat. For a moment, he thought of fixing the toilet right away. Then he thought, No, the blood comes first.

The blood on the floor around the table roughly approximated the shape of an elephant. It had dried and didn't seem so much like blood as cheap paint. It was smeared with footprints and those same feet had tracked blood all over the living room.

Charlie had been in the house about five minutes when the phone rang. It was a reporter from Albany. Charlie said he didn't want to talk, then unplugged the phone.

For several hours, Charlie scrubbed the floor. When he finished, he began on the table. He used a wire brush to scrape the blood from the cut made by whatever implement had removed McClatchy's head—meat cleaver or samurai sword. The cut was an inch deep and about a foot long. In order to find a round oak table that he liked, Charlie had driven to nearly every used-furniture and antique store in Saratoga and Washington Counties. The cut was very white, while the rest of the surface was dark brown. Charlie considered filling it with plastic wood. Then he wondered if he would ever be able to look at the table without remembering how McClatchy's corpse had been sprawled across it.

The police had taken McClatchy's belongings. The only trace of him besides the cut on the table was a lot of missing food and a ring of black bristles in the sink where he had shaved. Charlie stared at the bristles, thinking that the face that grew them was now off on an adventure of its own, God knew where.

At five o'clock Charlie decided to deal with his other major problem and called John Wanamaker in Santa Fe. Wanamaker was staying in a boardinghouse and Charlie had to wait several minutes until he was brought to the phone.

"Sorry to take so long, Charlie. I was asleep."

Charlie immediately felt guilty. "You having a hard time?"

"Not so bad, but I had to sit up with mother last night. The doctors say she's sinking fast."

There was static on the line. Charlie had never been to Santa Fe and wanted to ask Wanamaker what he could see from his window. He imagined miles of sand spotted with cactuses and maybe armadillos. "I guess you have no idea when you're coming back," he said.

"No, the doctors say it could be at any time. I mean, I can't hurry her up, Charlie." Wanamaker's voice sounded muffled, as if it came from under a pile of blankets.

"I'm sorry, John, I didn't mean to imply that."

"That's okay. I guess I'm a little on edge. How are things in Saratoga?"

"Great, John, they couldn't be better." Even as he said it, Charlie asked himself why he was lying.

After hanging up, Charlie walked out onto the dock in front of his house, looked at the lake and thought about Black Jack Ketchum. All around the border of the lake he saw flashes of fall color. For most of his life, or at least since the age of twelve, Charlie had read about outlaws, robbers, bandits, kidnappers, gamblers, murderers and the history of the West. He found it comforting. Here was a world where the sequences of cause and effect were clearly understood. A man robbed a bank. He was pursued. He was either caught or got away. If he got away, then he robbed another bank. And in times of stress or whenever he felt anxious, Charlie would consider these bad fellows of the past and think of their stories. It was like knitting. As Charlie thought of how this one was hung or how that one had escaped to rob again, his own anxiety seemed to slip away. He grew calm and ready once again to shoulder the burdens of his life.

When Black Jack Ketchum stood on the scaffold waiting to be hanged, a priest had asked if he could do him any little favor. "Go get a fiddle, padre," Black Jack had said, "and we'll all dance. I want to die as I lived."

Not that Black Jack had done much dancing. The eight-and-a-half-foot drop ripped off his head and it had to be sewn back on for the funeral. Charlie wondered what would happen to McClatchy's head if it showed up after he was buried, whether it would get a separate little grave. Then he wondered at the preposterousness of cutting off the head in the first place.

Chapter Four

The front-page article in the *Daily Saratogian* said that Charlie and McClatchy had been good friends ever since they had both been employed by Lew Ackerman's Lorelei Stables some years earlier. Then it went on to recount how Charlie had been seen talking to underworld figures shortly before McClatchy's death. The insinuation was that not only had Charlie known about the race fixing all along but that he had betrayed his friend to the very people he was to testify against. Charlie had driven into Saratoga around six o'clock Tuesday evening just to see what the paper had to say.

Peterson had not specifically accused Charlie of disclosing McClatchy's whereabouts. What he said was: "Either the murderers followed him to Bradshaw's or Bradshaw possibly told someone. A lot of people would have paid good money to know where McClatchy was hiding. It'd be a temptation."

A further paragraph said that while the New York grand jury was scheduled to continue, McClatchy's death would definitely hamper the prosecution. The head itself was still missing. The article concluded with a brief biography of McClatchy, which revealed that the last time he had raced was in Saratoga fourteen months before.

Charlie read the article sitting in his Renault, which was parked in front of the Grand Union supermarket. When he finished, he walked over to his office to find Victor. All along the street he felt people were staring at him.

Victor was sitting behind the desk looking through a pile of eight-by-ten photographs. When he saw Charlie, he shook his head. "Charlie, here I am trying to set up a decent business and you got to wreck it by getting your name spread all over the newspapers."

"No jokes, Victor."

"Vic."

"All right, all right."

Charlie picked up one of the photographs. It showed a fat man of about sixty and a girl about seventeen crouching on a rumpled bed. Both were naked and appeared very startled. Charlie couldn't imagine what the picture was for and continued looking through the others. All showed the man and girl with different expressions of surprise and attempting to cover themselves.

"What are these?" he asked.

Victor grinned. "Aren't they beauties? Jesus, Charlie, I was so fucking pleased. I mean, you work and work and when it pays off you feel like a million bucks."

"What are these pictures?"

"Me and Rico got them."

Rico Medioli was another ex-stable guard and friend of Charlie's, a man in his mid-twenties who had spent about half his life in jail.

"That still doesn't explain what they are. Who's the old man?"

"That's Ryan Mitchell. You know him, he's got a shoe store out at the mall. His wife thought he was fooling around so she paid us to find out. I don't know who the girl is, some Skidmore bimbo. Kinda cute, hunh?" Victor looked at her appreciatively, then began sucking his teeth.

"You mean you photographed these yourself?"

"Sure. They were cooped up in a motel on the road to Glens Falls. I borrowed this camera with a motor drive from a guy at the paper. Rico and I waited outside till we heard heavy breathing, then he kicked open the door. Fucking eeks all over the place. We were gone in about five seconds."

At first Charlie didn't think he had understood, then he thought he understood too much. He didn't feel so much angry as exasperated. Slowly he picked up the top picture and tore it into four pieces. Then he began tearing up the rest.

"You ever hear of blackmail?" he asked. "You're lucky he didn't shoot you. What other cases are you working on?"

Victor looked unhappily at the torn pictures. "Are you really pissed?" he asked. "Maybe you're just upset because of McClatchy."

"I told you I didn't want to do work like this. It's humiliating."

"I wasn't going to blackmail the guy. His old lady wanted some dirt so I found it."

"Just tell me about your other cases."

"Well, there's a high-school girl who's run away from home. Probably she's shacking up with a boyfriend. Then there's a lady who wants some letters back from a guy, a local lawyer."

"What kind of letters?"

"You know, the kind that say, 'I kiss your feet,' only she don't feel like that any more so she asked me to try and get 'em back, even offer money if I have to. So far the lawyer says no. Most likely he wants her to raise the ante. Then there's a clerk out at the mall who's maybe lifting a little merchandise and I get to stand around and watch him. And there's an insurance company that wants some arson investigation on a guy whose bar got torched. That one's a little tricky. I mean it's all cinders to me. But the night before the fire the guy removed the color TV so I figure that's a bad sign. And then there's Marotta. He's the last, not counting the old fart and the Skiddy."

It occurred to Charlie that since Victor had taken over the detective agency, business had picked up by more than two hundred percent. "You tell Eddie Gillespie to follow Marotta again?" he asked.

"Yeah, except Marotta hasn't left the house all day."

Charlie tried to decide if that meant anything. Maybe Marotta had the flu or had slipped on a cake of soap in the bathtub and had broken his leg. On the other hand, Peterson and Hank Caldwell had presumably interrogated him, so Charlie guessed he was just lying low.

"By the way," said Victor, "there was an old geezer in here looking for you. He stopped by twice. I tried to call you but your phone was busy all afternoon. You running a bookie joint or something?"

"I unplugged it because of reporters. Was he a big man, almost bald, maybe seventy-five?"

"That's him. Pretty jumpy." Victor had retrieved a few fragments of the photographs and on the desk's green blotter he had lined up four little breasts.

"What did he want?"

"Beats me. Maybe he was peddling Girl Scout cookies. The last time he stopped by was around six. He said he was going to drive out to your house."

"I must have passed him on the road. Hand me the phone book, will you?"

Rodger Pease appeared not to have a telephone. It was now past seven. Charlie thought again of Rodger's various eccentricities and hoped his business could wait until tomorrow. He and Victor had intended to have fried chicken at Hattie's Chicken Shack, but as Victor locked up the office, Charlie suggested they have dinner at his house instead. After the article in the *Saratogian,* he wanted to avoid public places.

"You clean up McClatchy's blood?" asked Victor as they walked back to Charlie's car.

"Of course. What do you think I did all afternoon?"

"And you're sure there's not a drop left, not a single drop?"

"Positive."

"What about a smell, is there any kind of funny smell?"

"Of course not."

"What d'you have to eat?"

"Steaks."

"You really know how to take advantage of a guy, don't you?"

As they drove back along Broadway to Lake Avenue, Charlie saw his cousin Robert standing in front of the boutique owned by Charlie's ex-wife and her sister Lucy. Robert, who sold insurance and real estate, was married to Lucy; Charlie often suspected that his ex-wife had agreed to marry him only because she wanted to be related to his respectable cousins. Wearing a tweed jacket and smoking a pipe, Robert stood with his arms folded, looking as if he owned half of Saratoga. If he saw Charlie in the Renault, he gave no sign of it.

Charlie pointed him out to Victor. "You know what would happen if my cousins found out about those pictures?" he asked.

Victor slouched down in his seat and put his feet up on the dashboard. "The trouble with guys like your cousins," he said, "is that they're the ones, when they were teenagers, that got scared off about masturbating."

"What do you mean?" asked Charlie.

"Like maybe they were scared about getting warts on their palms or black hair, you know, that black hair you're supposed to get all over your hands? They were scared that people would look at their hands and say, 'Hey, I know what you've been doing.' So they withheld themselves. Well, it does a lot of damage."

"What sort of damage?" asked Charlie, turning onto Lake Avenue.

"I mean all that sperm accumulates. It doesn't just go away. There gets to be a coupla quarts of it. And after a while it leaks into the brain. Sperm brain. It's a known fact. It rots out the white cells or whatever. I mean you take a smart kid with lots of promise and the whole world before him, then you let him develop a terror of furry palms and before you know it sperm brain sets in and he's no good for anything. You can see them on the street as adults. Their lives over, their senses dulled."

"How can you recognize them?" asked Charlie.

"They're the ones saying, 'Quack, quack,'" said Victor. "Just like your cousins."

It was completely dark by the time they reached Charlie's house. A cold wind blew across the lake and the leaves in the driveway seemed to scurry around their feet. Victor hung back by the car. "I tell you, Charlie, if I stumble over that head, I'll never forgive you."

Charlie started to reply, then noticed a piece of paper fluttering from a nail on his front door. Removing it, he went inside and flicked on the lights. It was a note from Pease: "Charlie, I must see you right away. I'll be at home." There was an address on Ward Street near the harness track, Saratoga Raceway.

"What's up?" asked Victor. He stood in the doorway, looking suspiciously around the room and sniffing.

"It's a note from Pease. I think I should go over to his house."

"What about the steaks?"

"Maybe we can eat them later."

Victor groaned. "Let me get something from the refrigerator. You don't want me to die on you, do you?"

Five minutes later, they were driving back to Saratoga. Victor was trying to balance a chunk of salami, some crackers, a piece of cheese and a beer. "I feel I been had," he said. "Just don't hit any bumps, this is my best sweat shirt. Who is this guy Pease?"

The road along the lake was empty and Charlie drove fast. "A friend of my father's. You know how I told you that my father was a crazy bettor? A lot of those stories came from Pease."

"If he was such a good friend, why didn't he keep your old man from putting a pill in his noggin?"

"Guess he wasn't able to."

Pease had a very small white house about half a block from the main stabling area of the harness track. All the lights were on at the track, making a white glow in the sky; and as Charlie drove up Ward Street, he heard a gathering human roar as the first race came to a close. Charlie only went to the harness track once or twice a year. He told himself it was because the front runners always won, that the sulkies blocked the trailing horses. But actually he felt that an interest in the harness track was somehow disloyal to his love of Thoroughbred racing.

Charlie pulled into Pease's driveway. Parked near the house was a rusty Dodge Dart with a bent hanger for a radio antenna. The house was dark, but through a downstairs window they saw a flickering candle.

"Isn't that touching," said Victor, getting out of the car.

Charlie and Victor stood on either side of the Renault, looking at the small light surrounded by the black of the window.

"What's that smell?" asked Victor.

Suddenly the candle seemed to expand a millionfold, filling the window with light, then flame, blowing out the glass and frame itself with a whoosh that expanded into a roar as the house exploded. Charlie raised an arm to cover his face. Immediately, it was as if a great hand was lifting him and throwing him back. He landed on his side in the street and rolled. The air was filled with light and noise. Charlie kept thinking something had gone wrong with the candle. He tried to stand up, stumbled, then crouched at the curb as glass and bits of debris rained down on top of him. In the glare of the flaming house, he saw Victor sprawled on his stomach behind the Renault.

Painfully, Charlie got to his feet. "Victor!" he shouted. His voice was overwhelmed by the roar of the fire. Shielding his face, Charlie made his way across the street to where Victor was just getting to his hands and knees. Charlie saw that Victor's face was bleeding. The house was full of orange and red flame that pushed out of the windows, licked up the walls and swept over the roof. Billowing skyward was a cloud of black smoke. Little fires kept springing up on the grass.

Charlie pulled Victor to his feet. "You all right?"

"I been better. Why don't you move your car before you lose it."

Charlie ran around to the driver's side, yanked open the door and got in. The windshield was smashed and a layer of debris covered the hood. The Dodge Dart was already burning. Charlie backed his car across the street. In the distance, he heard sirens. Victor joined him, wiping the blood from his face with a dirty handkerchief. The small house was completely wrapped in flames. Charlie rubbed his shoulder. His face burned in the heat. He knew that if Rodger Pease was in the house, he was already dead.

Three hours later, Charlie and Victor were in Peterson's office in police headquarters. Charlie sat in a straight chair next to the desk, slouched down on the tip of his spine with his legs straight out in front of him. Although his predominant feeling was grief for Rodger Pease, he was also bored and out of sorts. Victor was studying some photographs of Irish setters on the side wall. His face was spotted with half a dozen small bandages. Both men had gone from the fire to the hospital and it was from there that Peterson had collected them two hours before.

"Charlie," said Peterson, "if this guy, Pease, had something to say about McClatchy, I don't know why you didn't come to me right this afternoon."

"I didn't think it was important until I got the note."

"Did the note say anything about McClatchy?"

"No, but Pease had asked about him earlier."

"So it's possible," said Peterson, fiddling with the silver revolver on his watch chain, "that the reason he wanted to see you might have had nothing to do with McClatchy."

"It's possible," said Charlie.

"Hey, Peterson," said Victor, "what do you do with all these dogs?"

If the police chief had a single passion, it was for the Irish setters that he had raised and trained during the fifteen years Charlie had known him. On the walls of Peterson's office were color photographs of his eight champions, plus pictures of other winners, citations, letters of commendation from the American Kennel Club and dozens of different colored ribbons. Peterson looked at Victor as if he couldn't remember what he was doing in his office.

Victor had picked up a sort of inverted golden flowerpot topped by a little golden dog. He was swinging it idly.

"Put that down before you break it," said Peterson.

Victor drew back his arm as if to pass the trophy to Charlie like a football. Then he shrugged and put the trophy back on top of a bookcase with a thump. "If you don't want me here," he said, "then why don't you let me go home?"

Peterson ignored him and turned back to Charlie. "What did Pease want when you saw him at the Backstretch?"

"I told you, he wanted to know if I'd said anything to Marotta about Jimmy McClatchy."

"And what did you say?"

"I told him I had never mentioned McClatchy to anyone."

Peterson stood up, then raised himself onto his toes. "You know, Charlie, Caldwell wants you locked up. I tell him we don't have the evidence but he says, what the hell, we could keep you in the slammer for a coupla of days. By any rights I should do it. I should probably lock you up until your lawyer can get you out. You and your bozo buddy. But your cousins are good friends of mine, Charlie. They're men I both admire and respect. . ."

"Where is Caldwell?" interrupted Charlie. He had no wish to hear about his cousins.

"Down in New York," said Peterson.

"Is he running this case or are you?"

"Well, Charlie, you know how it is. These things become a kind of joint effort."

"What about your stolen cars?"

Peterson looked at Charlie as if trying to decide whether Charlie were having a joke on him. Peterson disliked jokes. He was saved from having to make up his mind by the ringing of the telephone.

As Peterson answered the phone, Charlie got to his feet and wandered over to the window. It had started to rain and the streets were black and shiny. Peterson repeated the word Yeah into the mouthpiece half a dozen times. Victor continued to study the photographs of the Irish setters.

"You know," said Victor thoughtfully, "some people have sex

with dogs. I never could see it myself. Dog lovers, they call them. It must take a special kind of personality."

Peterson hung up the phone and began writing something on a note pad. After a minute, he said, "It seems the explosion was caused by gas. All four burners and the oven were left on. Pease's body was found next to the stove. There was a dog there too, I don't know what kind. The gas built up and when it reached the candle in the other room, bingo, an explosion. The point is that it looks like suicide."

"Then why was he looking for me?"

"Don't be so innocent, Charlie. You're an old hand at this. How many suicides have you known who left word someplace, hoping that some good samaritan would come along and rescue them?"

The fact of the phone call made Rodger Pease's death real in a way that not even the fire had done. Charlie told himself that Pease was his friend, that he had known him all his life. He knew that Peterson was partly bullying him with his suicide theory. Peterson could argue that if Charlie had been faster and more responsible, then Pease might have been saved.

Unfortunately, Charlie felt pretty much the same way. He knew that if he had sought out Pease right after Victor had mentioned that Pease was looking for him, then he might have reached the old man in time. Not that Charlie believed the suicide theory. He had little doubt that Pease had been murdered and that the murder was connected to McClatchy. It struck him that Pease was almost the last person in Saratoga, apart from his family, who had known his father.

"What if he was already dead when the explosion occurred?" asked Charlie.

"You mean murdered? Who'd bother to kill an old geezer like that?"

"Maybe he knew something about McClatchy?"

"Charlie, I'm not going to be bullheaded about this. If there's a link between Pease and McClatchy, I'll find it. But right at this moment Pease looks like a suicide. He's an old guy, no friends, no money, no job, nothing but his old dog. Who can blame him?"

"Hey, Peterson," said Victor, "you ever hear of sperm brain?"

"Be quiet, Victor," said Charlie.

"What's sperm brain?" asked Peterson, puzzled.

"Never mind," said Charlie. He realized that because of McClatchy and because he had been seen talking to Marotta, he had no credibility. True, he and Peterson had been disagreeing for over fifteen years, but occasionally the police chief had believed him, even respected him. Now it seemed that the very fact that Charlie was saying that Pease had been murdered was reason enough for Peterson to believe something different.

"Are you going to do an autopsy?" asked Charlie.

"I guess so, why?"

"Let me know if you find any gas in his lungs."

Charlie walked to the door. He half-expected Peterson to call him back, but when he looked at him he saw that Peterson was rearranging the dog trophies that Victor had disturbed. Charlie opened the door and went out.

"Hey," said Victor, "wait for me."

As Charlie went downstairs, he thought that the suicide theory was especially convenient for Peterson because it allowed him to separate Pease's death from McClatchy's. If Pease was a suicide, then Peterson could continue to concentrate on his stolen cars, leaving McClatchy to Hank Caldwell, who presumably thought the murderers were someplace downstate.

"Wait up," said Victor.

Charlie paused on the sidewalk. The rain had mostly stopped and the air smelled of wet brick.

"What did you mean, gas in his lungs?" asked Victor.

"If there's no gas, it means he was already dead."

They stood in front of city hall at the corner of Broadway and Lake. "You think Pease killed himself?"

"No, I don't," said Charlie, "but maybe I believe that because I don't want to believe he committed suicide."

"That's pretty complicated," said Victor. "What do you plan to do about it?"

Charlie watched a souped-up '36 Ford rumble past on Broadway. He decided it had been built from a fiberglass kit and for some reason that depressed him.

"I guess I'm going to poke around a little," he said.

Chapter
Five

The ball-cock assembly, new tank ball and lift wires took Charlie over two hours to install. Even so he had to give a slight flick of the wrist and several wiggles of the flush handle before it would work properly. He knew that he would be the only one who could operate it, that he would spend a huge amount of time telling guests just how to flick their wrists in order to keep the lift wires from getting entangled. But for the moment, it was done and he could turn his attention to the death of Rodger Pease.

He had brooded about Pease ever since he left Peterson's office the night before. He had brooded about him all morning as he delivered milk. Then, while repairing the toilet, Charlie told himself he had to drive over to Pease's house and look around. What "look around" meant he had not yet decided.

Taking an apple from a bushel basket near the back door, Charlie put on his blue windbreaker and left the house. He had borrowed Victor's yellow Volkswagen until the windshield could be replaced on the Renault. For years it had been Charlie's Volkswagen and he had sold it to Victor after his friend had convinced him that he would be happier with the red Renault, which was newer, more comfortable and which should have been a better car. Maybe it would have been a better car if it started one hundred percent of the time. As it was, it started ninety-five percent of the time and Charlie felt he had been duped.

It was nearly two o'clock when Charlie reached Pease's house. Not that there was much house left. Instead, there was half a wall, some pipes, charred timbers, mounds of soggy debris and a brick chimney rising up like a single finger. The Dodge Dart had also burned and stood black and dismal on four flat tires. Charlie got out of the Volkswagen, trying to visualize the tidy house he had seen on the previous evening and thinking what a difference it might have made had he arrived five minutes earlier.

Pease's house had been situated between a vacant corner lot and a three-story brown house with a long front porch and rusty screens. Its paint was blistered from the fire and if the wind had been stronger, the brown house might have burned.

Charlie climbed the steps of the front porch and knocked on the door. The floor of the porch was littered with toys and the bottom part of a broken broom. A middle-aged woman in a pink bathrobe answered the door. Her hair was in curlers and she had some sort of white cream on her face.

"I'm all done talking to the police," she said.

Charlie gave her one of his cards, which identified him as Charles F. Bradshaw of the Bradshaw Detective Agency. "I just have a couple of questions," he said. From inside the house came the whistle of a teakettle.

"Like what?"

"Did you know Mr. Pease next door?"

"Never spoke to him. Old men like that, they never wash."

"What about visitors," asked Charlie. "Did he have any visitors yesterday afternoon?"

"I was out all day yesterday." She made it sound as if she had been unconscious. The teakettle continued to whistle.

"Did you ever notice anyone over there? Did he have any friends, anyone who came to see him?"

"No, I never saw anyone. I'll say this for him," the woman added, "he was no trouble. Sometimes his dog barked but in general I never heard any noise. The only time I saw him was when he took that dog for a walk. Twice a day, morning and evening, like clockwork."

After asking the woman to call him if she remembered anything else, Charlie crossed the street. It was another warm fall day. From the shed rows by the harness track came the smell of horses and manure. A string of clouds like small white boxcars trailed across the sky to the east. Charlie climbed the steps of a small gray house and rang the bell. A dog started yapping, then a man about Charlie's age opened the door. He was wearing an undershirt, baggy green pants, and had a cigarette stuck in the corner of his mouth.

"Yeah?" he said.

Charlie gave him one of his cards. "You see anyone across the street yesterday, maybe late in the day or early in the evening?"

"Not me, Jack, I didn't see anything." The man started to close the door. Charlie noticed that he was wearing bright red slippers.

"How about friends?" asked Charlie. "Did the man across the street have any visitors?"

"Not that I ever saw."

"Rudy," called a woman's voice from inside, "Rudy, who're you talking to?"

"Some private dick," shouted the man. "You got any more questions?" he asked Charlie.

"You ever talk to Pease?"

"Never. Didn't even known that was his name till the cops told me."

A woman in a blue bathrobe appeared behind Rudy's shoulder. She too had curlers in her hair and Charlie wondered if anyone on Ward Street ever bothered getting dressed.

"What's he want?" asked the woman, looking suspiciously at Charlie.

"He's asking about the guy across the street."

Charlie guessed the woman had thought he was after Rudy. Once she realized that Rudy was safe, she cheered up. "Wasn't that a shame," she said. "Why'd a nice old man like that want to go and blow himself up?"

"You ever see any people over there?" asked Charlie. "Or know if he had any friends?"

"Never saw a soul," said the woman. She kept patting at her curlers, which contained little pinwheels of black hair. "But one time we saw him in a bar with an old woman. You remember that, Rudy? They seemed pretty friendly."

"How long ago was that?" asked Charlie.

"'Bout a month ago. You know the Towne Bar over on the next street? It was over there. They might know something."

The waitress at the Towne Bar hadn't heard about the fire, didn't recognize Pease's description and seemed to think Charlie was making it all up. She was an attractive young woman with thick brown hair that fell to the middle of her thighs. Its weight pulled back her head, making her keep her chin slightly raised so that she looked regal or conceited. Charlie couldn't decide which. He wanted to ask her how heavy it was but instead he concentrated on convincing her that he had to find out about Pease. After he had told her this for the tenth time, she called the owner out of the kitchen. He was a man of about fifty who wore aviator glasses and a baby-blue cowboy shirt with pearl snaps.

"An old guy, you say?"

"Tall," said Charlie, "and big like, well, a sack of potatoes. He was supposed to have been in here with an old woman."

Two girls were playing pool. Neither of them looked eighteen. One had no teeth. She kept laughing, showing her pink gums.

"Yeah, I remember a guy like that," said the man. He glanced down at his cowboy shirt and unsnapped the top two snaps, exposing curls of black hair. "Funny old geezer. Used to come in here with this old woman who was even taller than he was. I tell you, they were quite the couple. Even saw them dancing once. I figured it was his wife but then I said something and the woman said they weren't married. After that I didn't see them again. Her name was Flo something, I don't know her last name. Maybe Maggie does. Hey, Maggie, come out here a minute."

A heavyset woman with damp-looking pink cheeks came out

of the kitchen wiping her hands on a white apron.

"What was that woman's name," asked the man. "Flo something, that used to come in here with the old guy?"

"You mean the one you insulted?"

"Who insulted? I never said a thing."

Maggie looked at Charlie, then curled her lips scornfully. "This old fool told them he thought it was swell to see an old married couple who still liked each other. He made a big deal out of it, kept buying them drinks. After that they never came back. I don't know her name, just Flo, like the old fool says, but she told me once that she lived in a rooming house over on Ludlow, because that was the time I was thinking of moving out, and she said it was clean but cheap. Don't ask me if she lives there now. I was so mad at the old fool when they stopped coming back. I knew he had upset them. They'd sit over there in that corner booth, talking with their heads close together and sometimes holding hands. It was a pleasure to see them."

Charlie had left the Volkswagen over on Ward Street and he walked back to retrieve it. Then he drove to Ludlow, which was behind the Fassig-Tipton stables where the yearlings were auctioned each August. There were three rooming houses on Ludlow and the old woman, whose named turned out to be Flo Abernathy, lived in the third. It was a large Victorian house with a sort of turret running up one corner. Flo Abernathy had the turret room on the second floor and the turret itself was full of flowering plants.

Flo Abernathy was at least three inches over six feet, with long white hair done up in a French roll and pinned to the back of her head. She had a long, narrow face and wore a floor-length blue dress with a string of pearls. At first she had not wanted to let Charlie in, but then she seemed to recognize his name. She asked if he would like a cup of coffee and went off to prepare it before he could answer. Her whole body was narrow, like the spine of a book, and she held herself very straight when she walked.

Charlie sat uncomfortably on an antique chair with a wicker seat. In his lifetime, he had broken nearly a dozen chairs like this one by leaning back or stretching or sitting down too abruptly. The blue walls of the room were covered with photographs. Some were of people—Charlie recognized several of Rodger Pease—but there were others of houses, a lake, a couple of racehorses and an elaborate rose garden with Greek pillars and statues.

Flo Abernathy returned with a tray on which were two cups of coffee, a silver cream pitcher and sugar bowl and a little silver plate of chocolate-chip cookies. The room was crowded with furniture, as if the furniture of a dozen rooms were being stored here. Covering the floor were a number of overlapping carpets of the kind that Charlie's mother called Turkey carpets. The windows had red curtains and the afternoon sun filled the room with pinkish light.

Flo Abernathy handed Charlie a cup of coffee and sat down. "Rodger and I were to meet last night. When he didn't appear, I walked by his house. Then I called the hospital and a nurse told me he was dead."

"Had you known him long?" Charlie sipped the coffee, then put his cup and saucer on a little round table. He always felt inadequate in the face of other people's grief. It made him dislike himself.

"We had been friends for forty-five years. I heard on the radio that the police suspect it might have been suicide. It wasn't, of course. But the police are apparently looking for his next of kin. He had a wife who moved to Miami in 1953. I don't know if she's still alive. I suppose after this much time it doesn't much matter, although she would be pleased to hear that he was dead and I was left by myself." Miss Abernathy sat with her cup and saucer in her lap. Charlie doubted that her back was touching the back of her chair. She stared into her cup as she spoke. Then she looked up at Charlie. She had dark blue eyes that matched the blue of her dress.

"What makes you think he didn't commit suicide?" asked Charlie.

"We had talked about suicide in the past. We both had. But

after discussing it, we decided it would be wrong for one of us to abandon the other. Until recently we had been very happy. Then something happened to upset him. I don't know what. But he seemed frightened. I considered going to the police. Do you think I should? I would much rather they didn't know of my existence. I would hate to have my name appear in the papers."

Charlie remembered a wealthy family in Glens Falls by the name of Abernathy and he wondered if this woman was related. Then he tried to imagine her involvement with Pease over a period of forty-five years. In the corner, partly hidden by a painted screen, was a brass bed. Charlie tried to think of Pease with his sack-of-potatoes body making love to the tall, delicate woman who sat beside him.

"You have no idea why he was frightened?" asked Charlie.

"No, we rarely discussed our difficulties. It's foolish perhaps but we had a sort of game. We would never talk about the outside world, or at least very little, but would try only to talk about each other. And memories, of course."

"How did he earn his money?" Charlie considered taking a cookie, worried that it would make him seem frivolous, then took two.

"He received a small amount from Social Security, very small, and he supplemented this by being what they call a ten-percenter."

Charlie had almost guessed as much. Ten-percenters were people who cashed in tickets for bettors who wanted to avoid paying taxes on their winnings. Anyone who won over six hundred dollars had to fill out a tax form, and sometimes a person would turn to a ten-percenter instead of filling out the form and putting himself in a higher tax bracket. The tax system, however, was in the process of being changed and next season the taxes would be deducted directly at the window. In the past, ten-percenters had been made up of the unemployed and the elderly—people like Rodger Pease whose taxes would be little affected by a winning ticket. For their services they charged ten percent, although Charlie knew it was often less.

"How long had he been doing this?"

"About fifteen years, ever since he had found it difficult to obtain other work. He also worked at the harness track, but it was with the Thoroughbreds in August that he had the best luck. Once he even tried it down at Belmont but he found it too hard to break in. Here at least he was well known."

"You have any idea who he cashed tickets for?"

"No. As I say, we rarely talked about that part of his life. I knew that he did it and that was all." Miss Abernathy paused and looked away. During their whole conversation, her eyes had been brimming with tears. Now she reached into her pocket, took out a white handkerchief and pressed it first to one eye, then the other. "Excuse me," she said.

Charlie nodded and concentrated on the flowers in the turret. He was what he thought of as an emotional joiner: at the sight of someone else's tears, his own eyes would invariably moisten. He hoped he wouldn't do anything foolish.

"I wonder, Mr. Bradshaw," said Miss Abernathy after a moment, "if you could find out about the funeral. I don't think I should go but I would like to send a wreath. I'd also like to pay to have him buried in Saratoga and pay for a headstone as well. I'm sorry to trouble you with this but you've been very kind. What I want is for you to buy two adjoining plots in the cemetery. Could you possibly do that for me?"

Charlie started to ask why she needed two, then stopped himself. "Certainly," he said.

"It's a shame about the dog. He was such a smelly old thing. I would never let him come up here but now I'd be happy to have him. The terrible thing about a fire is that it's so complete. I have nothing but a few pictures."

Charlie finished his coffee and stood up. Her grief made him feel claustrophobic. He wanted to get away, yet at the same time he condemned himself for his cowardice. "Don't worry about the funeral stuff," he told her. He tried to nod reassuringly but guessed he was just dumbly bobbing his head.

Half an hour later Charlie was back at the wreckage of Pease's house digging through the debris with a borrowed shovel. So far he had found a couple of badly scorched books and a heavy blue mug. A few cars slowed as their drivers stared at him curiously. Charlie dug at the ashes, heaved charred boards out of the way and grew increasingly filthy. It was the murder that made him angry: the fact that someone felt that he or she could erase Rodger Pease as if he were no more than a stick figure on a blackboard.

Charlie guessed that the link between McClatchy and Pease had to do with Pease being a ten-percenter. It made him want to know more about that August more than a year ago, which had been the last time McClatchy had raced.

The shovel clanged against something metallic and Charlie bent over to see what it was. Brushing away the ashes, he found a metal horse about fifteen inches high. He wiped it off on his pants and saw that it was made of brass—a brass horse with a racing saddle. He put it on the grass next to the books and blue cup. He decided he had to go over to the *Daily Saratogian* to look through the newspapers for that last August. Then he realized the paper was the worst place to go unless he wanted to deal with a lot of questions about how he had betrayed Jimmy McClatchy to the Mafia. After a moment, he thought of someplace else.

At six o'clock, Charlie was banging on the screen door of a rundown Victorian house on the west side of Saratoga. Most of the screening had long since rusted away, but the frame made a loud noise when Charlie hammered on it and after a couple of minutes he began shouting as well. "Felix, I know you're in there. It's Charlie Bradshaw. Open up before I kick down the door!" Cradled in his left arm, Charlie carried a bag containing twenty-five pounds of dry cat food and a dozen cans of soup.

It was a square, two-story house with a high attic. Once it had been painted a cream color but most of the paint had peeled. Some of the windows had brown shutters. Other shutters had fallen off and were scattered across the lawn. The grass around the house was knee deep and Charlie doubted it had been cut for years. All the windows were covered with tattered green shades.

"I'm counting to three, Felix, then I'm kicking down the door. One . . . Two . . ."

The door flew open and five cats rushed past Charlie, raced down the steps and across the yard.

"Now look what you made me do!" shouted an angry voice.

Charlie hurried through the door and slammed it behind him.

"Back, kitties, back!" shouted the voice.

The room, a kitchen, was almost dark and Charlie could barely see about twenty cats nervously prowling back and forth in front of the door. Immediately, Charlie felt he was about to sneeze. Then he did: a loud, wet, two-shout sneeze that sent the cats scurrying into the darkness.

"You've scared them," said the voice petulantly.

"They'll get over it. Can we have a little light, Felix?"

"There's some in the other room." Felix had a high, querulous voice that seemed accustomed to complaining. "Would you have really kicked in the door?"

"I expect so. I did it once before, remember?"

"But you're not a policeman now. If you'd kicked down my door, then all my cats would have gotten out."

"Maybe they don't like it here," suggested Charlie. He had followed Felix through a dark hall to a front room, which was dimly lit by light coming around the edges of the green shades.

"Of course they like it here. You frightened them, that's all."

Felix was a small, wizened man with patches of straggly white hair and a pair of knobbly hands that looked like claws. He wore a constantly startled expression as if someone had just shouted, "Hey you!" or "Watch out!" Charlie thought Felix had the whitest skin he had ever seen and he doubted that it was ever touched by sunlight. He wore blue dungarees and a wrinkled white shirt that appeared ten sizes too big for him. His neck stuck up through the collar like a pencil through a doughnut hole.

The room smelled of cats and a hundred different kinds of dirt. The cats kept rubbing themselves against Charlie's ankles. He sneezed again and a dozen cats fled the room. One time, as a policeman, Charlie had been able to keep the authorities from locking up Felix and condemning his house as a health hazard;

but whenever he saw the filth and the fifty or sixty cats, Charlie worried that he might not have done the right thing.

Charlie handed the bag of groceries to Felix. "Here's some food," he said.

Felix put the bag on the table, then took out the cat food and soup. "It looks like a bribe. What do you want?"

"I want to look through your *Racing Form*s."

"No, Charlie, they're brand new." Felix's voice rose about an octave. "It's not fair. Ask for something else instead."

"It won't do any good, Felix. I need to look at the *Racing Form*s for August of last year. I promise to be careful."

Felix walked to the other side of the room, muttering to himself. Charlie pressed his finger under his nose so he wouldn't sneeze, then sneezed away. Against two of the walls piles of newspaper were stacked to the ceiling. A tunnel through one pile led to another room. The floor was covered with tin cans, pieces of torn fabric and spilled kitty litter.

Felix came back, still muttering. "I need more cat food, Charlie. They won't stay if I don't feed them."

"I'll bring another bag this evening."

"Are your hands clean?"

"Yes."

"If you tear any newspaper, do you promise to replace it?"

"I promise."

"Come with me," said Felix.

Charlie followed Felix through the tunnel of newspapers and up the stairs. Everywhere stacks of newspapers were piled to the ceiling. Looking through a doorway, Charlie saw a room heaped with bits of paper that he realized were losing tickets from the track. Another room was filled with magazines. Felix led the way to the attic. He walked with a sort of sideways stoop and kept glancing back to make sure Charlie wasn't touching anything. The cats were everywhere and all seemed intent on getting entangled between Charlie's legs. By the time they reached the right room, Charlie guessed he had sneezed fifty times.

The yellow attic room was filled with stacks of *Racing Form*s. Light from the setting sun streamed in around a torn shade that half-covered the gable window.

"This is my favorite room, Charlie. I'd be upset if you disturbed it."

"It's a very nice room," said Charlie.

"Don't humor me, Charlie. You just think I'm crazy."

Felix lifted a stack of papers, put them on the floor, then continued poking through more papers and muttering to himself. After several minutes, he turned back to Charlie. "All right, here is last August and the months before. Don't forget, they're all in order. Make sure you put them back where you found them. I'll leave you here. It would make me too unhappy to watch."

"You mind if I open the window?"

"I wish you wouldn't."

"I'm allergic to cats."

When Charlie was certain that Felix had gone downstairs, he opened the window, leaned out and breathed deeply. Down below, he saw two small boys pointing up at him. They seemed astonished. Charlie waved, then went back to the papers.

Charlie wasn't sure what he was looking for. Primarily, he wanted to see what sort of horses McClatchy had ridden that past August. Although McClatchy was not one of the popular jockeys, he had ridden once or twice a day for the entire month. Charlie first sought out the *Racing Form* for the last day of the Saratoga meet, then worked his way back. Toward the end of the meet, McClatchy had had a big win on a three-year-old colt by the name of Sweet Dreams in a $20,000 claiming race. The horse had had odds of 30 to 1 and paid fifty-six dollars. According to the Past Performance charts, Sweet Dreams had lost badly in his previous three starts, all of which had been $20,000 claiming races. Nor was there anything in his workout times that indicated any speed. A short article on Sweet Dreams the day after the win quoted the owner and trainer as saying that the horse was nervous in the gate but that he hoped the problem had cleared itself up. The article referred to another big win at the beginning of the month at odds of 25 to 1 with the horse paying forty-eight dollars on a two-dollar ticket. That had been in a $12,500 claiming race. But what interested Charlie most was that the owner and trainer of the horse, Willis Stitt, lived in Hoosick Falls, a town about thirty miles from Saratoga.

When he could no longer read by the light from the window, Charlie turned on a light hanging from a cord in the middle of the ceiling. It appeared to be a fifteen-watt bulb. Cats kept trying to snoop into the room and he shooed them away. After reading through the *Racing Form* for another two hours, Charlie learned that Sweet Dreams had run eleven times between April third and August twenty-sixth, losing badly in nine races and winning twice. McClatchy had been the jockey all eleven times: six races in Belmont, five in Saratoga. What also interested Charlie was that although he looked forward in the September and October issues, he found no further mention of the horse. It seemed that Sweet Dreams had quit racing at the same time as McClatchy.

Sweet Dreams appeared to be an average loser: Sweet Dreams out of Indian Maid and Buckdancer—neither parent rang any bells. Yet he had won two races at great odds. At that time it was not generally known that McClatchy pulled horses, while Willis Stitt's explanation about Sweet Dreams being nervous in the gate seemed sufficient reason for his uneven record.

But now, with Pease and McClatchy dead and Sweet Dreams's owner living only thirty miles away, Charlie decided he wanted to learn more about Sweet Dreams and Willis Stitt. McClatchy had had two other wins that August, plus several second- and third-place horses. But none of the horses had run at great odds or made a lot of money.

It was completely dark by the time Charlie left Felix's house. He first went to Star Market, bought four twenty-five-pound bags of cat food and took them back to Felix. The cats smelled the food and swarmed around Charlie's feet. Felix was moderately pleased but didn't think the cat food was worth the disturbance of his papers. He thanked Charlie but asked him not to come again.

Afterward Charlie drove over to see Flo Abernathy and to give her the books, blue mug and brass horse. The books were two novels about Horatio Hornblower. Flo stood in the doorway and held them, looking down at them for a long time. Charlie was afraid she might cry but she didn't. She just slowly nodded her head.

"I wanted to ask one more question," he said. "Did Rodger Pease do particularly well as a ten-percenter a year ago last August?"

The old woman thought a moment, then turned away and put down the mug, brass horse and books on a small table. "He did quite well that August. That's the last time he had much money. I remember he said his luck had changed. He was even planning to go back down to Belmont but then he didn't. I don't know why."

"Did he ever mention the jockey Jimmy McClatchy?"

"No, never. He never mentioned anybody's name. But that August was a good time for us. One night we even had champagne."

After leaving Miss Abernathy, Charlie spent about an hour searching the seedier Saratoga bars for an old acquaintance by the name of Maximum Tubbs. He finally located him in the Turf Bar on Caroline Street listening to scratchy Al Jolson records on the jukebox. When Tubbs saw Charlie, he slowly shut his eyes and looked away.

Maximum Tubbs was a small, dapper man who, Charlie thought, always looked ready, as if he were constantly calculating odds, doing sums in his head and preparing to place a bet. During August he seemed to live at the track. Otherwise, he was someplace shooting craps, playing poker or on a brief trip to Belmont or Aqueduct. He had soft little white hands that looked as if their only function was to handle dice, playing cards and money. He too had known Charlie's father. As a policeman, Charlie had arrested Tubbs for gambling about twenty times and each time he had felt embarrassed.

Charlie sat down on the stool next to Maximum Tubbs and inquired about his health and his fortunes. Tubbs grunted noncommittally, still not looking at Charlie. Undiscouraged, Charlie asked about Willis Stitt, Sweet Dreams and the sire and dam, Buckdancer and Indian Maid. Tubbs sipped his dry vermouth, then glanced at Charlie quickly. "Are you on a case?" he asked.

"I haven't decided. Do you remember Sweet Dreams?"

"It would be hard to forget him. He was a memorable horse. I was sorry not to have a little bundle on him. Since then, I've wondered if McClatchy hadn't been strangling him all along. As for Stitt, he runs a small claiming stable. Barely gets by." Tubbs glanced at Charlie again, growing more interested. "The other horses I don't recognize. What were their names again?"

"Buckdancer and Indian Maid." Charlie had bought several bags of peanuts and was wolfing them down. He had eaten nothing else since Flo Abernathy's cookies.

"They don't sound like winners to me. You want me to check?"

Charlie nodded.

"Any other little errands?"

"I guess not. What would happen if it could be proved that Stitt had McClatchy constantly pull that horse?"

"He'd lose his license and be charged with interfering with a sporting event. Also the IRS would probably take an interest in him."

"Would it mean a jail term?"

"It would depend on how good a lawyer he had."

Charlie couldn't imagine killing two men over what was essentially a nickel-and-dime issue, no matter how much money had been won. "Don't tell anyone I've been asking, okay?"

Tubbs lifted his chin and looked at Charlie over the tip of his nose: half-scornful, half-amused. "You're not very popular right now, Charlie. I doubt I'll brag about knowing you. In fact, I probably shouldn't even be seen talking to you. I take it you don't think McClatchy was killed by his New York buddies?"

"I'm not sure what I think."

"You know, Charlie," said Maximum Tubbs, suddenly looking embarrassed, "I'm not one of those people who think you said anything to Marotta."

Charlie started to speak, then found that he couldn't. Instead, he roughly patted Maximum Tubbs's shoulder and hurried out of the bar.

By now it was nine o'clock and Charlie decided to walk over to Victor's apartment to see if his friend would give him a sandwich. After Felix's house, one more cat wouldn't hurt. But as Charlie crossed Lake Avenue by the police station, he saw that the lights were on in Peterson's office. He remembered that he still had to find out about the funeral arrangements for Pease's body, and as he entered the police station he half-decided to tell Peterson what he had learned about Pease, Willis Stitt and the horse, Sweet Dreams.

Peterson was in his office with the FBI agent, Hank Caldwell. The door was open and when the two men saw Charlie they looked at him with a mixture of curiosity and indignation. Peterson sat at his desk, which was bare except for a brass nameplate that said he was Director of Public Safety. "You got something you want to tell us?" he asked.

"I wanted to find out about the funeral arrangements for Rodger Pease."

Caldwell sat in a straight chair next to Peterson's desk. After having looked once at Charlie, he had turned to an inspection of his fingernails. He wore a gray suit and his thin face and pointy nose seemed as smooth as polished stone.

"Charity case as far as I can see," said Peterson. "We'll probably send him over to Mitchell and Sons in a day or so. He had no bank account and the house was rented."

"Will it be a public funeral?"

"Who'd want to go?" asked Peterson.

"There's a wife in Miami," said Charlie.

Peterson looked at him for a moment. "She died two years ago," he said.

"You going to try and fool around with this case, Bradshaw?" asked Caldwell.

Charlie ignored him. "Have you found out anything else about Pease?"

"Like what?" asked Peterson.

"Like how he died."

"He died in the fire. But since you're so eager to know, I guess there's no harm in saying that he'd taken a pretty strong sedative. We think he didn't want to stay awake waiting for the gas to take effect."

"You still don't think he was murdered?"

Caldwell got to his feet and slowly walked over to Charlie. Then he reached out and took hold of one of the buttons on his shirt right above his chest. He tugged it slightly. "You ever hear of interfering with a police investigation?" he asked. "We don't need much evidence to lock you up for that one."

Charlie thought about the horse Sweet Dreams, thought about how McClatchy must have held him back for all but two races, then he thought about how Pease must have cashed a whole handful of winning tickets and that whoever had gotten the money had probably killed him. There were little white marks around Caldwell's nostrils. His face looked so rigid that Charlie wanted to reach out and touch it, just to see if the skin was really as hard as it looked. Then he thought better of it and, with a quick backward movement, he pulled himself free and left the room.

Chapter
Six

Thursday morning Charlie lost a filling while eating a doughnut. He had been delivering milk and had stopped at the Schuylerville bakery. It was a large doughnut, maple flavored, packed with cream and when the filling popped out of an upper left-side molar, Charlie had considered it a judgment. When he touched it with his tongue, the hole felt as deep as a one-quart bottle. He called his dentist in Glens Falls, but the earliest he could see him was Monday afternoon.

It was late by the time Charlie got back to the barn and he would have to rush if he wanted to go swimming. Consequently, it was with a sinking heart that he saw his cousin James's big white Oldsmobile, with his cousin patiently waiting in the front seat, parked next to the yellow Volkswagen. For a moment, Charlie considered driving straight to Saratoga in the milk truck. Then he decided against it. His tooth had begun to hurt and he wished his life were simpler.

James was five years older than Charlie. During the years he had been a carpenter, people called him Jim or Jimmy; but now that he had his own construction company, everyone called him James. He was president of the local Lions Club, a leading Rotarian and a seven-time recipient of the Little League Booster Award. Additionally, he held it as a matter of religious faith that a mentally healthy person needed no more than four hours sleep a night. James often seemed to worry that Charlie might be making life difficult for Chief Peterson, whom he described as a "personal friend," with the result that Charlie would spend some moments trying to define "impersonal friend."

James remained in his car while Charlie unloaded the milk truck. He appeared to have a small microcassette recorder and was talking into it, presumably dictating material that would later be transcribed by his secretary. James wrote weekly letters to a wide number of Congressmen and imagined himself a political watchdog.

When Charlie finished, he walked over to James's car. His cousin got out to greet him. James was several inches over six feet, athletic, and his almost rosy face was accentuated by thick silver hair. He stuck out his hand. "Charlie, I've driven out here so that we might have lunch."

Charlie shook his hand. "This is really a treat," he said.

The dairy ran a restaurant around the corner and they strolled over in that direction. James walked with one hand resting lightly on Charlie's shoulder. "Tell me," he said, "what have you heard from your mother?"

"I got a card yesterday. She plans to stay in Atlantic City for a few more days."

"She's a great woman, Charlie, but I'm afraid she requires a little looking after."

They took a booth by the door and the waitress brought them menus. James ordered a fruit salad with cottage cheese. Out of perversity Charlie ordered a hot-fudge sundae. The ice cream was extremely painful on his tooth, forcing him to eat only with the right side of his mouth. This required him to tip his head a little to the right in order to chew and some ice cream dribbled out onto his chin. James kept looking at him.

"Charlie, I wanted to talk because I've been hearing things that have made me unhappy. Astonishing as it might seem, I've heard you had some involvement with the deaths of two men. Charlie, at the age of forty-eight aren't you too old to be playing cops and robbers?"

"Forty-six."

"Pardon me?"

"Forty-six, I'm only forty-six." Charlie wiped some fudge sauce from his lower lip.

His cousin looked at him skeptically. "Charlie, I think it's time to give up this crazy detective agency. I've talked to the people at Wholesome Dairy and they're prepared to offer you a permanent position."

"I don't want to be a milkman," said Charlie. What irritated him most was that no matter how hard he tried, he always seemed to revert to his childhood relationship with James: that of an eight-year-old being corrected by a thirteen-year-old.

"It's a respectable job and it would mean a lot of security. Your mother may need taking care of. She might be coming back to Saratoga completely penniless. She's in her mid-sixties, Charlie, you can't let her go on being a waitress forever."

"I don't like being a milkman," said Charlie. He watched his cousin eating and disliked how he took small bites and chewed very carefully. He suspected that his cousin's teeth were perfect.

"You know, Charlie, Chief Peterson is a personal friend of mine and he told me you might even face criminal charges. Already your name has appeared in the paper several times. Charlie, I don't suppose you remember your father as well as I do, but I remember the kind of chances he took and how people talked about him. He was not a man who commanded a lot of respect. I even remember one time when he spent five hundred dollars in order to smuggle whiskey into the old county jail."

Charlie pushed away the last of his hot-fudge sundae. He wondered why he allowed himself to be so bullied by his family. Practically on the spur of the moment he decided he had to talk to Willis Stitt. He got to his feet and tossed a five-dollar bill on the table.

"James," said Charlie, "I'm glad my father bought whiskey for the jail. It makes me proud."

"That's not a very grown-up way to feel, Charlie," said James.

Charlie tried to think of some crushing response, but he didn't particularly dislike his cousin. He just felt suffocated by him. "Thanks for your concern," he said at last. Then he left the restaurant.

But as Charlie drove the yellow Volkswagen over to Willis Stitt's stable in Hoosick Falls, he continued to worry about his mother, his cousins, his tooth, his semirepaired toilet and even the smashed windshield on the Renault, which was supposed to have been fixed the day before but still wasn't ready. All he really wanted was to coach Little League baseball, go to horse races and spend a lot of time with Doris Bailes. But the Little League Association saw him as a corrupter of the young, racing season was over and he had no chance to court Doris in ways he felt appropriate. Besides, since McClatchy's murder, Charlie wasn't even welcome in the Backstretch anymore.

The sky was lumpy gray, like a tumble of gray blankets heaped on a bed. Leaves gusted down from the trees and the fields of cornstalks on either side of the road looked dismal. Then Charlie thought of his father smuggling whiskey into the jail. James had criticized his father as a man who took chances, but any gambler took chances as long as he thought he might win.

One of the Charlie's Saratoga heroes was Bet-A-Million Gates, the turn-of-the-century gambler and stock-market tycoon who had made his first fortune selling barbed wire to Texas cattle ranchers. Bet-A-Million would spend whole nights playing faro at the Canfield Casino, wagering up to $10,000 on each turn of the card.

"That's the way I bet," he would say. "For me there's no fun in betting just a few thousand. I want to lay down enough to hurt the other fellow if he loses, and enough to hurt me if I lose myself."

Charlie liked someone who took chances, who believed in winners. He wanted to be that way himself. But it was hard to take chances when the toilet needed fixing, your fillings fell out and your relatives kept urging you to become a milkman.

Willis Stitt's stable in Hoosick Falls was about a mile from the farm where the painter Grandma Moses had lived. Her grandson ran the farm now and had a vegetable stand where Charlie bought tomatoes whenever he drove over to Bennington or took long summer drives through the country. It made him vaguely feel as if he were patronizing the arts.

The stable consisted of two red barns in need of paint and reshingling, a long red shed row and a shabby-looking Cape Cod house. Even the surrounding elms and maples seemed in disrepair, with a lot of dead branches and their leaves half gone. Leading to the house was a long gravel driveway and as Charlie turned up it, he saw a small circus tent behind one of the barns. It had alternate green and white stripes and seemed so out of place that he couldn't imagine its purpose. Between the barns was a corral with a wooden fence surrounding half a dozen horses.

Charlie parked the Volkswagen and got out. From the direction of the circus tent came the sound of a Strauss waltz played by a circus band. He heard a door slam. Charlie looked to see a young man in jeans and a blue sweat shirt coming toward him from the house.

"You Willis Stitt?" asked Charlie.

The man shook his head. "Nah, he's inside." He turned and shouted toward the house. "Hey, Will, somebody's here!"

"Thanks," said Charlie. "By the way, what's in the tent?"

The young man glanced toward the tent as if looking at something unpleasant. "That's Artemis. She's wacko." Without bothering to explain, he jogged off toward the corral.

The house door banged again and a rather pudgy man of about thirty-five came trotting down the steps. "You Mr. Emerson?" called the man. He had thick black hair, a wide owl-like face and a goatee.

"No, my name's Charlie Bradshaw." Charlie gave him a card. "You're Willis Stitt?"

"That's right," said the man, looking at the card. He seemed disappointed.

"I wonder if I could ask you some questions?" asked Charlie.

"I guess so," said Stitt. "What's it about?" Stitt wore jeans and a red-and-blue-plaid Western shirt that was too tight, so that the fabric around the pearl snaps was all stretched. Although he wasn't particularly cordial, neither did he seem suspicious.

"I wanted to ask you about a horse of yours named Sweet Dreams," said Charlie. As he pronounced the horse's name, it seemed to Charlie that Stitt stiffened slightly.

"What about him?"

"Did he run at all after that Saratoga meet over a year ago?"

"No. He injured his leg a few weeks later and I haven't raced him since." Stitt looked into Charlie's face as if trying to see behind it. After a moment, he took out a pack of cigarettes and offered one to Charlie. When Charlie refused, Stitt took a cigarette for himself and lit it with a kitchen match which he struck on his thumbnail.

"How'd he injure his leg?" asked Charlie.

"He hit his right foreleg on the door of his stall, breaking the pastern joint."

"Can it heal?"

Stitt shrugged. "He won't race again."

"The horse had an interesting record," said Charlie. "He raced only eleven times, is that right?"

"Yeah."

"And he won two races at great odds, how do you explain that?"

"I don't know how much you know about horses, Mr. Bradshaw, but there's a lot of chance involved. Sweet Dreams hated the gate and then a couple of times it didn't seem to bother him. If I'd kept racing him, maybe he would have turned into a good horse."

"You make a lot of money on those two races?"

Stitt shook his head. "No, nothing on the first race, maybe I had ten dollars on the second."

"How come you didn't race him as a two-year old?"

"I didn't think he was ready."

The Strauss waltzes were still coming from the circus tent. Beyond the tent to the east, the Green Mountains were covered in cloud.

"You know a man named Rodger Pease?" asked Charlie.

"Never heard of him."

Charlie felt he was lying. It wasn't that Stitt seemed tense; rather, he seemed to be forcing himself to appear relaxed. Stitt ground out his cigarette on the heel of his boot, then glanced over toward the man in the corral.

"Pease was a ten-percenter who worked at the track," said Charlie. "He was murdered on Tuesday. His house blew up and he was inside it. What about Jimmy McClatchy, you know him?"

"Sure I knew McClatchy. He used to ride for me." Stitt paused, then looked at Charlie more carefully. "You're the guy he was staying with, aren't you? I knew I'd heard your name before. Charlie Bradshaw. People say you sold him out. How come you're over here bothering me?"

Charlie didn't feel like answering that at the moment. "You have any idea why someone would want to cut off his head?"

"No, no idea. You still haven't said why you came over here."

"McClatchy was the only jockey you used on Sweet Dreams. How come?"

"I used him a lot over the years. He didn't charge as much as some of the others."

"You know he strangled horses?"

"I heard rumors, but you hear that about everyone. When the news broke about the Atlantic City scandal I was as surprised as anybody." Stitt took out another cigarette and lit it. "You still haven't answered my question."

Stitt seemed genuinely uncertain as to why Charlie was trying to connect him to the dead jockey. He took a large puff of his cigarette and blew smoke from his nose. Charlie decided that Stitt had begun to seem frightened, but of what he couldn't determine.

"Isn't it coincidental that Sweet Dreams and McClatchy stopped racing at the same time?" asked Charlie. "Maybe McClatchy also held back Sweet Dreams for all but those two races. Maybe you made a killing on those races and maybe Pease cashed the tickets."

Stitt pushed his face toward Charlie's. "Are you suggesting I might have murdered them?" He seemed both puzzled and angry. "You better get out of here, Mr. Bradshaw. If you have any charges to make, why don't you go to the police?"

"What about Monday," insisted Charlie. "Can you tell me what you were doing during the time McClatchy was murdered?"

Stitt ground his cigarette out on the gravel. "Get out of here, Bradshaw."

The music had stopped in the circus tent. A drop of rain fell on Charlie's wrist, then another on his bald spot. "Okay, Mr. Stitt, I just wanted you to know the kind of questions you could expect from the police."

"I've been here all week," said Stitt, "and I can prove it if I have to. Why should the police want to talk to me anyway?"

Charlie smiled and shook his head, as if to indicate that they both knew very well why the police should want to talk to him. It seemed to Charlie that Stitt's fear came partly from confusion, as if he wasn't sure what exactly had happened. He appeared to be indifferent to the deaths of McClatchy and Pease, yet nervous about Charlie's questions concerning Sweet Dreams. Stitt's black hair was long, brushed back over his head and Charlie guessed it was one of his little vanities.

"Where's Sweet Dreams now?" asked Charlie. "I wonder if I could look at him." He knew he was pushing his luck but he wanted to see what would happen.

"Bradshaw, you've got no legal right to ask me anything. Why don't you get out of here?"

"Just let me see the horse," said Charlie.

Stitt turned quickly toward the corral where the young man was doing something to the watering trough. "Hey, Tony, come here and help me with a problem!"

"Forget it," said Charlie. "I was just leaving." As he drove out of the driveway, he saw Stitt still staring after him.

At three o'clock Charlie arrived at Mitchell and Sons Funeral Home to arrange Rodger Pease's funeral. Ten minutes later he was walking back to his car, unhappy with himself for not finding out how much Flo Abernathy wished to spend. Did she want Pease buried or cremated? If buried, did she want the seven-hundred-dollar or seven-thousand-dollar casket? Then there was the headstone and the double cemetery plot. Charlie left saying he would return the next day.

He drove to the Backstretch, where he was to supposed to meet Victor at three-thirty. As he crossed Broadway it began to rain. Only the left-hand wiper seemed to work and it didn't wipe so much as bat fretfully at the raindrops. Charlie parked next to the Backstretch, then got soaked as he ran to the door.

Besides Doris, there were four people in the bar and again Charlie sensed that they looked at him with suspicion and dislike. Although he was used to the disapproval of his cousins' friends, the dislike of people whom he had considered good acquaintances was unpleasant and made him feel lonely.

"Want a beer?" asked Doris. She smiled and when Charlie reached out his hand, she took it and pressed it. She wore a red blouse and a string of yellow beads. Charlie was struck by the whiteness of her teeth. They made his own damaged molar begin to ache. Taking a couple of napkins from the container on the bar, he wiped the rain from his face and hair.

"No, let me have a cup of coffee. Has Victor been in?"

"I haven't seen him."

"Will you have dinner with me Saturday night?" asked Charlie.

When Doris smiled, the top part of her cheeks bunched up in a way that reminded Charlie of half a plum or peach. It was a physical characteristic that he had admired in his favorite actresses of the 1940s.

"Sure, I'd be glad to go to dinner."

"Maybe we'll drive down to Albany. I don't seem too popular around here."

Doris put a mug of coffee on the bar in front of Charlie. "That's true enough," she said. "I just heard about that other man this morning. Did he really commit suicide?"

"I think he was murdered," said Charlie. "You know, when McClatchy showed up at my house he said he had hitchhiked, but it seemed unlikely that he could catch a ride along the lake on a Sunday night. Also, I never heard a car. It seems possible that he went to Pease's house first and then Pease drove him to my place. Maybe he meant to stay with Pease and Pease refused. I don't know, but Pease clearly knew something about McClatchy that no one else did and I'll bet he knew what McClatchy intended to do in Saratoga."

"And what was that?" asked Doris.

But before Charlie could reply, Victor hurried into the Backstretch. His brown sport coat was dripping wet and his hair was plastered down over his forehead. Glancing at the other men in the bar, he wiped the rain from his face with his hand, then gave Charlie a military salute.

"Well, there he is," said Victor, "Saratoga's own pariah and black sheep, Mr. Charlie Fucked-Up Bradshaw himself. Take a bow, Mr. Bradshaw, and say hello to the folks."

"Lay off, Victor."

"Vic. 'Lo, Doris, aren't you afraid of blowing your reputation being seen with this guy? Jesus, Charlie, everywhere I go I hear a bunch of assholes saying what a bad hat you are. Wasn't your fuckin' fault that the old man's house blew up."

Charlie saw that Victor had a large purple bruise under his left eye. "What happened to your face?" he asked.

"Someone punched me. Can you believe it? Laid his whole fuckin' fist on the sacred flesh."

"Why'd he punch you?" It occurred to Charlie that he himself had been the reason. Perhaps someone had insulted him and Victor had protested. Charlie prepared himself to be deeply touched.

"He caught me lookin' through his desk," said Victor.

Charlie stopped feeling touched. "You're lucky he didn't call a cop," he said.

Victor shoved his thumbs through his belt loops and gave his pants an upward tug. "He told me to wait in his office. Is it my fault I can't be trusted? It was that lawyer. Leakey. I offered five hundred dollars for those letters and he turned me down. Hell, for five hundred dollars I was tempted to write them myself. Anyway, he went out for a second, so I took a gander at his desk. Nothin' there but some pencils and a pistola. Guess I'm lucky he didn't shoot me. By the way, some guy by the name of Maximum

Tubbs called you. Says you should call him at the Turf Bar. You sure got queer friends."

Charlie called Maximum Tubbs from the pay phone at the back of the bar just where the smell of stale beer met the smell of soy sauce from the Chinese restaurant. As Charlie waited for Tubbs to come to the phone, he could just make out the scratchy voice of Al Jolson singing, "How I love ya, how I love ya."

"Say, Charlie, I found out about those nags. Neither was worth a cheap cigar, if you ask me. The mare, Indian Maid, wasn't so bad but Buckdancer was a real loser. Not a drop of blood in him. Can't see why anyone would want to use him for stud. As a teaser, sure, but not for stud."

A teaser was a stallion used to excite the mare to see if she was ready to breed.

"Hell," said Tubbs, "I'm surprised that Sweet Dreams could find his way around the track. Half-dog, that's what he looks like to me."

Chapter
Seven

The driver's seat on the milk truck—actually it was a sort of perch—had a broken spring and whenever Charlie hit a particularly bad bump, the spring would jab him. Saturday morning, Charlie hit a lot of bad bumps.

The previous night he had again talked to John Wanamaker, who said there was nothing new to report except that his mother's endurance was making a kind of medical history. Charlie said he was glad to hear it, that maybe she would get better. Wanamaker said no, she was already nine-tenths dead. All that was left, he said, was that bright spark of intelligence that makes the difference between human beings and animals.

"So when will you be coming back, John?" Charlie had asked.

"As soon as I can, Charlie. You know, this afternoon, I was sitting by my mother's bedside listening to her faint breathing and I thought, It would be so simple, all I would have to do would be to cover her face with a pillow and my mother would sleep in peace."

Charlie was shocked. "Don't do anything rash, John."

"I'm glad you understand, Charlie."

As he drove back to the barn, Charlie asked himself what had been his criteria for ever hiring John Wanamaker as a guard at Lorelei Stables. He had hired him solely because an earlier Wanamaker had once been owner of the Grand Union Hotel, the largest of Saratoga's grand hotels, which had rooms for 1,500 guests, over a mile of broad piazzas, and had its own church and opera house on the grounds. Charlie's mother once worked there as a maid.

John Wanamaker was not related to his famous predecessor, nor had he heard of him. Wanamaker himself was an ex-burglar and alcoholic who had become a born-again Christian in prison and was subsequently paroled into Charlie's care. Although in the beginning he had always carried his Bible on his rounds as a stable guard, he soon gave it up, becoming a lapsed-again Christian. Charlie imagined Wanamaker's mother living on year after year, as articles about her were published in popular-science magazines and Wanamaker himself appeared as a featured guest on the nightly talk shows: the man with the immortal mother.

By eleven o'clock Charlie had returned the milk truck to the barn and a half hour later he was ready to drive back to Saratoga, where he hoped to go swimming. He still had the yellow Volkswagen, much to Victor's dislike. The man responsible for fixing the windshield of the Renault had come down with the flu. Come hell or high water, Charlie had been told, he would have the Renault Monday afternoon, exactly at the time he was supposed to see the dentist in Glens Falls.

Charlie's tooth had settled down to a dull ache. As he took the back road out of Schuylerville, he told himself that what he disliked most was his inability to keep his tongue out of the hole. He constantly fiddled with it. His dentist was an old resident of Glens Falls and, besides fixing his tooth, Charlie hoped he could tell him whether Flo Abernathy was related to the wealthy Glens Falls family of the same name.

Charlie had spent much of Friday taking care of Pease's funeral, which had required a dozen trips between the funeral home and Miss Abernathy's turret room on Ludlow. Miss Abernathy had wanted everything just right and as Charlie drove back and forth he decided she must have a little money. Although the final funeral arrangements were modest, the bill had come to nearly five thousand dollars. The funeral itself would be Tuesday morning, out of the Episcopal Church, and as far as Charlie could figure, he and Flo Abernathy would be the only mourners.

Charlie had also spent some time on Friday learning about Willis Stitt. He discovered that Stitt had moved to Hoosick Falls eight years ago from Long Island, where he had worked as an assistant trainer. It seemed that in 1972 Stitt's wife had died in a car crash and he had become the beneficiary of her small inheritance. He had used the money to open the stable, but although he had had several winning horses, he appeared to be losing money and had probably gone through most of his wife's estate.

Stitt appeared to have few friends, rarely came to Saratoga and hadn't remarried. He also bred horses in a small way and the most interesting fact Charlie had learned was that Stitt was using Sweet Dreams for stud. Given Sweet Dreams's lineage, it seemed unlikely that the foals were worth much.

Charlie parked in front of the Y, checked his wallet and watch at the desk, then went into the locker room. Several men glanced at him but no one spoke. Quickly, he changed into his suit, then showered and went into the pool area. There was no sign of George Marotta and Charlie wondered if he had given up swimming for good. Eddie Gillespie was still watching Marotta's house and had seen Marotta walking from room to room. He left his house only to go to the restaurant, and then only late at night. Charlie assumed that Marotta's actions were governed by fear, but of what he couldn't determine. Certainly it was something more than the disapproving looks of his fellow swimmers.

Charlie smeared saliva into his goggles, then dove into the medium lane. Kicking his way back to the surface, he began to swim almost automatically, following the black line from one end of the pool to the other. As he swam, he thought about Willis Stitt. It occurred to Charlie that since McClatchy had been granted immunity by the grand jury, he had been in a perfect position to commit blackmail. If he had really held back Sweet Dreams, he could confess that fact without fear of prosecution. How simple then to come to Saratoga, contact Stitt and demand money. Charlie had read in the paper that McClatchy was receiving eight hundred dollars a month from the Federal Witness Program. McClatchy had expensive tastes and Charlie doubted that eight hundred dollars would go far.

The problem was that Stitt didn't seem like a murderer. Even if he had engaged in pulling Sweet Dreams, the criminal charges were rather trifling. He might be finished as a trainer but given his lack of success such a reversal might be all for the best. Furthermore, even though Stitt had known that McClatchy was staying with Charlie, it hadn't been McClatchy's name that made him nervous, but Sweet Dreams's.

Charlie continued to slog through the water, trying to kick his feet hard enough to keep his legs at the surface. Every so often a faster swimmer passed him and briefly the water filled with turquoise bubbles. When he had finished his seventy-two lengths, Charlie rested a minute, then climbed out of the pool, feeling clean and virtuous.

He showered, then in the locker room he tried to start up a conversation about the World Series with a fellow who was assistant coach of a local Little League team. The man appeared not to hear him. His name was Raymond Sharp and each year he tried to get the kids to call him Razor Sharp.

"What do you think about Philadelphia?" Charlie asked.

Raymond Sharp stood at the mirror tying his tie, which was blue with the initials RS repeated over and over in an overlapping pattern. The three other men in the locker room tried not to look at them. Forget it, said Charlie to himself, just forget it.

That Saturday afternoon Charlie staked out a house for Victor, who was trying to locate a sixteen-year-old runaway expected to visit her boyfriend. It was the sort of work Charlie was worst at and after two hours of fiddling with his bad tooth and musing about the whereabouts of McClatchy's head, he fell asleep. An old car accelerating down the street woke him at five o'clock. His neck was stiff and he had a stomachache. The house—a cheap, two-story house covered with brown shingles—looked deserted, although Charlie knew that in the time he had been asleep several elephants could have tripped in and out. Instead of being upset, he found himself wondering why Willis Stitt was using Sweet Dreams for stud.

Charlie started the Volkswagen and drove back to the office. That evening he would take Doris out to dinner. They would drive down to Albany, maybe even see a movie. He would be constantly aware of her presence, would keep touching her, holding her coat, touching her arm or hand. He would forget about Rodger Pease and his funeral, the milk truck, the imminent arrival of his mother, his bad tooth and McClatchy's missing head. The sky had grown dark and it began to rain. With every leaf that swirled down from a tree, Charlie felt a wrench. He parked on Phila and hurried up to the third floor.

Victor was sitting with his feet on the desk. "Did she show up?" he asked.

"I didn't see her."

"You look like you been asleep. Your eyes are all baggy." Victor leaned forward and stared at Charlie.

"That's true," said Charlie. "I fell asleep."

"Hey, look," said Victor, "I'm the last guy to complain. Forty winks is forty winks."

"It was half the afternoon," said Charlie. "I'm sorry."

Victor linked his hands behind his head, leaned back in the swivel chair and raised his eyebrows. "As long as her old man didn't see you, what's the diff? But I should say, Charlie, that old eagle-eye Gillespie never but never falls asleep. He might smoke a little reefer or take a nip now and then but he's always wide-eyed. By the way, you better keep your coat on. Some guy wants to see you."

"Who?" asked Charlie.

"Some guy named Willis Stitt. He's over at the Roosevelt Baths. Room 14. He said he'd be there until about five thirty. I was going to come over and get you if you didn't show up. Good thing I didn't catch you napping."

"Why does he want to meet there?" asked Charlie, half to himself.

"That he didn't divulge," said Victor. "Maybe he wants to keep it quiet or maybe he's a regular. You know, soaking in that funny water and having some ex-wrestler beat up his decrepit flesh. Is he mixed up with this McClatchy business?"

"McClatchy rode for him." Charlie stood by the desk, feeling undecided about what he should do.

"I don't want to tell you your business, Charlie, but don't go riling up Peterson again, will you? He could make it hard for us to keep working."

"Did Stitt say what he wanted?"

"Nah, hardly said anything at all. Just that it was important. What's his voice sound like anyway?"

Charlie had put his blue jacket back on and was zipping it up. "I don't know, a regular voice, neither high or low, no discernible accent. Why?"

"The guy's voice on the phone was sort of low and muffled, like he was talking through a damp rag."

"Are you telling me he was trying to disguise his voice?" asked Charlie.

Victor took a dirty red handkerchief from his back pocket, blew into it and speculatively eyed the results. "I wouldn't go so far as to say that," he said, "but if he *was* trying to disguise his voice, that's how it would sound. What do I know, maybe he was just scared."

Charlie stood for a moment, then went to a small safe in the corner, knelt down, spun the dial several times and opened the door. The safe was empty except for a snub-nosed .38 revolver. Charlie took the revolver and stuck it in his belt.

"Want me to come along?" asked Victor.

"No, I don't think there'll be any trouble."

"Just packing the pistola to feel like a big guy, right?"

Charlie didn't answer.

It was raining even harder when he hurried across Phila to the yellow Volkswagen. Accelerating up Putnam, he circled around the block to Broadway. The street lights were all coming on, even though it was only five fifteen.

The Roosevelt was the last of the baths that remained open year round. Two others had closed down permanently and the Lincoln Baths were only open in the summer. For nearly two hundred years the springs had been the main reason that people came to Saratoga, but now they were mostly an oddity. The baths were run by the state and Charlie guessed that they operated at a loss.

Charlie drove up Broadway to the Avenue of Pines. The wind had blown a few small branches across the road and the Volkswagen bumped across them. In the glare of his headlights, the trees looked shiny and new. Charlie drove around by the theater and tennis courts. The park with its semi-Georgian buildings was deserted. Charlie drew up in front of one of the four Greek columns supporting the portico of the baths. Built in the 1930s, the Roosevelt baths occupied a U-shaped, red brick building with a gray slate roof. Each wing had about twenty rooms where a visitor could bathe in a tub of carbonated water heated exactly to body temperature, receive a massage, then doze while wrapped in warm sheets on a narrow cot. Charlie had gone once. It made him feel tubercular.

Charlie passed through the tall glass doors to the lobby. A young woman in a glass reception booth glanced up, yawned, then went back to her book. He turned right past her desk to the men's wing, then turned left down the long green hall, which was partly blocked by large laundry hampers overflowing with white towels. The air felt damp. A fat man wearing white trousers and a white T-shirt sat on a bench fanning his face with a copy of *Racing Form*. He belched faintly as Charlie passed. Some doors were open and Charlie saw white-haired men lying on metal cots. Through one door he saw a naked one-legged man lying on a massage table. The stump of the man's leg pointed toward the door like a cannon. A faint humming noise came from the phosphorescent lights. They made the air itself seem green, as if the hall were under water. At the far end of the hall was another door that led out across the lawn to the performing-arts center. The door was open and through it Charlie could see the dim shapes of trees blowing in the wind.

The doors along the hall were numbered and Room 14 was on the left near the back. Charlie knocked but there was no answer. He waited a moment. From another room someone began whistling *The Streets of Laredo*. Charlie tried the knob and the door opened.

The room was about ten feet by ten feet with white tiles going halfway up the wall, then peach-colored paint after that. Along the left wall was a low white bathtub filled with what looked like seltzer water. Against the wall opposite the door was a hospital cot with a rumpled gray blanket, as if someone had just been sitting on it. Above the cot was a window looking out onto the darkened and rain-soaked lawn. It was slightly open. The room was lit by a single light set into the ceiling. On a coat tree in the corner hung a man's leather jacket.

The room was empty. Charlie glanced around, shutting the door behind him. It was very quiet and his rubber-soled shoes made a squeaking noise on the tiles. Some water and wet towels on the floor showed that the tub had been recently used. Past the tub was another door. Charlie walked over and opened it.

It was a bathroom. Willis Stitt sat on the floor, leaning back against the toilet. His black hair hung in damp strands across his forehead. Hearing the door, he slowly looked up. His cowboy shirt was unbuttoned and there were two red holes in his chest. Blood was seeping from both in a pair of upside-down Ys. A revolver lay on the floor next to his leg.

Stitt tried to focus on Charlie. His mouth was open and a little blood trickled over his lip and into his goatee. He appeared to be listening to something far away. Slowly he raised his right arm, propping his elbow in his lap so that the forearm stood straight up and his fingers pointed to the ceiling. He relaxed his wrist and his hand fell to the left. Once more he raised his hand, pointing his fingers at the ceiling, then again he let it fall to the left. He did it a third time. It was as if he were waving. Charlie stared at his face but there was only that listening expression and a look of surprise. Stitt began lifting his hand a fourth time.

Suddenly Charlie leaped sideways, pulling his revolver from

his belt. An instant later the room seemed to explode behind him and Charlie felt a hot tug at his left arm. Falling to his knees, he twisted and fired twice at the open window. One of the ricochets whined around the room. Charlie reached up and flicked out the light. The room smelled of gunpowder. Holding his revolver with both hands, he kept it pointed toward the window as he got to his feet. The window formed a gray rectangle in the darkness. Charlie moved toward it until he could see trees and the women's wing across the lawn. Poking his gun through the torn screen, Charlie looked out. At first he saw nothing. Then he saw someone in a light-colored raincoat running across the grass toward the performing-arts center.

Shoving the gun back in his belt, Charlie ran to the door. His arm was beginning to hurt but he ignored it. He yanked open the door and ran out into the hall. Half-sliding on the tiles, he turned toward the door at the end of the hall leading out to the lawn. He guessed that the person was running toward the parking lot at the performing-arts center and he thought he had half a chance to catch him.

At that moment, something hit him from behind, sending him flying to the floor and crashing into a hamper of towels. There was the smell of sweat and the soft feel of damp flesh. Before Charlie could think what to do, his good arm was wrenched behind him into a hammerlock. He wanted to tell whoever it was to stop. Then the person grabbed a fistful of his hair and began pounding his forehead against the floor. The last thing he remembered was the way his teeth banged together each time his head smacked the tiles.

The bars of the Saratoga jail were painted medium green and the cots were covered with brown blankets. As Charlie sat on the edge of a cot three hours later, he tried to calculate how many people he had put into these cells. Maybe a thousand, maybe more. He had never expected to be here himself. On the wall above the toilet, someone had written, "What train's going to come to carry me across so wide a town?"

Stitt was dead and Charlie was accused of his murder. Of the person in the raincoat, there was no sign. Charlie kept trying to tell various policemen about him, but his words were met with skepticism and silence. Although Charlie felt generally unhappy, his major distress had come from being unable to pick up Doris Bailes at seven o'clock.

He had yet to see Peterson and had been booked by his old friend Emmett Van Brunt, who had refused to speak except to ask his name, address and occupation. When Charlie said he was a private detective, Emmett had made a sort of choking noise, which Charlie realized was meant to be laughter. He even had to give Emmett his belt and shoe laces, and it was only grudgingly that Emmett had let him keep the new sling that supported his left arm.

Charlie had first been taken in handcuffs from the Roosevelt Baths to the hospital where his arm had been bandaged. The bullet wound in the fleshy part of his upper arm was a clean hole and would heal in a couple of weeks. It hardly even hurt. What hurt was his forehead where the fat masseur had hammered it against the floor. The bruise was covered with a thick pink piece of adhesive and Charlie kept picking at it. The bandage felt as large as pillow and there was a loud ringing in Charlie's ears.

Around nine o'clock, Emmett returned to take Charlie upstairs. His black horn-rim glasses had slipped down his nose, making him appear professional. "The chief wants to see you," he said. He unlocked the cell door, then stood back as if expecting Charlie to jump at him.

Charlie remained seated on the edge of the cot. "I want to make a phone call," he said.

"You can make it after you see the chief."

"Emmett, I get to make it right now."

"You calling a lawyer?"

"What's it to you?"

Emmett led him to a small office and pointed to the phone. "No more than two minutes," he said.

Doris answered right away and when Charlie said hello she

made a growling noise. "Where are you?" she asked. "I've already chewed off my lipstick twice."

"In jail. Peterson thinks I killed someone."

"Did you?"

"Of course not."

"So we'll have dinner some other night?"

"I hope so. By the way, could you call Victor and tell him that if he doesn't hear from me tonight, then he should have a lawyer over here the first thing Monday morning."

"You mean you'll be there all weekend?"

"Possibly. If I'm charged, they won't set bail until Monday."

"What about the milk?"

Charlie had forgotten about the milk. He found himself imagining a giant milk bottle about ten stories tall. "Tell Victor that if he doesn't hear from me tonight, then he should call the dairy tomorrow." Charlie was sure it would mean the loss of that job, which meant Wanamaker would be fired.

"Anything else?"

"No, I guess not." Charlie could just make out the sound of her breathing. It was a steady, comforting noise. He wanted to tell her how much he regretted missing their dinner but Emmett Van Brunt was standing about two feet away and looking at his watch.

"I'm sorry about tonight, Charlie. I was looking forward to it."

"So was I," said Charlie. "I can't tell you how much."

After Charlie hung up the phone, Van Brunt led him upstairs to Peterson's office. Actually, he walked several feet behind him and kept his hand on his revolver. Charlie wanted to tell him that he was behaving foolishly, that they had known each other for years. But he knew it would do no good. He had the fleeting sense that perhaps he was wrong after all, perhaps he really *was* a criminal or at least a sort of social failure. Then he decided there was no future in that kind of thinking. Even if he was as bad as people thought, he still had to stick by himself.

When Charlie entered Peterson's office, he found the police

chief staring at him from behind his desk. His bushy eyebrows looked bushier than ever. Peterson shook his head. "Looks bad, Charlie, really looks bad."

"I didn't shoot him, if that's what you think." Charlie was amazed that he was actually being accused of murder.

"Now, Charlie, let's not get off on the wrong track. This isn't an interrogation. Stitt was a friend of McClatchy's. So maybe he thought you were responsible for his buddy getting killed. All right, so he decides to get even. He gets you over to the baths and draws a gun. Too bad for Stitt you got a gun yourself, right? Hey, Charlie, who's going to blame you? Someone sticks a rod in your face and you blast him. Let's call it second degree."

Charlie sat down in the straight chair in front of Peterson's desk. On the edge of the red blotter was a rosewood box with the profile of an Irish setter carved on the lid. The box contained cigars. Charlie took out a cigar and sniffed it. His head hurt and the ringing in his ears seemed worse. He returned the cigar to the box. "Where's Caldwell?" he asked.

"Somewhere downstate. I been trying to reach him on the phone."

"You doing ballistics tests?" asked Charlie.

Peterson stood up and shoved his hands into the side pockets of his suit coat. "It's all part of the routine," he said.

"Stitt was shot by somebody standing outside the window," said Charlie. "Did you look for footprints? The ground was pretty wet. There's bound to be some."

"I haven't got a full report yet."

"No? Then send me back downstairs until you do. Either that or let me go home."

"I can't send you home, Charlie, this is serious."

"Then put me back in a cell so I don't have to listen to you."

Peterson leaned above Charlie like a great blue tree. Charlie guessed he was meant to feel intimidated. But he had known Peterson too long for that. Instead, he straightened the sling supporting his left arm. It would probably make driving the milk truck even more difficult.

"Hey, Emmett," Peterson shouted, "put Bradshaw back in his cell."

"You got a magazine or something I can read?" asked Charlie.

"What do you think this is," said Peterson, "a lending library?"

As Charlie was led back downstairs, he passed several cells occupied by drunks and petty thieves. Charlie knew four of them and they greeted him warmly. "That's Charlie Bradshaw," said one drunk, "he's as good as gold."

Once in his cell, Charlie asked himself what would have happened if he hadn't taken his .38 to the Roosevelt Baths. Presumably the person at the window would have shot him, then tossed the gun inside. There already had been a revolver next to Stitt and the presence of the two corpses and two guns would make it appear that Charlie and Stitt had shot each other. Of course, fingerprint and paraffin tests would show that neither man had fired a gun but perhaps Peterson wouldn't have bothered with the tests. Charlie, however, doubted that. Peterson sometimes might be mistaken but he wasn't a total incompetent. Charlie asked himself if he believed that one hundred percent. Not quite, he decided. It depended how eager Peterson was to solve the crime.

Then Charlie wondered what his cousins would say when they learned he was in jail. He was sure they wouldn't be surprised. It was as if they already knew there was a jail cell in his future and the only question was precisely when it would appear. He could hear his cousins saying how he had been offered the path of virtue and had turned it down.

Charlie gingerly touched the bandage on his forehead. He tried to forget his difficulties and soon found himself thinking about Butch Cassidy, one of the leaders of the Wild Bunch, who at one time had tried to set aside the fast life and seek a pardon from the Governor of Utah. He had grown tired of being chased all over simply for robbing a few trains. He wanted to settle down. It seemed to Charlie that he understood just how Cassidy felt. Cassidy had even agreed to take a job as express guard on the Union Pacific in order to scare off those same outlaws who had been his partners a few weeks before. Unfortunately, the plan fell through when Cassidy, in need of spending money, robbed the train in Tipton, Wyoming. Once more Cassidy was hounded all over the West. In search of a little peace and quiet, he hid out for three months in Fanny Porter's Sporting House in San Antonio, Texas, where the only violence he engaged in came from learning how to ride a bicycle. But then he became the greatest cyclist in San Antonio and the whores leaned from their windows and cheered when Butch Cassidy rode by waving his derby hat.

Shortly after eleven p.m., Charlie was taken back upstairs to see Peterson. He had been asleep and would have preferred to stay asleep.

Peterson stood next to his trophy case with one hand resting on the marble statue of a dog. "Charlie," he asked, "what made you so interested in Stitt in the first place?"

Charlie remained by the doorway. "You get the test results?"

"Ballistics show your gun didn't kill Stitt. It was the other gun, but there were no prints on it. We also found footprints, and a masseuse in the women's wing says she noticed a man out on the lawn, although it was pretty dark and she couldn't give much of a description, just that he was wearing a tan raincoat."

"So that means I can go?"

"Tell me what made you interested in Stitt?"

But Charlie was tired of being helpful. "Maybe I wanted to sell him some milk," he said.

Peterson cleared his throat and looked disappointed. Then he carefully put the statue of the dog back in the trophy case and locked the door. "This is no joking matter, Charlie. Whoever killed McClatchy and cut off his head has been sending out photographs. I mean, photographs of the head by itself, just sitting on a table. The Jockey Guild got one, so did the *New York Post* and the federal prosecutor in Brooklyn."

"Is that what Caldwell's dealing with?"

"I talked to him half an hour ago. He said the pictures were mailed from the City. You shouldn't be so hard on him, Charlie. It's not as if he was just some FBI agent up from Albany. He was in charge of McClatchy. That was his big case. Caldwell thinks I should keep you for the weekend, but I don't know. I mean, you're clearly meddling, but I've got no real grounds. You know that two Mercedes were stolen last night, two big fuckin' Mercedes? You got to stop fiddling with this case, Charlie. I know you were upset about McClatchy. Maybe you didn't say anything to Marotta, I don't know. Caldwell swears you did. I bet I been on the phone to your cousin James half a dozen times. You got two choices, Charlie, either you drop the whole thing and Caldwell lets you go, or you keep messing around and Caldwell puts an interference charge on you."

Peterson stood behind his desk, leaning forward with his hands on the blotter. Charlie felt almost sorry for him. Then he remembered how Stitt, dying on the bathroom floor, had tried to warn him. And there was also Rodger Pease, who had come looking for him and whom Charlie hadn't found in time.

"I appreciate your concern," said Charlie, "and if I was just working to clear my own name, then maybe I'd forget it, but I've got a client."

Peterson eyed him suspiciously. "Who is it?"

"I'm not at liberty to say, but I'll talk to the client and if the client gives me permission, then I'll tell you."

"I think you're lying," said Peterson.

Chapter Eight

"*By a string, Charlie,* my poor mother's hanging by a string. You expect me to desert her, to leave her in some strange hospital surrounded by people who don't care if she lives or dies?"

"No, John," said Charlie, "I was simply wondering if you had any better idea when you might be coming back to Saratoga." It was ten o'clock Sunday morning and Charlie's sole pleasure came from knowing he had waked Wanamaker up.

"I told you, Charlie, I'll come back as soon as I can. The doctors say they never seen anything like it. I know you want her dead but it's really a miracle, a God-given miracle."

"I don't want her dead, John, I only want to know how much longer I've got to deliver milk."

"That's up to the Lord, Charlie. But just believe me when I say I'll be back as soon as I can."

Ten minutes later Charlie was driving the yellow Volkswagen over to Ballston Spa to see Eddie Gillespie, the ex-car thief and stable guard who had been following Marotta. It was difficult to drive with his left arm in a sling and he kept having to steer with his knees. Charlie told himself he truly didn't want Wanamaker's mother to die. If she recovered, he would be delighted, but he had taken the milk route for four days and here it was already four weeks.

The morning was so bright and sunlit that it appeared to have been specially polished by the previous day's rain. Charlie estimated that the colors were at their peak—the maples had turned a startling red, the birches were a dozen shades of orange. The entire Hudson River valley between the Green Mountains and the Adirondacks seemed to flicker with color. As for Charlie, his appreciation was tempered by his injuries and preoccupations. Tilting the rearview mirror to the left, he again inspected the bandage on his forehead. The intense pink of the previous evening was slightly soiled and spotted with drops from the grapefruit he had eaten for breakfast. The bandage, he thought, occupied his forehead in the way an oven door occupies the front of a stove. As for his preoccupations, two truths had become obvious: one, he had fully committed himself to the investigation; two, he appeared to be losing. That, however, would have to change, which was why he wanted to see Eddie Gillespie.

Ballston Spa was a small town about six miles to the southwest, which had once attempted to compete with Saratoga as a place of pleasure. But although Ballston Spa was nice enough, it had failed as a fashionable resort. Charlie tended to think of it as the town that had lost, which made it, he felt, a suitable home for Eddie Gillespie, another loser.

It wasn't that Eddie Gillespie was bad. Charlie could point to no one who was kinder or more generous. The problem was that Eddie Gillespie seemed unable to resist temptation, and since the age of fifteen his prime temptation had been driving stolen cars at speeds in excess of 120 miles per hour.

Recently, however, Eddie had been able to balance his desire to race stolen cars against his disinclination to go to jail. As a result, he had turned his attention to milder temptations: girls, alcohol, drugs and sleeping late in the morning. It was to that last temptation that Eddie Gillespie was submitting himself when Charlie found him at his mother's house at eleven o'clock Sunday morning.

Eddie was twenty-five, had tousled black hair and appeared to be naked under the covering of a none too clean white sheet.

Charlie sat on a chair covered with a substantial mound of Eddie's clothes—mostly T-shirts advertising rock-and-roll bands. On the wall above his bed was a poster from a Rolling Stones concert, showing a red mouth and a long protruding tongue.

"I guess you caught me at a bad moment, Charlie. What happened to your forehead?"

Eddie sat up in bed and pulled the sheet up to his middle. He took a Lucky Strike from the pack on the bedside table and lit it. Some sparks fell onto the sheet and he patted them out. He had a round, open face with a wide nose and a constant wondering expression.

"I ran into a door. Are you still following Marotta?"

"Finished last night. Vic said we'd used up all the money." Eddie's chest was covered with curly black hair. He began scratching it. From downstairs came the sound of a vacuum cleaner.

"I want you to keep following him for a while. You don't have to do it all the time. Just make sure he knows you're there."

"Did his old lady cough up some more dough?"

"You'll be paid okay."

"He still hasn't left the house except to go to his restaurant."

"Doesn't matter."

Eddie blew a series of smoke rings toward the ceiling. "That's fine by me, Charlie. It's just the kinda work I like, sittin' in a car listenin' to the radio. Like I'm your friendly and dependable private eye."

"There's some other work I'd like you to do for me as well," said Charlie, "which is a little more complicated."

"Is it dangerous?" asked Eddie.

"Not really. Have you ever delivered milk?"

"Milk?"

"That white stuff that comes in bottles that you put on your cereal each morning."

"I don't eat cereal. What's it got to do with milk?"

"Let me tell you more about it," said Charlie.

It had taken a great deal of persuading before Eddie Gillespie had agreed to deliver Wanamaker's milk. Charlie had had to suggest it was a special undercover job for the detective agency. Beyond that he had been forced to offer Eddie six dollars an hour, which was two dollars an hour more than Charlie was making himself. However, it would be worth the extra twelve dollars a day not to get up at four thirty in the morning. He gave Eddie a map of his route and various warnings about dogs and bad bumps, and after Eddie had sworn to do his best, Charlie left, thinking it might be a perfect match. After all, Eddie liked driving around in vehicles that didn't belong to him.

From Ballston Spa, Charlie drove over to Doris's apartment in Saratoga Springs. She lived on the third floor of a yellow Victorian mansion on Circular Street. She wasn't home. Charlie imagined that she had gone out with another man the previous evening and had been seduced. Maybe she had fallen in love, maybe she was already engaged. From Doris's, he drove over to Ludlow to see Flo Abernathy.

As Charlie climbed out of the Volkswagen, he heard the sound of someone playing the clarinet. He paused for a moment on the sidewalk. The music was quiet, almost melancholic. The Sunday-afternoon street was very still, while the sunlight through the multicolored leaves made the air shimmer and dance. Charlie entered the rooming house and went upstairs. It turned out to be Miss Abernathy playing the clarinet. She sat in the turret with her back to Charlie, surrounded by flowering plants. She hadn't heard him knock and when he touched the door it had opened. The music, she told him later, was part of a clarinet sonata by Brahms. Miss Abernathy wore a black dress and the sunlight streamed over her shoulders. Charlie realized she was wearing mourning. He didn't find it strange that she was playing the clarinet but the music made him sad. He stood in the doorway as she sat perfectly straight in her chair and when she had finished, he said, "Excuse me."

She turned but didn't seem surprised. Perhaps she had heard him knock after all. She came over and shook his hand and again her superior height made him feel timid. Above her left breast she wore a cameo in a gold setting, showing a woman's profile.

"Would you like some coffee?" she asked.

"That'd be fine," said Charlie.

She left him to go over to the kitchenette, which was half-concealed behind another screen. Both this screen and the one by the brass bed were Oriental and had pictures of mountains, golden clouds and cranes flying. Up the side of one mountain wound a procession of men with triangular hats. At least fifteen small tables stood around the room and all were covered with various objects. On the table nearest Charlie was a ship in a bottle with tiny black cannons and gossamer rigging. Behind it were two glass snowstorms: one showed a polar bear on its hind legs, the other had a miniature Christ on the cross.

Flo Abernathy returned with the silver tray, silver cream pitcher and sugar bowl, coffee and a small plate of chocolate-chip cookies.

"Is this a social visit?" she asked.

"I'm afraid not. I need a favor."

"And what's that?" She poured him a cup of coffee.

"I need you to hire me as a private detective."

She paused, mildly surprised, then poured a cup of coffee for herself. "And why do I need a private detective?"

"To prove that Rodger Pease didn't commit suicide."

"But I already know he didn't commit suicide."

"Then to find out who killed him."

"I don't particularly care about that. He's already dead and the details surrounding that death can only be depressing."

Charlie sipped his coffee and burned his tongue. "I'm going about this in the wrong way. What I mean is that I've been trying to find out who killed McClatchy and Pease and a third man you don't even know about. Unfortunately, the police aren't happy that I'm doing it on my own. I have to have a client. Therefore, I'm asking you to hire me."

"Why not let the police take care of this business by themselves?" asked Miss Abernathy.

"Because they've got it all mixed up. They think that Rodger Pease killed himself and that McClatchy was killed by gangsters after I told them he was staying at my place. Partly I want to clear my own name. I mean, people will only be convinced I didn't betray McClatchy if I find out who actually killed him. Beyond that, I guess I just think it's untidy to have a bunch of unsolved murders."

Flo Abernathy glanced at the bandage on Charlie's forehead but didn't say anything. Then she glanced at his arm in its sling. She sipped her coffee and set the saucer on a table. "How much do you cost?" she asked.

"You can have my services for a five-dollar retainer."

"That doesn't seem like much."

"It'll do. All I need is a signed receipt."

"I think I can afford that," she said. "I've never hired a private detective before. And you promise to keep my name out of the papers?"

"I promise, but I might have to tell Chief Peterson if that's all right with you."

Twenty minutes later Charlie was driving out to Willis Stitt's stable in Hoosick Falls. He drove slowly, looking at the trees. Although the day was bright, it was also chilly and he kept his windows rolled up. Between the towns of Greenwich and Cambridge was a high ridge from which he could see panoramas to the east and west. Charlie pulled over to the side of the road. The yellow cornfields, cows in their green pastures, clusters of trees and the greater masses of woods with their leaves shading from green through all the gradations of yellow and orange, an occasional rise of smoke, red barns and white houses, winding roads and rolling hills—it occurred to Charlie that this had been his home for forty-six years. It seemed significant that it was fall, that the year was ending. In his ears he still heard the reedy sound of the clarinet as if the notes and swirls of the Brahms sonata were directing his attention across the landscape. Charlie thought of all the deaths—those of the season and those he kept stumbling upon. He asked himself if he truly expected to slow down the process of entropy. Perhaps only its unnatural forms. High to his left Charlie saw a ragged V of Canadian geese. They appeared to be flying north. His impulse was to urge them to correct themselves, to tidy up their pattern. Then he grinned at himself and started the Volkswagen.

Several cars were parked in front of Stitt's run-down Cape Cod when Charlie arrived. As he got out of the Volkswagen, two men walked up the driveway to meet him. One was the young man he had spoken to the other day. The other was older: a short, fat man wearing a Yankees baseball cap. As a Red Sox fan, Charlie felt an irrational wave of antipathy. From the circus tent, there again came the blare of a Strauss waltz played by a brass band. A black Saab was parked near the tent.

"What's on your mind?" asked the young man. He wore jeans, a brown sweat shirt and a jean jacket. On the front of the sweat shirt was a picture of a tyrannosaur.

"I wanted to ask some questions about your boss, Willis Stitt."

The fat man stuck his hands in his back pocket and stared up at Charlie. "We already spent a long time talking to the cops. Who are you?"

Charlie gave the man one of his cards. "I'd like to know who Stitt's friends were."

"We were his friends," said the fat man.

"Nah, Freddie," said his companion, "this is Charlie Bradshaw, he's the one who blew the whistle on McClatchy. Seems to me, Mr. Bradshaw, that if you'd stayed out of this, Willis would still be alive." In the corral a gray horse whinnied, then reared up and began pawing the air.

"I came here the other day to ask about McClatchy. I had nothing to do with his death, any death." Charlie wondered if either of these men could have been the figure outside the window at the Roosevelt Baths.

"Who're you working for?" asked the young man. He picked up a couple of pebbles from the driveway and began rattling them in his palm.

"A friend of Rodger Pease's."

"And who's that?"

"He got blown up in his house last week. Don't you remember him? He's the one who got paid to cash in the winning tickets on Sweet Dreams."

The young man stared at Charlie, then tossed the pebbles into the grass. "Like my friend said, we already told the cops all we know. You want to hear about it, then go to them. As far as I can see, you've been causing a lot of trouble. I didn't care two cents about McClatchy but if he was staying with you and you ratted on him, well, I don't like that. Then you came out here to see Willis and he got killed. I don't like that either. Now you're talking about some guy who got blown up in his house. Seems to me that you carry around a lot of bad luck. I don't like bad luck so why don't you get lost."

Charlie straightened the sling supporting his arm. It was light blue and he thought of how he would have to wear it for several weeks. "You mind if I talk to the person in the tent?" he asked.

"You mean Artemis? Why?"

"Maybe I like circus music."

"Look, buddy," said the fat man, "just beat it, okay?"

"I want to talk to Artemis," Charlie insisted. He had no idea who Artemis was. Presumably it was a woman's name and the worst she could do was to ask him to leave. On the other hand, maybe she could tell him a little about Stitt.

The young man glanced over at the tent, then looked back at Charlie. "Sure, talk to Artemis," he said. "You deserve each other. But when you're done, then get out. I don't want you hanging around."

Charlie walked toward the circus tent. Its precise green and white panels rippled in the wind. As he got closer, he heard the sound of horse's hooves galloping along in time to the music. Charlie passed through the opening of the tent, then immediately leaped out of the way as a huge, pinkish horse thundered by him.

Stumbling forward, he fell, then sat in the dirt and watched the horse continue its leisurely gallop around the tent. Standing on the horse's back was a small slender woman in a black leotard. She was staring at him. Her arms were folded, her feet were slightly apart and it seemed to Charlie she could have been standing on any street corner. She had what he thought of as finely chiseled features: a long, narrow nose; flat cheekbones; a high, clear brow. Her hair was the color of dark leather and fell in a wave across her forehead.

As the horse again bore down upon him, Charlie jumped to his feet and hurried into the center of the ring. The woman slowly bent over backward until both hands touched the horse's withers so that she was bent like a croquet hoop. Then she kicked up her feet and stood on her hands.

"You nearly bumped into Phillip," she said.

"Phillip?"

"This is Phillip." The woman patted the horse's rump, then somersaulted onto her feet again.

"Phillip nearly bumped into me," said Charlie. "Are you Artemis?" Charlie stood in the center of the ring, turning slowly in a circle, as the pink horse galloped around the tent. It was a big, thick, rectangular horse like a large loaf of bread with legs. Charlie considered how close Phillip had come to trampling him.

"Yes, I'm Artemis, although on the Continent I'm known as Lucette Bonchance. Have you come to book me?"

"Book?" asked Charlie, for whom the word meant to charge with a criminal offense.

"To offer me employment as an equestrienne."

"I don't think I need one," said Charlie.

Artemis did another somersault so that she was again balancing on her hands on the horse's back. "Regrettably, I hear that more and more often," she said.

Charlie wasn't sure what they were talking about. He decided to abandon that line of conversation and try another. "I'm here because I wanted to ask you some questions about Willis Stitt."

Artemis flipped herself over onto her feet and again crossed her arms. She was so slender that Charlie guessed he could count her ribs. She fixed her eyes on him, widening them slightly, then said, "Poor Willis never had this much attention when he was alive. It's a pity he couldn't be brought back for an hour to enjoy it. I'm sorry I can't offer you a place to sit. Perhaps you would like to sit up here with me."

"No, thanks," said Charlie. The tent was empty except for a large blue and red ball, half a dozen red Indian clubs and a small cassette recorder that was still playing the Strauss waltzes. "Did you know Stitt very well?" he asked.

"We had a brief affair some years ago but I grew bored with it. Willis had no sense of humor, no depth of character, and he snored. Therefore my contact with him became limited to my use of his stable, although occasionally we would go out to dinner. I'm only in the States two or three months each year. My actual home is in Vienna, although I also have a small house in Bennington. Too small for dear Phillip." As she talked, Artemis did a series of stationary cartwheels. The horse moved along as smoothly as a locomotive.

"The police were here to ask about Willis. Are you connected with them? I must say they were a trifle rude. The man in charge actually had the nerve to ask me to get down from my horse. I never get down from Phillip—well, hardly ever. When I'm in the States, we're inseparable. Poor Phillip has passed the age where he feels comfortable with circus life. The smell of the crowd upsets him. Whenever you pass through Vienna," said Artemis, "you must come and see me perform."

She kept widening her eyes and raising her eyebrows so that her face was constantly busy. It seemed to Charlie that he could almost see her think and it reminded him of a clear plastic model he had once seen of an internal combustion engine.

"I'd like to come to Vienna," he said, "but I'm not connected to the police. I'm a private detective."

"How romantic," said Artemis. "Is that where you received all your injuries?"

Charlie touched the pink bandage on his forehead. "I suppose so," he said.

"Are they a sign that you're winning or losing, or are you just very earnest?" As she had been talking, the waltz came to an end. Artemis gestured toward the cassette player. "Would you mind flipping that over? Phillip hates silence. My sense of private detectives derives strictly from low reading. Aren't you supposed to smoke a cigar?"

"They give me stomachaches," said Charlie as he turned over the cassette. "So you were still friends with Stitt?"

"After a fashion. I had come to regard Willis as a little brother: the sort of little brother that one loves and regrets, embarrassed to find him making mud pies. Poor Willis was always putting his hands in dirty places."

Charlie continued to turn slowly, following Phillip in his stately gallop around the ring. It made him dizzy. He found Artemis beautiful and compact, entirely without excess. Although he guessed that what she was doing was dangerous, his main impression was one of grace. Her features were sharp, almost strict, but she had a nice humanizing smile. Charlie imagined it charming the Viennese crowds. He expected that beneath her calm, she was something of a fanatic: the kind of person who in another life would have been a martyr or poet. He wondered if she ate and slept on Phillip's back. He imagined sandwiches and pizzas being delivered to the circus tent. Probably Artemis didn't eat pizzas. Probably she only ate croissants.

"Tell me more about Stitt," asked Charlie.

Artemis was standing on her hands again, then she arched her back and slowly raised her left arm so that she was balancing on just the right. "When they throw me roses," she said, "this is how I catch them." She lowered her legs, bending herself into another croquet hoop. "I was very fond of Willis but he was a man too easily satisfied with the second rate. He had no sense of personal dignity. You know how water seeks its lowest level? That's what Willis was like. He would often put on great airs, discuss art and literature, but basically he had no ideas that were not borrowed. His appeal was in a certain childlike quality. Often he reminded me of a boy about five."

"Could he fix races?"

"Do you mean cheat or repair?"

"Cheat."

"Certainly, if he could be sure not to be caught."

"Could he commit murder?"

"No, he had no passions or convictions. Essentially, there was nothing mean about him, nothing sadistic, and although he could be cruel, it was only out of selfishness or fear. Was he involved in a murder?" Artemis was now sitting cross-legged on Phillip's back with her elbows on her knees and her chin in her hands.

"I don't know," said Charlie. "He had employed a jockey by the name of Jimmy McClatchy and I think he paid McClatchy to hold back a horse. This McClatchy was murdered in my house about a week ago."

"I have always felt," said Artemis, "that if one hangs around with dubious types, then dubious things will happen to one. Do you think Willis killed this McClatchy? I can't believe he would."

"No, he didn't, but I think he knew who did and that's what got him killed. Another man was murdered as well, a ten-percenter by the name of Rodger Pease." Charlie went on to explain about McClatchy and the Brooklyn grand jury, what he had learned about Pease and Sweet Dreams, and how he had found Stitt dying in the Roosevelt Baths and had been shot at himself.

"You seem to have been having an exciting time," said Artemis. "The only one with whom I am personally acquainted is Sweet Dreams, who occupies the stall next to dear Phillip. A handsome horse but with little to say for himself."

"Is he lame?" asked Charlie.

"Not so one would notice."

"Do you know who Stitt's friends were?"

"Some. Occasionally Willis would take me to parties if I promised to behave. There was Ralph Conrad. I believe he was a businessman in New York. Then there was a doctor by the name of Jespersen, or perhaps he was a veterinarian. And Paul or Peter Reinhardt. He built houses. Let me see, there was a lawyer by the name of Leakey and another horse owner by the name of Perez."

Charlie wrote them down. The only name he recognized was Leakey but he wasn't sure where he had heard it. "Any others?" he asked.

"Yes, I expect there were quite a few. Willis trained horses for about half a dozen people and rented stable space to some others. He was a man who wanted to be liked. That seems such a simple desire, don't you think? Personally, I would rather be envied for something no one else could do."

Charlie thought about that for a moment. He wasn't sure he understood it. "Why does that young man outside dislike you?" he asked.

"He thinks it is my duty to go to bed with him, and I encouraged dear Phillip to run him down. Fortunately, the young man hopped out of the way. I've never cared for unmerited vanity. That was another of Willis's shortcomings. He believed that certain things were owed him simply because he was Willis Stitt."

They talked for a little longer about what Stitt did and who he knew, and at the end of it Charlie asked her to call him if she remembered any more names. He took out one of his cards and held it up for her as she rode by. Artemis did a backward flip, neatly picked the card from Charlie's fingers and tucked it down the front of her leotard.

As Charlie drove back to Saratoga, he thought that under different circumstances he could have easily developed a crush on Artemis. The results would have been disastrous. It would have been like a little pink pig becoming infatuated with a dove.

Chapter
Nine

"*I keep telling you,*" said Victor, "how do I know this joker was disguising his voice unless I know what his voice sounded like in the first place? Maybe he was born hoarse."

"You said he was disguising his voice," said Charlie.

"I said he might have been. Anyway, maybe it was Stitt who called after all. Maybe he wanted to talk to you in private, then got himself killed first. Who's to say?"

"But if it was someone disguising his voice," said Charlie as patiently as possible, "the reason would seem to be that he was afraid you might recognize his real voice, which would imply that person is a person you know or at least have talked to." Charlie leaned back in his chair and looked at Victor in what he hoped was a kindly manner. It was late Sunday afternoon. Charlie had returned from seeing Artemis half an hour before and had found Victor in the office. On top of the file cabinet was a stuffed parrot, which had not been there yesterday. Charlie was certain that Victor was waiting for him to ask where the parrot had come from but he refused to rise to the bait.

Victor locked his hands behind his head and eyed Charlie with displeasure. "For Pete's sake, Charlie, you don't have to talk to me like I was a moron. Either it was Stitt or somebody else. If it was somebody else, then that person might or might not have been disguising his voice. If he was disguising his voice, then either he was somebody I know and was afraid I'd recognize his real voice, or he was a lunatic. Personally, I think he was a lunatic but, hey, flip a coin and I'll go with the crowd."

"So it could have been Leakey since he's someone you've talked to before."

It had turned out that Roy Leakey, the lawyer named by Artemis, was the same lawyer whom Victor had been bothering about some old love letters and who had punched Victor for poking through his desk.

"If Leakey turns out to be the murderer," said Victor, "nobody will be happier than me. I'll even write to my Congressman and ask him to bring back the chair. But if it was Leakey who called, then I didn't recognize his voice."

"But if he was disguising it," suggested Charlie, "then how could you recognize it?"

Victor threw up his hands and slapped them down on the desk. "You got me. I've fallen prey to your spider logic once again. Okay, so it might have been Leakey, but I've also talked to Marotta. So maybe it was him that called."

"Fine," said Charlie, "but the point is you never talked to the others. You never talked to this Ralph Conrad or Reinhardt or Jespersen or Perez..."

"Hold it," said Victor.

"What?"

"I talked to Jespersen."

"How come?"

"He's Moshe's vet. Jesus, Charlie, don't you remember anything? Remember I said his old lady wanted me to get some dirt on him and I said I couldn't. I mean, a good vet is more important than a client."

"What did she want you to do?"

"We never got that far, but I think she wanted me to dig around and see how much money he has. I figured she suspected she was getting stiffed out of a little alimony. I sympathized but my hands were tied."

"Well," said Charlie, "I'll talk to Leakey, Marotta and Jespersen tomorrow. I've got a dentist's appointment in the afternoon but I might be able to see them first. After that we'll decide about those others. By the way, I talked to Eddie Gillespie this morning and told him to keep following Marotta."

"What for? We used up all his old lady's bread. Who's paying for it?"

"We will. There's a chance he had lunch with me in order to keep me away from my house, so if he's guilty, then maybe we can startle him into doing something drastic."

"No freebee tail jobs, Charlie. How we supposed to make an honest buck? Anyway, if he really killed three people, then it seems a little iffy to try and make him mad."

"Eddie won't be doing it for long." Charlie decided not to mention that he had hired Eddie Gillespie to deliver milk as well. He glanced again at the parrot on the file cabinet. It had blue and red feathers and looked as if something had been chewing on its tail. Maybe it was a cockatoo. He imagined asking Victor about it and then being hit with some punch line. Charlie disliked being the butt of Victor's practical jokes.

"I also have some good news," said Charlie. "We now have a client for the McClatchy stuff. She's a friend of Rodger Pease's and she's hired us to investigate his death. Put this in the safe, will you?" He handed Victor the check he had gotten from Flo Abernathy.

Victor looked at it. "Five fucking dollars. Is this what you call good news?"

"It might keep us out of jail."

"Hey, Charlie, if it comes to a showdown between working for five dollars or going to jail, I'd rather go to jail."

The next morning Charlie was roused at eight o'clock by a night letter from his mother. She was on a winning streak and wouldn't arrive until Wednesday. She asked if he knew anyplace in Saratoga where she could buy a roulette wheel. Charlie didn't. He thought of her cutting a swath through Atlantic City: a sixty-six-year-old lady with $40,000 looking for trouble. She sent Charlie her best and asked him to touch rabbit fur.

Charlie wandered into the bathroom and looked at himself in the mirror. The pink bandage was turning gray. Carefully, he peeled it off. Underneath, the skin was shiny red and developing a scab about two inches across. It looked like he had had a third eye which he had chosen to have surgically removed. He decided not to replace the bandage. Both his forehead and arm would keep him from swimming for at least two weeks. The arm had settled down to a dull ache and what Charlie minded most was the nuisance of the sling.

Charlie went into the kitchen and made himself some coffee and two pieces of toast with apricot jam. The previous evening he had taken Doris over to Skidmore College to see a double feature with Fred Astaire and Ginger Rogers. He had found the movies very restful. Nobody had been hurt. Nobody had died. During the 1940s, Charlie had seen a movie every week. Maybe five hundred movies and at least a quarter had been musical comedies. Even before wanting to be a third baseman, Charlie had wanted to be a tap dancer. Sometimes he still found himself in that musical-comedy world, as if his expectations about life had been shaped by Judy Garland, Gene Kelly and Ray Bolger. It meant believing that bills would be paid, that pretty girls would love you back, that the guns would be loaded with blanks.

Charlie took his toast and cup of coffee and walked out to the end of the dock that extended about ten feet into the lake. The water sloshed peacefully at the wooden pilings. Although cool, it was another sunny morning. A little mist rose off the water and obscured the far end of the lake near Kaydeross Park. Some mornings Charlie could see herons. He saw none today. The lake was ringed with trees at the height of color, but already a border of brown leaves littered the shore.

Charlie shivered and went back inside. He worried that Eddie Gillespie wouldn't make much of a milkman. Better get dressed and find Roy Leakey so that he wouldn't be wasting the morning.

His dentist's appointment was at three and would probably take the rest of the afternoon. Then, tomorrow morning at nine, was Rodger Pease's funeral.

His meager bank account worried him, and Charlie was afraid he would have to take a mortgage on the cottage. With any luck, the Pinkertons would offer him a job, but even as he thought it, Charlie hoped they wouldn't.

After the Pinkertons had blown up the house of Jesse James's mother in Clay County, Missouri, Jesse had gone to Chicago to get revenge. Later he said he had trailed Allen Pinkerton, head of the agency, for four months, intending to shoot him. Then he gave it up and went home.

"I wanted him to know who did it," Jesse said. "It wouldn't do me no good if I couldn't tell him about it before he died. I had a dozen chances to kill him when he didn't know it. I wanted to give him a fair chance but the opportunity never came."

Roy Leakey's law office was on the second floor of a building directly behind the Adirondack Trust and across from the post office. The walls of the waiting room were walnut paneled and hung with pictures of racehorses and ballet dancers. Charlie had plenty of time to study them in the forty-five minutes he waited. Even though Victor had described Leakey as "a mean son-of-a-bitch," all Charlie knew was that he was a lawyer who had some love letters sent to him by a woman who had hired Victor to get them back.

Shortly after ten, Leakey opened the door to the waiting room and stood glaring at Charlie. He was a slender, muscular man of about thirty-five with short dark hair and a dark, tanned face. He wore a rust-colored suit that looked expensive, and he had light gray eyes that Charlie thought of as cold. At least they were looking coldly at him at that particular moment.

Leakey cocked a finger and pointed it in Charlie's direction. "I want you to tell your bozo friend that if he doesn't stop bothering me, I'm going to get an injunction and slap his ass in jail. Is that clear?"

Charlie had been sitting in a chair by the window reading *Sports Illustrated*. Slowly, he got to his feet. "Do you mean Victor?" he asked.

"I mean that fat, frog-faced guy I caught rifling my desk."

Charlie glanced at the young secretary, who was reading a movie magazine. She didn't seem to notice her employer. Perhaps he was often like this.

"I'm not here on Victor's business," said Charlie. "I wanted to ask you some questions about Willis Stitt." He wondered again if Leakey could have been the figure outside the window at the Roosevelt Baths.

"Stitt?"

"Yes, I found him right after he'd been shot."

"You're *that* Charlie Bradshaw?"

Charlie wondered how many Charlie Bradshaws Leakey expected to find in Saratoga.

"You must be even more of a crook than your asshole friend," said Leakey.

The secretary continued to read her magazine. It seemed to Charlie that her refusal to look up was a commendable form of patience. He turned back to Leakey. "Have the police talked to you about Stitt?" he asked.

"No, why should they?"

"You knew him, he was a friend of yours. Now he's been murdered. Were you involved in any track business with Stitt? Looks like you like racehorses." Charlie nodded toward a photograph on the wall showing a horse and jockey in the winner's circle.

Leakey took a few steps into the waiting room and stood by the desk. His hands hung loosely at his sides as if he didn't know what to do with them. "Bradshaw, I don't want you here. If the police want to question me, that's fine, but you, you're nobody, nobody at all. And for your information, I wasn't a close friend of Stitt's. I did some tax work for him and maybe we had dinner a couple of times."

It didn't seem to Charlie that Artemis would have mentioned

Leakey's name if he was only a slight acquaintance. "What about Sweet Dreams?" asked Charlie. "Weren't you involved with Stitt over a horse named Sweet Dreams?"

"Never heard of him," said Leakey. "Or maybe I heard something, I don't remember. Stitt was always talking about horses. In any case, I wasn't 'involved' with him as you call it."

"I guess I've been told different," said Charlie. "Stitt and McClatchy were involved in racing Sweet Dreams and holding him back. They won twice at pretty hefty odds. An old ten-percenter by the name of Rodger Pease cashed in their tickets. Now all three are dead. I think there was a silent partner mixed up in this, someone who had a lot to lose if McClatchy mentioned his name to the grand jury."

"What would he have to lose?" asked Leakey. He had moved a few feet closer to Charlie and stood with his thumbs tucked under his belt.

"He could be disbarred for one thing."

Even as he said it, Charlie knew he had gone too far. He had been irritated with Leakey and wanted to give him a little verbal poke. Leakey immediately lunged at him, spinning him around and pushing him up against the wall.

"That's slander, Bradshaw." Leakey's mouth was about an inch from Charlie's ear. "If you ever come back here again, I'll throw you down the stairs. I hate little toads like you."

Using his bad arm, Charlie shoved himself away from the wall with enough force to send them both staggering across the office. He tried to pull his arm free of its sling but only managed to get it more entangled. He kicked backward at Leakey's shin. The secretary had stood up and was watching them impassively. When Leakey crashed against the opposite wall, Charlie was able to break free. He spun around and swung a fist at Leakey, who blocked it easily and gave him a little push toward the door.

"Get out of here, Bradshaw. I'm not going to fight a cripple."

Without glancing at Leakey, Charlie pulled open the door and went down the stairs, leaving the door open behind him. When he reached the bottom, he heard the door slam. The yellow Volkswagen was parked behind the post office. Charlie was breathing heavily and trying to make himself relax to the point where he no longer hated Leakey, where he could tell himself he was just doing a job. He got into the car and started it up. The Volkswagen needed a new muffler and roared. When he had sold the car to Victor, it had been on the condition that Victor would take care of it. But not only did it need a new muffler, the tires and the emergency brake were shot. There was also a funny clicking noise in the engine that didn't sound right. Victor was simply wrecking the car and Charlie meant to tell him when he picked up his Renault and returned the Volkswagen later that afternoon. Then Charlie stopped himself. The car didn't matter. Leakey didn't matter either. It was October, the leaves were beautiful and on Thursday he had been invited to have dinner with Doris in her apartment and who knew what might happen.

David Jespersen's office was on Clark Street near Five Points, an intersection on the south side of Saratoga where five streets came together. The building was a long, brick ranch house with white shutters and a chain-link fence in the back. Charlie heard dogs barking, the kind of barking that dogs at vets make when they think they recognize the sound of their masters' cars: I'm here, I'm here! A U-shaped driveway led up to the front door.

Charlie gave his card to the receptionist in the waiting room, then took a seat. His arm hurt and he hoped he hadn't broken open the wound by tussling with Leakey. Across from Charlie a middle-aged woman was rocking a small Boston terrier and whispering to it soothingly. Now and then the dog would lift its head and lick her nose. Next to her sat another woman with a cat-carrying case between her feet. From inside the case came the sound of mewing. Charlie felt his nose beginning to run. The walls were covered with pictures of dogs, cats, horses and health tips for keeping your pet happy. Above the receptionist's desk were Jespersen's credentials and diploma from Cornell.

After about ten minutes, Charlie was shown into Jespersen's office: a comfortable room with bookcases and soft leather chairs.

Jespersen had been sitting at a desk and stood up to greet him. He was a tall, slender man with a long face and a small, round chin like half a golf ball. His sandy blond hair was turning gray. He wore glasses with gold wire frames, which Charlie thought made him look grandfatherly. On the wall behind the desk were several pictures of men practicing karate in what appeared to be white pajamas. One of the men, photographed in the act of crashing the edge of his hand down on another man's shoulder, was Jespersen.

"I don't have much time, Mr. Bradshaw, perhaps you could tell me the nature of your visit."

His voice was cool but cordial. In the background, Charlie still heard dogs barking. He sniffed, then sneezed. Taking a tissue from a box on the desk, he blew his nose. "Allergy," he said. Jespersen waited.

"I'm the one who discovered Willis Stitt's body over at the Roosevelt Baths," said Charlie, "and I'm trying to find out some additional information about him."

"Are you working with the police?"

"In conjunction with them, yes. You were friends with Stitt?"

Jespersen crossed his arms and sat down on the corner of his desk. He wore a white laboratory coat, and sticking up from his breast pocket were about a dozen pens. "I took care of his horses, had dinner with him several times and perhaps invited him to a party or two. Did you know him?"

"I met him only briefly."

"He was a difficult man to be friends with, primarily because he wanted to be friends so badly. When he talked to you, it seemed his interest was caused more by his great need to be liked than by any true feeling. Unfortunately, this created a sort of barrier. I liked him, felt sorry for him, but he was really no more than a good acquaintance."

"What's the difference between an acquaintance and a friend?" asked Charlie.

"Let's put it this way," said Jespersen. "I would never have confided in Willis Stitt. When we were together, most of the time was spent discussing his concerns. In a true friendship, there must be more of a balance."

"Did you know Jimmy McClatchy?"

"The jockey? I've seen him ride, of course, but I never met him. Once or twice I saw him with Willis."

"What about Rodger Pease?"

"I don't recognize the name." Jespersen took a pack of Kents from under his laboratory coat, shook out a cigarette and lit it with a large brass lighter in the shape of a Model-T Ford. Instead of setting the lighter back on the desk, he glanced down at the flame, then ran it back and forth under his fingers very briefly before snuffing it out with his thumb.

"He was a tall, bulky-looking, balding man of about seventy-five. He hung around the track a lot."

"No, it doesn't ring any bells. Was he a friend of Willis's?"

"I believe they were business associates," said Charlie.

"Willis led a complicated life," said Jespersen. "He knew a lot of people, was involved in a lot of deals. Because of the horses, I saw him fairly often, but I never had the sense that I knew him."

"You think he could have held back horses in a race?"

"If he did, I knew nothing about it."

"Have you had any thoughts about his death?" Charlie looked again at the photographs of Jespersen practicing karate, and wondered why the veterinarian had chosen to hang them in his office.

"You mean who killed him? The newspaper suggested that his death was connected with McClatchy's death, whose death, according to the newspaper, was related to racketeering and race fixing. There was also some talk about organized crime. For all of Willis's desire to be liked, he was essentially a very private man. He could easily have known racketeers without my knowing about it. I was surprised, of course, but it didn't seem wholly improbable."

"What about the horse, Sweet Dreams? What can you tell me about him?"

"What's there to tell? He's a healthy four-year-old that broke the pastern joint of his right foreleg in his stall. A not-uncommon injury."

"How come Stitt was using him for stud if he was a mediocre horse?"

"He had a little speed. I gather his main problem was a nervousness in the gate. In any case, there're many racetracks in this country, Mr. Bradshaw. Sweet Dreams's progeny would be handsome, strong and fast enough to win at a few state fairs. Any more questions? I believe I have patients waiting."

"Do you know Victor Plotz?"

Jespersen shook his head, then pushed his glasses up onto his nose with his left forefinger. "I don't recognize the name," he said.

"He's a big man in his late fifties. He brings his cat to you. A one-eyed cat named Moshe. He works for me."

Jespersen laughed. The sound reminded Charlie of paper being crinkled. "I remember the cat. I even remember the man. Something of a joker, isn't he? I had no idea he worked for you. He spent a lot of time trying to convince my receptionist to go out with him. She finally had to ask me to intervene."

"That's Victor," said Charlie.

Chapter Ten

Peering into the mirror, Victor Plotz leaned over his bathroom sink and placed a round Band-Aid in the center of his right cheek. It covered a small cut—the last of several needing bandages—which he had received when Pease's house had blown up a week earlier. Victor then turned his attention to the bruise under his left eye where Leakey had punched him. He touched it gently. It was still tender but the purple was fading.

Victor liked his face. It reminded him of potato sculptures he had made years ago in grade school. All the individual features were oversized: lips, nose, ears, mouth, baggy eyes. Even his pores were deep and cavernous. Consequently, he regretted this sudden collection of cuts and bruises, and their presence made him doubt the wisdom of his recent choices. After all, there were only so many bruises a single face could tolerate without a drop in aesthetic appeal. It seemed that his first loyalty was to his own appearance, and that being the case, then maybe he should stay in bed.

Victor felt torn. As a matter of professional pride, he thought he ought to put enough pressure on Roy Leakey to persuade him to return those love letters. On the other hand, Leakey had already punched him once and, if he had actually killed three men, there seemed no limit to the damage he could inflict. Perhaps he should forget about Leakey and buzz over to the Pyramid Mall and stake out the suspicious salesclerk. That, however, was dreary work. He stood and stared at the salesclerk; the salesclerk stood and stared at him. After eight hours, Victor would have nothing to show for it but sore feet.

It was nine o'clock Tuesday morning and, glancing out the window, Victor decided it was going to rain. He went to the closet, took out a rather dirty tan raincoat, then headed for the door. Victor had a third-floor apartment in the Algonquin, an ornate redstone building on Broadway in downtown Saratoga. He hurried down the stairs and by the time he reached the sidewalk, he had decided to see Leakey one more time. First, however, he would visit his client. Her name was Ruth MacDermott and every time Victor saw her, he became short of breath. She was a tall woman with a mass of red hair and great long legs. Maybe she was forty. Her best feature, Victor was convinced, was a large bosom and a fondness for low-cut dresses that exposed milky-smooth breasts dotted with a few freckles.

The yellow Volkswagen was parked around the corner on Grove Street. Victor had retrieved it from Charlie the previous evening and had spent an inordinate amount of time listening to how he should treat it better. Charlie had been in a bad mood, having just spent two hours at the dentist.

Grove Street was a steep hill that dead-ended at Maple, the next street. The Volkswagen was the only car on the block, and pointed downhill. It was a tidy car, Victor thought, and he had agreed with Charlie that he should give it special attention.

The sky was dark gray and the wind was tugging leaves from the trees. It was a dreary morning and Victor was glad he hadn't gone with Charlie to Rodger Pease's funeral. As he reached the Volkswagen, Victor happened to notice that his right shoe was untied. Pausing, he put his foot up on the back bumper. Victor was wearing blue basketball shoes with high tops. He tied the shoe, then, as he straightened up again, he saw that the Volkswagen had begun to roll forward.

"Hey," he shouted.

The Volkswagen rolled into the middle of Grove Street and began coasting down the hill. Running after it, Victor managed to grab the back bumper. For a moment it seemed he might be able to stop the car, but then he was pulled forward onto his knees and forced to let go. He jumped to his feet and began to run. He never bothered to lock the Volkswagen and he thought if he could just reach the door, then perhaps he could jump inside.

"Stop!" shouted Victor.

There was no one else on the street. For a few seconds, Victor gained on the Volkswagen, but then it picked up speed and steadily drew away from him. Victor was running as fast as he could down the center of the street, with the tails of his raincoat flapping behind him. He disliked running, disliked all forms of physical exercise, and he began to worry about how he would stop. Beyond the intersection at Maple was a vacant lot and the car rushed toward it.

"Watch out!" shouted Victor.

The Volkswagen rushed across the intersection, hit the curb, bounced, rose in the air and then, inexplicably, continued to rise as a great orange ball of flame erupted from underneath its front end. Immediately, the car began to fly apart as the orange flame swept over it. Both doors sailed off. Bumpers, tires, fenders and hundreds of unidentifiable parts separated from the flaming mass of the body and rose up in high arcs above the vacant lot.

Victor, still running, forgot he was running, until he collided with the force and noise of the explosion, which stood like an invisible wall across the street. He smashed against it and was hurled back into the gutter. Landing on his side, he rolled head over heels across the pavement, as dirt and chunks of debris pelted down upon him. Then, for a moment, he lay still, making a silent inventory of all his moving parts. The wind had been knocked out of him, his face had scraped against the pavement and there were dozens of small pains that might become serious. He was about to try to get to his feet when his attention was distracted by the squeal of brakes.

Lifting his head, Victor saw a large blue car at the bottom of the hill fishtailing toward the burning back half of the Volks-wagen. As the blue car swung to the left, its right rear fender smashed against the wreckage. Then it bounced over the curb, ran down a stop sign and came to a halt halfway across Grove Street about ten feet from where Victor lay sprawled. Victor realized it was a police car. Then he saw Chief Peterson climb from the front. Victor put his head back down on the pavement. He didn't feel ready to talk to policemen. The remnants of the Volkswagen were burning fiercely, sending a great cloud of black smoke into the gray sky.

Victor squinted through half-closed lids and saw Peterson hur-rying toward him. At first he thought the police chief intended to help him. Then Peterson began to shout.

"You crazy fool, you nearly killed me!"

Victor dragged himself to his feet. His raincoat was ripped up the back to the collar. His hands and wrists were scraped from where he had hit the pavement. Bits of gravel were embedded in the cuts on his face. There was a tear in his trousers, and blood was coming from a cut on his left leg. His anger, however, temporarily allowed him to forget his bruises.

"Why should I waste a perfectly good car on an asshole like you?" he said.

Peterson stopped a few feet away and stood breathing heavily. His moment of terror had left him looking rumpled, as if his blue suit was too large or he had slept in his clothes. "Then why did it nearly hit me?" he said.

"That's kismet, bad karma, tough luck. How should I know? But you only got a dented fender and I lost my whole fuckin' car. If you had any decency, you'd stop your paranoid blowin' and call an ambulance. Then you'd find the homicidal lunatic who tried to kill me."

Victor had a hatred of hospitals dating from those last years that his wife had been sick. He hated the smells, the hushed voices, the urgent requests for doctors over the PA system. On the other hand, he liked the nurses. He liked teasing them about their starched white dresses to get them going, as he called it. But this morning, he felt so shaken by the narrowness of his escape that he didn't even try to get any telephone numbers.

Thirty minutes after Victor's arrival by ambulance, Chief Peterson appeared and began badgering him about the explosion. It turned out that some sort of device had been attached to the underside of the car. Peterson insisted that Victor must know who had put it there.

"I'm a man with a million friends," said Victor. "Wherever I go, I set little children's hearts a-singing. Believe me, if I knew who blew up my car, I'd be happy to tell you."

"But it must be connected to something you're working on."

"That seems like a safe bet. I been watching a clerk over at the Pyramid Mall who snitches ties. Maybe it was him."

Peterson and Victor were in a small room attached to the emergency ward of Saratoga Hospital. A young blond nurse was putting a bandage on Victor's forehead. Her starched bosom was so close to his face that it made his teeth ache. Peterson stood by the door.

"I don't want to joke with you, Plotz. Was it connected to something Charlie's doing?"

Victor glanced down at the bandages on his wrists and another on his leg. His left shoulder was sore and his face burned. "Hey, Peterson, I know nothing about it. I walked to the car, it started to roll, then it hit the curb and blew up. That's all I know. Okay, somebody stuck a bomb underneath. Don't bother me with dumb questions, go find him."

"Where's Charlie?"

"He went to Pease's funeral."

But at that moment, the door was pulled open and Charlie hurried into the room. Pushing past Peterson, he went to where Victor was sitting on the edge of the bed. "Are you all right?" he asked. "I just heard about it. Did the Volkswagen really blow up? Are you okay?"

"I may have some dimples I didn't have when I woke up this morning," said Victor, "but otherwise I'm pretty perky."

"What happened?"

"Like you say, the Volkswagen blew up. Fortunately, I wasn't in it." Charlie wore a brown suit, a narrow brown tie, and Victor thought he looked like a high school teacher.

"Why'd it blow up?"

"Peterson says there was a bomb in it. I don't know, maybe the tires were overinflated."

Charlie turned back to Peterson. "What about you? I heard you cracked up your car."

Peterson rubbed his chin. He seemed unsettled and lacked his normal self-assurance. "I'm okay," he said, "but your friend here nearly killed me."

"Peterson thinks it's a plot," said Victor. "Can you believe it? He thinks I wrecked the Volkswagen just to needle him."

"All right, all right," said Peterson, "I was upset."

It seemed to Charlie that Peterson was still upset, but because of Victor's joking he couldn't determine the seriousness of what had happened. "What about the car," he asked, "can it be fixed?"

"Not unless you're a whiz at putting ten million tiny pieces back together again," said Victor. "At one moment, it was a self-respecting Volkswagen. In the next, it was two thousand pounds of confetti."

"Can't you shut this guy up?" asked Peterson. "I mean, a car explodes right in the middle of Saratoga and all your buddy can do is laugh. It's my job to find out who did it. Am I going to get any cooperation? Charlie, is it something you're working on? Is it Stitt?"

"I don't know," said Charlie. He didn't want to tell anything to Peterson. "Where's Caldwell? Still downstate?"

"Yeah, he's in New York. He's supposed to come back today. Charlie, stop fooling around. Who blew up the car?"

"How should I know? I wasn't even there." Charlie picked up Victor's raincoat. When he saw how it was torn and ripped up the back, he looked at Victor's bandages more closely. After a moment, he turned back to Peterson. "Have you learned anything new about McClatchy and Stitt?"

Peterson seemed unhappy. "You know how these things go, Charlie. We've been talking to a lot of people, collecting a lot of information. Caldwell insists it's tied up with Marotta."

"And you've got your stolen cars."

"You know what the FBI's like. It's Caldwell's show. Are you going to tell me about the Volkswagen?"

The nurse had left. Victor sat on the edge of the bed, holding his head in his hands. When he shut his eyes he could see little flashing lights, like on the screen of a video game.

"I know nothing about it," said Charlie. "But I'm the one who's been driving that car all week, so I guess the bomb was meant for me. Caldwell says I told Marotta about McClatchy, then some racketeers killed McClatchy and cut off his head. Maybe those same racketeers are trying to blow me up."

"You don't believe that," said Peterson.

Charlie undid the top button of his shirt and loosened his tie. "So what? That's what Caldwell will believe and, as you said yourself, it's his show."

"Don't joke with me, Charlie. I mean, I might like to see you move away from Saratoga but I don't want you dead."

Charlie was almost touched. "That's nice of you, Chief, but you know me—I just deliver milk, and Victor here investigates suspicious salesclerks and runaway schoolgirls."

Peterson made a disgruntled noise, then opened the door. "Even when you worked for me, you were a smooth liar. By the way, you're going to be in some trouble about that milk route of yours. I was just coming to find you when that damn car blew up."

"What do you mean?"

Peterson sucked his teeth, then took a pocket watch from his vest pocket and checked its time against the clock on the wall. "The Schuylerville police called me," he said. "Your apprentice milkman was clocked driving his milk truck at 68 miles per hour through downtown Schuylerville at eight o'clock this morning The chief also said he was drunk and disorderly."

That Eddie Gillespie might not make a top-notch milkman, Charlie had expected. Still, he hoped for a few days relief from the milk truck and, who knows, perhaps during that time, Wanamaker's mother would die and Charlie could lay down this particular burden forever. These hopes had proved ill-founded.

By eleven o'clock Tuesday morning, Charlie and Victor were driving in the Renault over to Schuylerville. It was drizzling slightly and Charlie wished he could check into a motel and sleep for a week.

"You know," said Charlie, "I'd like to turn this car around and drive all the way to Key Largo. I bet you could get some rest there."

"Forget it," said Victor. "You got to find the fellow who tried to blow me up. What kind of hotshot detective are you anyway?"

Charlie looked over at his friend. Victor had a large bandage on his left cheek and another on his forehead. Charlie's own forehead was still sore and his wounded arm ached and felt stiff. Together they looked like a Band-Aid commercial. As for being a hotshot detective, Charlie wondered if he shouldn't remain a milkman after all.

"You know what I did last night?" asked Charlie. "I spent some time finding out about Roy Leakey. I learned that he's been a lawyer here for five years, that he passed his bar exam in 1974, that he spent six years in the Army and four of those years in Vietnam as a demolitions expert."

"So you figure he knows about bombs?" said Victor.

"That's right."

"You think he did it?"

"Maybe. On the other hand, maybe it was meant to look like he did it or maybe it was meant to look like Marotta did it."

"Why Marotta?"

"Racketeers are supposed to like bombs. Anyway, Leakey could easily have seen me driving the Volkswagen. And that's also true of Jespersen."

"What're we going to do about another car?" asked Victor.

It began to rain harder. Half the road was covered with brown leaves. Charlie thought of how much he had liked the yellow Volkswagen. "I'll borrow the milk truck," he said.

"Won't you feel foolish driving around Saratoga in a Wholesome Dairy milk truck?"

Charlie grinned. "If whoever is committing these murders thinks he's dealing with idiots, then maybe he'll take more chances."

This didn't please Victor. "Hey, Charlie, your murderer took a pretty big chance in blowing up the Volkswagen. If he starts taking even bigger chances, then I'm going to be spending a fortune on cotton gauze and Mercurochrome. Why rile him up?"

"Because I want to catch him," said Charlie.

Victor yawned, then scratched his scalp. "You know, I've learned several things in this detective business. Like I've learned you can approach a problem like Sherlock Holmes and crush the enemy with superior brain power or you can try using your method."

"And what method is that?" asked Charlie.

"It's like the clown in the carnival that sits up on a perch over a tub of water. He keeps insulting people and making them really mad until they throw the ball at the target and send him splashing into the water. That's what you do, you rile up Leakey or Jespersen or Marotta or whoever until they come after you. But, well, there's only one trouble with that."

"What do you mean?"

"The consequences are a lot more serious than a tub of cold water." Victor glanced out the window at the gray fields, then shifted painfully in his seat. Maybe it was better to watch the crooked salesclerk after all. "So how was the funeral this morning?" he asked.

"Sad."

"Were you and that old lady the only ones?"

"No, there were about a dozen people. All elderly and living in rooms somewhere, all full of stories about Saratoga in the '20s and '30s. Several of them knew Flo Abernathy. You know, I asked my dentist about her yesterday. She's the daughter of a guy who used to own a big chunk of Glens Falls. She'd been a student at Skidmore in the '30s and then quit. She wanted to be a singer. Her family just wrote her off."

"What happened to her singing?" asked Victor.

Charlie shrugged. "She sang in some local clubs, but I guess she wasn't good enough. Luckily she inherited some money from her mother, but it seems she's been out of contact with her family ever since. There's a brother that's living, also some cousins."

"If she's got money," said Victor, "maybe she can pay us more than five dollars."

"I want to find out who killed Pease for my own reasons," said Charlie. "The money's not important."

"Not me," said Victor, "if I can't do it for money, then let me do it for revenge. I didn't like that car blowing up in my face and if the lunatic who did it turns out to be Leakey, then I'll be one cheerful fella. Did I ever tell you about my happiest moment of revenge?"

"No, but I take it you're going to tell me now," said Charlie. He pulled out to pass a slower car. Victor waited until the Renault was back in the right-hand lane.

"This concerns a girlfriend I once had that some greaser stole away from me," Victor said. "It was a sad time and I was very unhappy but the lady said how she really liked the greaser, and that I should let bygones be bygones and bite the bullet or some shit like that. Well, this was back in the days when I was a young guy selling men's clothing and I was fool enough to say okay.

"But then one night I'm sitting in a local bar and in comes this greaser and he sits down beside me and says, Hey, I feel pretty bad about this myself, but what the hell, love is love. I'd had a couple of drinks and was ready to forgive and forget so, like a dumbo, I say, You know, Agnes—that was the young lady's

name—Agnes likes little treats like flowers and candy, and if
you're going to steal her from me, then you got to treat her right.
And the greaser says, I appreciate you telling me and I'll try to
do the proper things. He's very polite. I think he worked for a
funeral home or something. Then he says, Is there anything else
she likes? And I say, She likes sleeping late on Sunday mornings
and she likes a good back rub when she just gets home from
work. Wow, says the greaser, I really appreciate your telling me
this, what else?

"But then I stop and say to myself, Hold up, what are you
doing giving this tub of lard such a load of information? Hasn't
he robbed you of your heart's desire? All this time the greaser
keeps saying, What else, what else? So I say, You know, our
Agnes, she's got some pretty queer tastes. And the greaser, he
leans over and says, Ohhh? And I say, Nah, I can't tell you this,
it's too intimate. The greaser is leaning over so far that he's
practically in my lap. Tell me, he says. And I say, I can't, it was
a secret shared between Agnes and me. And the greaser says,
You can trust me not to abuse your confidence, or some shit like
that. So I say, You know how excited our Agnes can get when
it comes down to actual lovemaking? Yeah? says the greaser.
Well, I say, I made this little discovery that drove her absolutely
crazy with passion. Tell me, begs the greaser.

"But I wasn't ready, so I tell him it's like a sacred pact, a
trust, something that had happened during a holy moment and
in no time at all he's panting like a dog. Okay, I say, right
when we were making love, right when I could tell she was
ready, really ready, right when she was trembling like a spring
leaf, I reached over to a cup that I was keeping next to the
bed and at the last possible moment, I took an ice cube and I
slipped it into her ass."

"Jesus, Victor," said Charlie.

"That's right," said Victor, "that's what I told him."

"What happened?"

"Well, two days later I heard this guy was in the hospital with
some kind of strain."

"Strain?"

"That's what I said. When he tried that little number with the ice cube, our Agnes leaped sideways about as fast as a cat touched by a hot match. That's what did it. Yanked his root half fuckin' off."

Chapter
Eleven

Jesse James had not been the only outlaw tormented by the Pinkertons. They had hounded poor Butch Cassidy over the entire United States when all he wanted was to settle down and raise a few cows. Worse, they had forced Cassidy, along with the Sundance Kid and Etta Place, to flee the country and try to make a life for themselves in Argentina, where the government had given them four square leagues in Cholilo, Province of Chubut, District 16 de Octubre. They bought thirteen hundred sheep, five hundred head of cattle, thirty-five horses and tried to make a go of it.

But even in Argentina they weren't safe. Two years later, in March 1903, Pinkerton operative Frank Dimaio arrived in Buenos Aires and began plastering the country with Wanted posters. Cassidy and Sundance were forced to sell their ranch to a Chilean beef syndicate and start robbing banks, beginning with el Banco de la Nación in Mercedes where they got $20,000, but killed the bank manager. Butch was nearly forty. He'd had only five years of living without fear and constant worry. Once again, Charlie asked himself, how could he work for the Pinkertons?

It was Tuesday night and Charlie was trying to pay some bills and balance his checkbook. If he didn't work for the Pinkertons, then maybe he could get a job as a guard in a supermarket. He couldn't think of anybody famous who had ever held up a supermarket. On the other hand, considering the state of his finances, maybe he should just remain a milkman.

Eddie Gillespie was still in jail and Charlie had had to deliver the milk that Gillespie hadn't bothered to deliver himself. On Monday it turned out that Gillespie had skipped about half the houses. He also hadn't emptied the truck and instead of delivering fresh milk Tuesday morning, he had simply used the milk left over from the previous day, which had gone sour. Charlie knew he could get the money to bail Gillespie out of jail, but he didn't feel like it. Maybe tomorrow or the next day.

For much of the evening, Charlie had been trying to call John Wanamaker in Sante Fe, but without success. Somewhat guiltily, he wondered if this was a sign that Wanamaker's mother had died.

Charlie got to his feet and began to gather up his papers. He had been working at the dining-room table and as he stood next to it, he let his finger trace the groove in the wood caused by whatever instrument had cut off McClatchy's head. And where was the head? Why was someone sending photographs of it to the Jockey Guild and various newspapers? Surely that was more interesting than delivering milk or guarding eggs in a supermarket.

It was eleven o'clock. Charlie decided to make himself a cup of peppermint tea with honey, then go to bed. But as he was putting his old checks and bank statement into an envelope, there came a loud knock at the door. This made him jump because he hadn't heard a car. It reminded him of the night that McClatchy had appeared. Again the person knocked. Quickly, Charlie went into the kitchen, opened a drawer full of dish towels and took out a revolver. Then he returned to the living room.

Opening the door, Charlie found a middle-aged man in a gray overcoat and black cap who looked vaguely familiar. He had just been raising his hand to knock again. Charlie held the revolver out of sight against his leg. The man had a big smear of a nose that looked as if lots of people had taken swings at it.

"What's up?" asked Charlie.

"Someone wants to see you," said the man. "I'm the chauffeur."

"What if I don't want to go?" said Charlie.

This seemed to please the chauffeur, who smiled. "Mr. Marotta said I wasn't supposed to take no for an answer."

Charlie considered showing the man his gun, then changed his mind. "Let me get my coat," he said.

Charlie followed the man out to an old black Cadillac parked along the road. The man held open the back door. "I was hoping you'd make trouble," he said. "Jimmy McClatchy was an especial favorite of mine."

"He must have lost you a lot of money," said Charlie, getting into the car.

The chauffeur settled himself in the front seat and started the engine. Then he turned around in Charlie's driveway and headed back toward Saratoga. "I don't mean I ever bet McClatchy to win," said the chauffeur. "It's just that it's good to know who the losers are."

"I never thought of it that way," said Charlie.

"That's the trouble with you punks," said the chauffeur. "You never think."

Marotta's restaurant was five miles west of Saratoga on a country road with several dairy farms. It was a long yellow building and on either side of the front door were two Roman pillars made from a combination of plywood and plaster. The Roman decor was continued inside with more pillars, reproductions of statues like the Discus Thrower and a wall mural of the Coliseum. Red tablecloths covered the tables and bunches of red plastic grapes dangled from the archways. Although the restaurant could have easily seated three hundred people, on this evening it was practically empty. Three waiters in black suits with white napkins over their arms stifled yawns as they watched the color television in the bar, where one cowboy was jumping up and down on another cowboy's hat. The bartender gave Charlie a small wave. Before quitting the police department, Charlie had arrested this man about five times for cashing bad checks.

The chauffeur led Charlie to a table next to the empty dance floor and said that Marotta would be out in a minute. A black piano player in a tuxedo was playing Cole Porter songs.

As Charlie removed his blue jacket, the maître d' approached almost on tiptoe. "Mr. Marotta says you may order whatever you like." The man was dignified and expectant.

"Just a beer, I guess."

"We have fresh oysters."

"That's okay, a beer's fine."

"Domestic or imported?"

"Domestic's okay with me."

As the man disappeared, Charlie wondered if he had turned off the stove before leaving the house. He had been intending to make tea and couldn't remember if he had actually put the kettle on to boil.

Marotta appeared five minutes later. He wore an immaculate gray silk suit with the tip of a red handkerchief poking out of the breast pocket. On the little finger of his left hand was a large gold ring with a blue stone. He nodded to Charlie but didn't offer to shake hands. As he sat down, a waiter brought over a tray with a glass, a small bottle of Saratoga Vichy and a little silver bowl with several wedges of lemon. Marotta poured himself some Vichy and added a few drops of lemon. His fingernails were perfectly groomed and Charlie imagined him spending an hour every day with a beautiful manicurist. Marotta sipped the Vichy.

"I realize," he began, "that Chief Peterson and half of Saratoga believe you told me about Jimmy McClatchy and that this led to his death. I also realize that you and I are the only two people who know for certain that this is not true. We talked, if I remember right, only about my wife and the fact she was paying you to have me followed. I asked you not to discuss the subject with anyone and it seems you haven't. I appreciate that. I also asked you to stop having me followed. This you have failed to do. Although I haven't noticed anyone today, there was a young man sleeping in a car in my parking lot for much of last night."

"He's in jail," said Charlie. He finished his beer and wondered if he should ask for another.

"Jail?"

"That's right, he was pulled over in Schuylerville for doing 68 miles per hour in a milk truck."

Marotta pressed the bump on his nose between his thumb and index finger. He seemed on the verge of asking what Gillespie had been doing in a milk truck. "So he won't be following me?" he asked.

"I don't know about that," said Charlie. "I might bail him out tomorrow." It seemed that Marotta was frightened and Charlie couldn't imagine why.

"Haven't you run through the money my wife gave you?"

"I'm paying him myself." The maître d' drifted near their table and Charlie signaled to him. "Get me another beer, will you?"

"Why are you paying him to follow me?" asked Marotta. He had started to lift his glass of Vichy and now held it frozen between the table and his mouth.

"We both know I told you nothing about McClatchy," said Charlie. "But there's still the chance you already knew that McClatchy was staying at my place. Maybe somebody told you to keep me occupied while they went out there and cut off his head."

Marotta put down his glass and began to look angry. "You know the trouble I'm in because of that damn lunch with you? I've had the FBI and Peterson out here a dozen times and I've had that dope sleeping in my parking lot. Everybody knows he's working for you and everybody knows that you're investigating these murders. Consequently, they think I'm involved."

He took another sip of Vichy and looked over at the piano player, who had begun to play "Moonlight in Vermont." The maître d' brought Charlie's beer. By now all the other tables were empty.

"Let me tell you my problem," said Marotta. He paused, then leaned slightly over the table. "Over the years I've heard rumors that I am in some way connected with organized crime. This is greatly exaggerated but it's what people like to talk about. Recently, however, people have begun to say that you are having me followed precisely because of this connection. This upsets me. Perhaps I do have a few friends who got in a little trouble a long time ago. One of the main reasons I'm their friend is because I have no bad marks. And maybe I'm useful to them in various ways. They're not going to like my being followed. That punk kid and your friend Victor Plotz have no subtlety. In no time at all my friends will hear about them. I can't afford that. Plotz and that kid could make my friends drop me like a hot brick. If that happens, I lose the restaurant and go broke."

Marotta seemed to expect Charlie to say something, but Charlie drank a little beer instead. He felt foolish for having brought the revolver. Certainly Marotta was more afraid of him than he had been of Marotta.

"Okay, so this afternoon I hear about Plotz's car getting blown up," said Marotta. "People are already saying it's the Mafia and that the reason the car was blown up was because Plotz was messing with me. This could ruin me, Charlie."

Off to the side of the restaurant, Charlie could see five waiters watching them. It occurred to him they were worried about their jobs. "So what do you want?" he asked.

"How much did my wife pay you to have me followed?"

"One thousand."

Marotta took a billfold from his breast pocket, counted out ten one-hundred-dollar bills and tossed them on the red tablecloth.

Charlie looked at the money. "Keep it," he said. "Neither Victor or Eddie Gillespie will bother you, but I don't want the money."

"I want you to have it," said Marotta.

Charlie shook his head. He wished Marotta would put the money back in his pocket. "No, I appreciate the offer but it's not necessary."

Marotta retrieved the money and stuck it in his side pocket. Then he again massaged the bump on his nose. He had dark brown eyes that rarely seemed to move. He looked at Charlie for several moments, as if trying to decide something about him. "For your information," he said at last, "I want to tell you that racketeers or gangsters or whatever you call them were in no way connected with McClatchy's death. Maybe if you told me what you've found out, I could give you some help."

Charlie hesitated. He knew that just because Marotta claimed not to be involved didn't mean it was true. "Do you know a Saratoga lawyer by the name of Roy Leakey?" he asked.

"Not very well. I know he likes horses and women and has a temper. The one time he was out here he got so drunk I had to ask him to leave."

"What about a veterinarian by the name of David Jespersen?"

Marotta thought a moment. "He also likes horses. A lot of people do in Saratoga. I've heard he's involved with a young woman who owns a boutique downtown. Her name's Kathy Marshall and the store's called something like the Blue Lion."

Charlie knew the store. It was next door to the store owned by his ex-wife and her sister. Since Charlie tried to avoid those two women whenever possible, he rarely walked around on that part of Broadway. "Wasn't Jespersen recently divorced?" asked Charlie.

"About two years ago, I gather. He started up with Kathy Marshall about a year before that. She's got a lot of money from someplace. They got together when he ran for city commissioner."

"I didn't know about that."

"He nearly won and I've heard he wants to run again. Kathy Marshall also likes horses. She's even bought a few. Maybe Jespersen was involved with that since he can't race horses himself."

"What do you mean?"

"It's illegal for vets to own Thoroughbreds and race them at tracks where they do any work. That's a New York State law. It's considered a conflict of interest. Jespersen works for about half a dozen trainers every August. And he does some work at Belmont as well."

"What about a horse named Sweet Dreams?" asked Charlie. "You ever heard of him?"

"Never. Should I have?"

Charlie told Marotta about Sweet Dreams's eleven races, and that McClatchy had ridden him each time. "He was owned by

Willis Stitt," said Charlie. "That's the guy who was murdered at the Roosevelt Baths on Saturday."

"I'd met Stitt a couple of times," said Marotta, "but didn't have any sense of him as a person. What kind of breeding does Sweet Dreams have?"

"Not so hot. A mare named Indian Maid and the stallion was Buckdancer. Neither horse ever did anything."

"You have a blood test done?"

"No." It had never occurred to Charlie.

"There's a fair chance that Sweet Dreams was a mediocre horse that McClatchy strangled. On the other hand, maybe he's a ringer. There's been a lot of trouble because of that horse. I'd guess there's more involved than just holding him back. If he was a much better horse than his breeding indicated, then he'd stand a better chance of winning. What's he doing now?"

"They're using him for stud."

Marotta finished his Vichy, then poked at the wedge of lemon with a black swizzle stick with the name MAROTTA printed on it with gold lettering. "If I were you, I'd see about a blood test. Maybe Buckdancer's not the sire after all."

"How would I find out about that?"

"Get the Bureau involved."

"The FBI?"

"No, the Thoroughbred Racing Protective Bureau. It's part of the Thoroughbred Racing Association. They police about sixty tracks. Their offices are in Lake Success near Belmont on Long Island."

Chapter
Twelve

Charlie held the handset of the telephone a short distance from his head and squinted at it in irritation. "What do you mean you can't investigate without grounds. I'm giving you grounds."

There was a mild belch, then a voice answered, "That's not good enough. You tell me this horse is a ringer and we should take a blood test. We can't just rush in because you say so."

The man on the other end of the line was Lenny Ravitz at the Racing Protective Bureau. Charlie had been arguing with him for about fifteen minutes. It was early Wednesday afternoon and Charlie was in his office. On the other side of the desk, Victor was cutting out a string of paper dolls. Charlie kept staring at them. He'd never seen buxom paper dolls before.

Charlie gripped the handset a little tighter. "Look at the horse's record," he said. "McClatchy was strangling it."

"Maybe he was, but that doesn't prove he's a ringer. Don't you remember Carry Back?"

"Who?"

"Carry Back, by Saggy out of Joppy, a horse with no breeding and no style that won the Derby and the Preakness in 1961. What I'm saying is that blood mostly counts but sometimes it doesn't. Possibly Sweet Dreams is like that: a fluke."

Ravitz had a very slow, raspy voice and Charlie kept losing

patience with it. On the file cabinet, the beady black eye of the stuffed parrot seemed to be mocking him. He still hadn't asked Victor where it had come from and didn't plan to.

"You ever hear of Roy Leakey, a Saratoga lawyer?" Charlie asked.

"No, should I?"

"I'm not sure," Charlie said. "Doesn't it mean anything that Stitt was using the horse for stud?"

"Not necessarily. Anyway, we can't go in there without grounds. Look, don't think we don't have a strong interest. If we had a blood sample and checked it against Buckdancer and it turned up wrong, then that would give us the edge to go in and demand an official sample."

"So how would you get a blood sample?"

"That's for you to figure out," said Lenny Ravitz.

"Why do you have a strong interest?"

Ravitz made a snorting noise into the phone. "We've received two snapshots of McClatchy's head. Just the head, by itself, on some kind of table with a hole in the forehead and the eyes a little open and stupid looking."

After Charlie hung up, he sat staring out the window, trying to decide what he should do. Across the street was a dentist's office and Charlie could see some poor fellow sitting in the dentist's chair with his mouth open. It made his jaw ache. His own dentist had found three cavities on Monday afternoon and Charlie's mouth still felt stretched and tampered with.

"So what did he say?" asked Victor, wadding up his chain of paper dolls.

"He wants me to send him a blood sample."

"Let me and the boys do it."

"He wants a sample, not a bucket."

"Charlie," said Victor, "you got to learn to trust me. I've your best interests at heart." Victor stood up and put on his ripped tan raincoat, which had been restitched up the back with black thread. The two bandages on his face and the others on his wrists made him look particularly fragile. His gray hair stood out about three inches from his head in all directions, making his head look like a gray dandelion clock.

"Where're you going?" asked Charlie.

"That MacDermott lady called me. She says she's got some information about those love letters she sent Leakey."

"Be careful with Leakey," said Charlie.

"Believe me, the picture of that Volkswagen blowing up will be forever stamped on my brain. Did Peterson tell you anything new?"

"No, nobody saw anyone tampering with the car. Caldwell isn't convinced the explosion was connected with McClatchy. He asked Peterson if you'd ever been mixed up with organized crime."

"Sure," said Victor, "I used to sell them little girls. Maybe I slipped them a goat by accident. What's with this Caldwell anyway?"

Charlie straightened the sling supporting his left arm. The arm felt stiff and itched under its bandages. "He's got one idea in his head and can't get rid of it. I think even Peterson's beginning to disagree with him."

Victor paused in the doorway, then gave a little salute. "Wish me luck with this MacDermott lady," he said, "I think she likes me."

Shortly after Victor left, Charlie decided to drive over to the Backstretch and talk to Doris. He remembered her mentioning Jespersen's girlfriend, Kathy Marshall, and he wanted to learn more.

The milk truck was parked in a lot on the corner of Putnam. That morning in Schuylerville, Charlie had had to apologize to about twenty irate customers. Now they were only mildly angry. Gillespie must have driven the truck through a field because it was spattered with mud, and weeds dangled from the bumpers. Charlie was sorry that he hadn't washed it before driving to Saratoga. As he climbed into the truck, he glanced around to see if anyone was looking.

After work that morning he had bailed out Eddie Gillespie, who had seemed contrite and subdued. His only explanation for drunkenly racing the truck through Schuylerville had been that he wasn't born to be a milkman. Charlie didn't feel he was born to be a milkman either, but he had been tactful enough not to say this. He had offered to drive Eddie home in the milk truck, but Eddie said he would rather hitchhike.

As Charlie drove over to the Backstretch, he kept wondering how he could obtain a blood sample. He knew that if he just broke into the stable and jabbed the horse, there would be trouble. Possibly he could ask someone.

Charlie had been correct about Doris knowing Kathy Marshall. "I worked for her for a couple of weeks after she opened the Blue Lion," she told him. "I liked her well enough but she was too bossy."

Charlie and Doris sat across from each other in a booth at the back of the bar. His shoes were on either side of hers and he enjoyed the illusion that he was containing her. The afternoon sun through the window gave a reddish tinge to her hair.

"Do you know Jespersen?" asked Charlie.

"I never met him. When I knew Kathy she was dating a lawyer."

"You know his name?"

"No, it was a few years ago."

"Was it Roy Leakey?"

Doris squinched up her eyes as she tried to remember. "Maybe that was it but I'm not sure. I never met him either. I know Jespersen's ex-wife a little. In fact, I told her to hire you."

"Me, what for?" Charlie had been drinking coffee and he set the white mug back on the table.

"She was trying to get additional alimony from her husband and he said he had much less money than she thought he had. Something like that. I remember she told me he was secretive with his money. She thought a private detective might help and I gave her your name. Did she call?"

"She called Victor once but never called back. Victor in the meantime decided he couldn't take the case because of a conflict of interest."

"What conflict of interest?"

"Jespersen takes care of Victor's cat. What's Jespersen's ex-wife like?"

Charlie's right hand was resting flat on the table. Doris reached over and slowly outlined his fingers with one of her own. "I like her. She married Jespersen when she was eighteen. I gather he gave her a hard time. We were both in the same exercise class at the Y. That was last year. I haven't seen much of her since except on the street or in a store."

"What about Kathy Marshall?" asked Charlie. "What's she like?"

"Ambitious and hard-boiled, but nice under all that. I guess her family has some money. She graduated from Skidmore about five years ago and opened the Blue Lion a year later. The last time I talked to her, which was last spring, she was busy buying a racehorse. I don't know if she did or not." Doris paused, noticed a speck of something on the front of her purple blouse and brushed it off. "But I'm certainly positive she wouldn't be involved in killing someone," she added.

"Stitt had a secret partner," said Charlie. "It might have been Leakey or Jespersen or it might have been someone else. Whoever it was had a lot to lose if McClatchy testified against him. What's interesting about all three murders and even the car being blown up is they were designed to point the blame at presumably innocent parties. Pease supposedly committed suicide. I supposedly killed Stitt. And racketeers supposedly killed McClatchy and blew up the car."

Some construction workers with yellow hard hats came into the Backstretch and Doris stood up. "I have to get back to work," she said. "Are you still coming to dinner tomorrow night?"

"What are you having?" Charlie couldn't imagine why she should think he would change his mind.

"Baked snake," said Doris. "I thought since you were delivering milk again you might not want to." She stood next to the table smoothing her dark gray skirt down over her thighs.

"I have to have something nice in my life," said Charlie. "If

I'm really lucky, maybe Wanamaker will come back from Santa Fe."

A few minutes later Charlie left the Backstretch to drive over to the Star Market to pick up some groceries. Again he began to brood about the blood sample. It was embarrassing. Here he knew the histories of a thousand desperadoes who had stolen everything from a Union Pacific locomotive to the Mona Lisa and he couldn't think how to swipe a teaspoon of blood.

The market was crowded and Charlie saw several people he knew. By their expressions, he realized he should have come at a less public time. The papers had reported Charlie's connection with Stitt's murder and the explosion of the Volkswagen. One had even printed his picture, showing him in a plaid winter hat with ear flaps. Charlie was certain he had never seen the hat before and couldn't think when the picture had been taken.

After wheeling his cart down several aisles, Charlie saw a rather small and familiar-looking woman staring at him fixedly. He looked away. He needed beer, bread, cereal, and Freihofer's fruit cookies. He hurried to get them. At the cereal shelf, he again noticed the small woman. She was attractive, in her thirties, and after a moment Charlie realized it wasn't that she was small, but that he was seeing her without her horse. Also she was wearing a skirt and brown sweater instead of a leotard. Charlie pulled his cart to a stop and clumsily said hello.

"I was wondering how many times I would have to wheel my Post Toasties past you before you realized who I was," said Artemis.

Charlie felt his face grow hot. "I didn't recognize you without your horse," he said.

"I left him in the car. He hates public places without his makeup."

Charlie was about to speak again when he felt a sharp pain in his left ankle caused by someone bumping into him with a cart. He turned to discover his ex-wife's sister, Lucy, who had married his cousin Robert. She was a tall, severe woman who always wore dresses and whose blond hair was sculpted weekly into extravagant designs by a local beautician named Big Ruby. Charlie was almost glad to see her since she owned the store next to Kathy Marshall's Blue Lion, and he wanted to ask her several questions. One look at Lucy's face, however, and he knew he could expect no help.

"I'm surprised to see you in Saratoga, Charlie," she said, "considering what's being said about you."

Charlie started to make some apology when he was interrupted by Artemis: "That's all right, dearie, I gave him ten cents to push my cart."

Lucy stared at Artemis in surprise, then, without answering, she continued down the aisle. Charlie realized that Lucy must have bumped into him on purpose.

"You have nice friends," said Artemis.

"She's sort of an ex-relative." Charlie looked at Artemis. She was perhaps five inches shorter than he was. Again, she struck him as very compact. Then an idea occurred to him about the horse Sweet Dreams. It seemed to leap into his head. "I don't suppose I could interest you in a little petty crime," he asked.

Artemis smiled and rose up on her toes like a ballerina. "On the contrary," she said, "petty crime is my middle name."

At eleven thirty that night, when Charlie ought to have been sound asleep if he hoped to face the next day with any enthusiasm, he stood whispering with Artemis near the closed flap of her circus tent. She wore a black turtleneck and black pants. Charlie guessed that her choice of clothing had been determined by movies she had seen about commando operations.

"From what I've read," said Artemis, "I think we should dig a tunnel. The best prisoners always escape through tunnels."

"Sweet Dreams is not a prisoner, nor are we going to rescue him," said Charlie. "Do you know where he's kept?"

"He was in the stall next to Phillip but they moved him the other day. Now he's in that little barn and I believe the door is locked. Shall we go see?"

Artemis led the way out of the tent. The air was cold and Charlie zipped up his jacket. High over the house shone a half moon but it scarcely gave enough light to keep him from stumbling over his feet. He had left the milk truck in front of the hotel in Cambridge where Artemis picked him up. She had offered to supply the syringe and even do the blood test. This pleased Charlie, who had no idea where to look for blood on a horse. Artemis said the jugular vein was the best bet.

"You know," said Artemis in a whisper, "if those two men in the house catch you, they are likely to do you damage."

"That had already occurred to me," said Charlie.

The door to the barn was locked by a large padlock and a shiny new hasp. Artemis flicked off her small pencil flashlight. "That was put on quite recently," she said.

Charlie took hold of the padlock and tried to twist it. Although it created a problem, Charlie felt encouraged since the lock indicated that Sweet Dreams was more valuable than he seemed.

"Do you have a crowbar?" he asked.

"I have even better," said Artemis. "Wait here."

Charlie waited. From the shed row came the occasional snort of a horse. Far away he heard a dog barking. The night was cloudless. Charlie found the Big Dipper and Cassiopeia, then began looking for Orion. He had left his .38 at home, not wanting to become dependent on it. He began to wish he had brought it.

After a few minutes, Charlie saw a black shape as big as a house lumbering toward him. It was the horse, Phillip, with Artemis on his back. She hopped off when she was next to Charlie.

"Here, you hold the light on the lock," she said.

Charlie did as he was told. Artemis took a length of rope, passed it through the padlock, then tied the rope around Phillip's neck. She moved briskly, like someone tidying a room. Making certain the rope was secure, she produced a carrot and gave it to Phillip who chewed it contentedly with a steady and peaceful slurping. When he was quite finished, she patted his forehead and said, "Up, Phillip!" in a kindly but commanding voice.

The huge horse heaved himself onto his hind legs. There was

a loud cracking and breaking as the door to the small barn was torn from its hinges.

"Do you see how convenient a properly trained horse can be?" asked Artemis. "Down, Phillip!"

Phillip plummeted back down to four legs and the door crashed to the ground. Artemis quickly unfastened the rope. "Now we must hurry. I'm sure those two men heard the noise. Sweet Dreams is in here." She led Charlie into the barn. "You listen for those men and I'll get the blood. Do you think I'd make a capable criminal? Perhaps my talents are wasted in show business."

It was only minutes later that Charlie saw the yellow beam of a flashlight. "It came from over here," said a man's voice.

Charlie hurried into the barn. "Artemis, they're coming."

Artemis emerged from the stall. "Here's the syringe," she said. "Presumably this is enough blood. There's a hayloft upstairs. You go and hide and I'll deal with the enemy."

"What if they hurt you?" asked Charlie, uncertain whether hiding in the hayloft was the right thing to do.

"I should like to see them try," said Artemis. "Hurry, I hear their catlike tread."

Charlie put the syringe in his breast pocket, removed his arm from its sling and began climbing the ladder to the hayloft. As he reached the top, he heard Artemis say: "Gentlemen, come see what my bad horse has done."

"Is that you, Artemis? What the hell's going on?"

"Jesus, Freddie, look at this fuckin' door. You do this, Artemis?"

"I'm afraid to confess it was Phillip. He bounced into it." Artemis spoke energetically.

"Bounced?"

"Sort of jitterbugged. Up, Phillip!"

"Jesus, Freddie, watch out!"

There was a loud whinnying noise from Phillip. From where Charlie lay, he could see the flicker of flashlights underneath the door of the hayloft. The floor was covered with several feet of loose straw. Already Charlie had straw down the back of his neck and up the legs of his trousers.

"Down, Phillip! I was taking Phillip for a short walk and we became separated in the dark. This always makes him anxious. I was standing by this door when we had our little reunion and the excitement was too much for him."

"You mean this horse just knocked the door down?"

"He was so pleased to see me," said Artemis.

"Let's look inside, Freddie."

Charlie began to burrow under the straw. He heard the men downstairs, then one of them climbed the ladder to the loft. Charlie held his breath as he saw the light flicker above his head. Then the light disappeared.

"Nothing up here."

"Hey, Freddie, what're we going to do about this goddamn door?"

"Nail it shut for now. We'll fix it tomorrow. There's a hammer and nails in the storeroom."

Charlie heard the men bumping around. Then the door to the barn was heaved back into place. This was followed by the sound of a hammer. Charlie counted seven or eight nails being driven into the door, he wasn't sure which.

"You want something else, Artemis?" asked Freddie.

"The sight of physical labor invigorates me."

"Why don't you take your damn horse back to your tent, Artemis?"

"Why don't you take your hand off my arm, pal, before Phillip steps on you?"

"Hey, Artemis," said Freddie, "let's go back to the house for a drink."

"You boys have a drink without me. Phillip and I still have work to do."

"Come on, Freddie, she's a looney."

"Well, good night, Artemis. Keep your horse under control from now on, will you?"

"I certainly shall. Goodnight, gentlemen."

As Charlie listened to the sound of departing footsteps, he climbed out of the straw and stood up, pressing one finger under his nose to keep from sneezing. Then he brushed himself off. It was completely dark in the hayloft. After a moment, he waded through the straw to where he had seen a door. It was a small door, no more than four feet high and fastened by a hook. He undid the hook and pushed the door open. As he did so, he saw a great black shadow as Phillip returned through the dark.

Charlie sneezed.

"Was I spectacular?" asked Artemis. She was standing on Phillip's back.

"Very good. If there was any money to be made as a private detective, I'd offer you a job. How do I get down from here?"

"You can lower yourself onto Phillip's back." Artemis and the horse were directly below Charlie. She briefly flicked her penlight on and off to show him.

"I'd rather not," said Charlie.

"Then you'll have to jump or learn to love that hayloft."

"Okay, okay, tell me what to do."

"Take off your shoes and hang them around your neck. Phillip dislikes the feel of shoes. Then slide out on your stomach and onto his back. Just be careful of the syringe. I don't have another."

Charlie sat down, took off his shoes, tied the laces together and hung them around his neck. The horse's back was about five feet below the door. Again taking his arm out of its sling, he turned around and eased his legs through the doorframe. As he lowered himself, Artemis guided his feet. At first he went bit by bit, but then he slipped and slid on his belly until his feet came down hard on Phillip's back. The horse shivered, but remained still. It felt to Charlie that he was standing on a warm and prickly sofa. Artemis took his arm so he wouldn't fall. Charlie stood for a second, then lowered himself to a sitting position. It still seemed like a long distance to the ground. Artemis made a clicking noise and the horse slowly walked forward. Charlie found himself wishing that Chief Peterson could see him. Then he started to slide off and squeezed his legs tightly against Phillip's ribs.

"I would have made a rotten cowboy," Charlie said.

"I don't like sitting so much myself," said Artemis. "That's why I stand."

Chapter Thirteen

V*ictor leaned back* in the swivel chair, gingerly lifted the .38 and looked down the barrel. Its interior was dark and gloomy. He decided to leave it in the safe. Leakey was presumably still at the movies at Pyramid Mall and even if he left early, he was unlikely to drive out to his cottage.

It was the cottage, really a cabin, that Victor had heard about from Ruth MacDermott the previous day: a two-room cabin on a pond in Greenfield a few miles north of Saratoga. Leakey seemed to use it exclusively for amorous adventures, and Ruth MacDermott said that was where Leakey was hiding her love letters.

Victor had already driven out to the cabin just to look at it— an actual log cabin set back from the road with a large fieldstone chimney and a screened-in porch. It was now nine o'clock Thursday evening and in about half an hour Victor meant to do some burglary.

Of course he hadn't told Charlie, who, unfortunately, believed that honesty was the best policy. Victor too thought honesty was a pretty good policy, but it wasn't the only policy. Far from it, there were lots of other policies almost as good.

Victor stood up and returned the .38 to the safe. He still limped from being hurled to the street when the Volkswagen had blown up. In the dark window, he happened to see his reflection and he paused to study it. Although his large bandages had been replaced by smaller ones, his injuries reminded him that Leakey had threatened to do him physical harm. Victor had no wish for further scars. On the other hand, he wanted those letters. It rankled that Charlie had not taken him to get that tablespoon of Sweet Dreams's blood. It seemed to indicate a lack of trust. Victor hoped to regain that trust, or at least some respect, this evening.

As for the blood, Charlie had sent it off to New York by an express bus. Lenny Ravitz at the Thoroughbred Racing Protective Bureau had said that Buckdancer's blood was on file, so it would be an easy matter to compare it with the sample taken from Sweet Dreams. All blood testing for the Jockey Club was done at a lab at the University of California at Davis. Most mares were already blood typed, as were about seven thousand stallions.

Victor took his raincoat from the hook behind the door and left the office. The red Renault was parked up on Broadway in public view where, he hoped, nobody would shove a stick of dynamite under its hood. Charlie had wanted to use it this evening but Victor insisted he needed it for work. This was true, but beyond this truth was Victor's determination never to be seen driving the milk truck. It was okay for Charlie. People already expected the worst of him. But what if one of Victor's girlfriends saw him tooling around town in a Wholesome Dairy milk truck? How could he keep up his reputation as a Casanova if the ladies thought he was peddling skim milk and yogurt?

Charlie had said he had a big date and didn't want to go courting in a milk truck. Victor had suggested he could put a mattress in the back.

"Come on, Victor," Charlie had complained, "this is an important relationship."

"They all are," Victor had told him.

It wasn't as if Charlie was taking Doris to dinner or to a movie. He intended to be at her apartment for the entire evening and had told Victor several times that he was not to be disturbed. Victor was only sorry that he hadn't had the chance to short-sheet her bed. Starting the Renault, Victor discovered that the headlights didn't work. He banged on the dashboard until they came on. Then he made a screeching U-turn and accelerated rapidly up Broadway.

Victor sympathized with Charlie's various problems. It depressed Charlie that his cousins thought him no better than a bandit and that people believed he had betrayed McClatchy to racketeers. It seemed to Victor that the farther you kept away from the dopes, then the better off you were. What was the good of having a fat ass if you couldn't tell the dopes to kiss it? And of course Charlie was sick of being a milkman. Who wouldn't be? But it was his own fault for taking the job in the first place. Ditto with McClatchy. Charlie wouldn't be in his present trouble if he had told McClatchy to hit the bricks. And now this afternoon Charlie had got a telegram from his mother asking if he could raise some money, which she might need in a hurry. Charlie had practically cried.

Victor drove first to Leakey's house on Underwood in northwest Saratoga. The house was a white split-level with green shutters. It was dark and there was no sign of a car. Then Victor drove over to the movie theater at Pyramid Mall to see if Leakey's BMW was still in the lot. It was. Victor decided there was no help for it but to break into the cabin. If he got arrested, Charlie would bail him out.

The cabin was on an unlit dirt road. Victor thought there were too many trees and not enough houses. Trees were all right in their place, in parks, for instance, but Victor disliked how they pushed their way all over the countryside. Furniture on the loose, that's how he saw them. Escaped pulp products, runaway picket fences. Here the trees pressed up against the road, forming a deep arch.

Victor drove past the turnoff to Leakey's cabin, then turned around. Parking the Renault some distance up the road, he took a flashlight from the glove box and walked back. Between the leaves, he could see a few stars. Victor heard an owl but for the most part he thought it was too dark and too quiet. His footsteps in the gravel seemed noisy and he was afraid they would attract attention. He imagined the woods full of animals and remembered stories he had heard about bears wandering down from the Adirondacks. Perhaps he should have brought the .38 after all. He kept the light off and flicked it on only occasionally to keep from falling into a ditch.

Victor reached the driveway to Leakey's cabin. He simply couldn't imagine anyone living out in the woods unless he had something to hide. Victor doubted he had ever spent more than a day of his life not surrounded by concrete and the bustle of a city.

The front door of the cabin was locked. Victor had expected that. After all, Leakey was no fool. Victor walked around the cabin trying all the windows. They too were locked. The cabin was a plain, rectangular building—the kind of log cabin that arrives in a thousand pieces on the back of a flatbed truck. Victor massaged the back of his neck and decided he would have to break a window.

After seeking out a fist-sized rock, he returned to the back of the cabin. First he tapped the glass with the rock. Nothing happened. Then he took out his handkerchief, held it against the window and hit the handkerchief. Still nothing happened. So much for being careful, he thought. Pulling back his arm, he threw the rock at the window, smashing a pane of glass above the latch. The noise seemed huge. He imagined all the bears perking up their ears. Quickly, he opened the window and crawled over the sill.

Once inside, Victor got to his feet and shone his flashlight over the room. Against the far wall to the right stood a large brass bed covered with what appeared to be a polar-bear rug. Near it was a pine bureau and vanity. The bedroom area was several feet above the rest of the room. On the lower level was a brown couch in front of the fireplace, then some stuffed chairs, several bookcases full of books and a rolltop desk. Hanging from the ceiling was a chandelier made from a wagon wheel.

Victor tried the desk first. It was full of little cubbyholes con-

taining letters but none were the right letters. He looked through
the drawers, even behind and under the drawers. Then he searched
the bureau, the vanity and the drawers of a table in the living
room where he found a deck of cards showing fifty-two different
naked ladies, which Victor put in his pocket. Then he searched
the closets and the pockets of all the jackets and coats. The floors
were covered with thick rugs that felt soft and spongy under
Victor's feet. Victor tried to stack all the clothes in a neat mound
but then he fell against them, knocking them over.

When he had finished with the closets, he began on the bookcases, first looking behind the books, then opening and leafing
through each volume. He piled all the books on the floor. Victor
had seen small safes disguised to look like books but all of Leakey's
books were authentic. The problem, as he saw it, was that Leakey
had no reason to hide the letters. If they were really in the cabin,
they would be in a fairly obvious place.

The kitchen was separated from the living room by a wooden
counter about waist high. Victor shone the light over the cabinets
and shelves, over the cans and boxes of food, Saltine crackers
and pea soup. He took everything out of the cupboards to make
sure nothing was behind them, then he looked in the stove. When
he had searched every possible place, he opened the refrigerator.
Its interior light seemed particularly bright after the dimness of
the flashlight. On the top shelf was McClatchy's head.

Victor leaped back, stumbling over a metal kitchen chair and
falling against the counter. The head was lying on its side and
McClatchy appeared to be drowsing. His thin lips were slightly
parted and his eyes were half shut. Victor saw a glimmer of teeth,
a glimmer of eye, as if McClatchy was studying the room through
half-closed lids. Occupying the center of his forehead was a bullet
hole. The neck ended in a precise cut, revealing the bone and
windpipe. McClatchy's brown hair was ruffled as if by a breeze.
His fat cheeks were paper-white. The light from the refrigerator
and the darkness of the room made the head seem as if it stood
on a small stage. Just beneath the head was a grapefruit and two
cans of Budweiser.

Victor scrambled to his feet and half-scrambled, half-tumbled backward toward the front door, keeping his entire attention on the head, as if without that attention McClatchy might wink one eye or open his mouth. Victor knocked over a lamp and another chair. Reaching the door, he unfastened the latch, backed hurriedly across the porch and stumbled down the steps. As he ran up the driveway to the dirt road, he glanced behind him and saw the light of the refrigerator and, he was certain, the round shape of McClatchy's head.

Victor ran up the road and at first couldn't find the Renault. For a terrible moment he thought someone had stolen it. But then he found it, yanked open the door and in his rush badly banged his knee on the steering wheel. He could hardly fit the key into the slot. Starting the car with a roar, he spat stones and gravel for twenty feet as he accelerated toward Saratoga.

As Victor drove, he realized he would have to tell Charlie. Never mind Doris and Victor's promise not to bother them, he still had to tell Charlie about the head. He tried to think of an alternative but there was none. It was just ten thirty. Perhaps Charlie and Doris were finishing dinner or watching the TV. But Victor doubted it.

The milk truck was parked several doors down from Doris's building on Circular Street. Pulling up to the front, Victor jumped out of the car and ran across the lawn. Doris lived on the third floor in an apartment that ran the length of the house. Victor hurried up the back stairs and knocked at the door. After a couple of minutes, Doris opened it. Her hair was rumpled and Victor knew they hadn't been watching TV. When she saw Victor, she raised her eyebrows.

"Is something wrong?" she asked.

"I've got to see Charlie."

"Wait here."

A minute Charlie appeared buttoning his shirt. He looked at Victor but didn't say anything.

"I've found McClatchy's head," said Victor. "It was out at Leakey's cabin. I wanted to know what I should do."

"What were you doing at Leakey's cabin?"

"Looking for those love letters."

"You broke in?"

"No, he sent me an invitation. Jesus, Charlie, don't you care about McClatchy's head? I found it. It was in the refrigerator with a bullet hole right smack in the middle of the forehead."

Charlie finished tucking in his shirt. He looked, thought Victor, as if he didn't care two hoots about McClatchy's head.

"You're not playing a joke on me, are you, Victor?"

"Charlie, for Pete's sake, I'm your friend!"

"I guess we better drive out there."

They drove without speaking. Victor became a trifle irritated. After all, he had risked his sanity, his very ability to sleep at night, just for Charlie's detective agency.

"Charlie, I wouldn't have bothered you if I hadn't thought it was important. I thought you'd want to know."

"That's okay," said Charlie, "you did the right thing."

"Were you in the sack?" asked Victor.

"I don't want to talk about it."

"Jesus, Charlie, how many times do I have to say I'm sorry?"

"Never mind. I'm glad you came. Did you find the letters?"

"Not a single one."

"How'd you get inside?"

"Busted a window."

Charlie made a groaning noise.

"Hey, it was a little window in back. You want I should leave him a couple of bucks?"

When they reached Leakey's cabin, Victor thought something was wrong but he couldn't quite put his finger on what it was. Charlie pulled up to the front, leaving on the headlights. The lights made the bare wood of the cabin look golden. When they got out of the car, Victor saw that the front door was shut. He started to say something about it, then changed his mind. He tried the front door. It was locked.

"The broken window's around back," he said.

Victor led the way with the flashlight. He almost expected to find it fixed and was relieved when he saw the glass smashed and the window open.

"See what a little window it is," he said.

"The size is not important," said Charlie.

Victor climbed through the window and Charlie climbed after him, bumping his head on the frame, then falling forward, hitting his knee on the floor.

"You okay?" asked Victor.

Charlie didn't answer. He got to his feet and looked around. "Where's the refrigerator?" he asked.

Victor flashed the light toward the kitchen. "In there. You do it. I don't want to see it again. Makes me want to puke."

Charlie kept looking around the cabin. Drawers were pulled out, books and papers were scattered across the floor, cushions were thrown around. "You sure made a mess of this place," he said.

"I'm an eager searcher. Just look at the head. Want me to find a paper bag for it?"

Charlie walked to the refrigerator. Victor remained about five feet behind him, trying not to look but looking all the same. Charlie opened the refrigerator door.

"What is it?" said Victor, who had turned away.

Charlie didn't answer.

"Come on, tell me," said Victor.

"The head's not there."

"You're fuckin' kiddin' me." Victor looked around Charlie's shoulder. The head was gone. He nearly pushed Charlie out of the way in order to make certain.

"I swear to you," said Victor, "the head was there on the top shelf."

Charlie knelt down and ran a finger over the shelf. "Well, there's no sign of it now."

"Hey, really, I wouldn't have dragged you out of the sack for a joke. Charlie, you're my buddy. The head was right there like

I said. Somebody was here. And when I left, the front door was open. Leakey's gone and swiped the head on us. Charlie, tell me you believe me."

Charlie shut the refrigerator door. "I believe you all right. Let's get out of here."

They drove back to Saratoga. Victor kept talking about the head, swearing he had seen it until at last Charlie told him to shut up. Charlie drove over to Leakey's house, which was still dark. Then he drove over to the Pyramid Mall, even though the movie had let out half an hour earlier. Leakey's car was gone.

"How'd you know he went to the movies?" asked Charlie.

"I followed him."

"Was he by himself?"

"Nah, he had a date. Hot little number in tight red pants."

"Did you bother to see if anyone was following you?"

"Why should anyone follow me?"

Charlie drove back to Doris's apartment. Looking up at her windows, he saw they were dark. He decided to go home.

"The way I see it," said Victor, "Leakey left the movie early, drove out to the cabin with this floozy and discovered someone had been there. So what does he do? He moves the head. Who could blame him?"

"Why'd he keep the head in the refrigerator in the first place?" asked Charlie.

"He had to keep it cool. I mean, a head once it's cut off is just so much hamburger. Probably he wants to take more pictures."

"So where's the head now?"

"Probably in his truck or maybe in his back seat or something."

"You've got all the answers, don't you?"

"Hey, Charlie, I'm a private detective. I gotta be on the ball."

Chapter Fourteen

The voice on the telephone coughed, cleared his throat with a long, gargling noise, then said, "Yeah, it's definitely not Buckdancer. No telling who it is but we've tipped off the Jockey Club. They're going to launch an official investigation." Lenny Ravitz began to cough again and Charlie pulled the phone away from his ear.

It was early Friday afternoon. Charlie had called the Thoroughbred Racing Protective Bureau from the office right after arriving from Schuylerville and the Wholesome Dairy. Because of his arm, he hadn't gone swimming. In fact, he hadn't gone swimming for over a week. This made him dislike himself. He imagined becoming so fat that no chair would fit him, that doorways would have to be specially widened.

"So the Jockey Club was interested?" asked Charlie.

"You bet. They're going to kick that horse right out of the Stud Book. And they'll also put a quick stop to the sale of his foals. Which reminds me, you know that guy Leakey you asked about? He's down as buying two of them."

"And now he can't race them?"

"Not on any Thoroughbred track he can't. They got no blood."

"You learn anything about Stitt?" asked Charlie. Victor sat across the desk listening and gently cleaning his ears with the eraser of a pencil. On top of the file cabinet, the stuffed cockatoo or toucan or parrot stared down at them. Charlie couldn't imagine why Victor had thought the office needed a stuffed parrot.

"Not much to learn. We thought there might be an angle on the inheritance, but his heir turns out to be a brother in Ohio. Teaches biology at some community college. Anything else?"

"Not right now. Let me know if you turn up anything new."

"Sure thing, and thanks again for the help."

As Charlie hung up the phone, Victor asked: "Who can't race where?"

"Your lawyer friend, Leakey. He bought two of Sweet Dreams's foals."

"You going to tell Peterson?"

Charlie looked out the window. It was raining and all his clothes felt damp. "I think I'll talk to Leakey first."

"Better take a gun," said Victor.

Charlie started to put on his jacket. "By the way," he asked, "where'd that bird come from?" He decided he had to find out one way or the other, even if it made him the butt of one of Victor's jokes. The bird was missing a lot of feathers and looked moth-eaten.

"What bird?" Victor glanced toward the ceiling.

"That parrot on the file cabinet."

"Oh, yeah, that showed up the other day. Didn't you get my note?"

"What note?"

Victor began rummaging through the papers on the desk. "Here it is. Your mother sent it from Atlantic City. You owe me fifteen bucks."

"Why?"

"She shipped it collect."

Charlie took three five-dollar bills from his wallet and tossed them on the desk. "Any idea why she sent it?" he asked.

"Not me. Maybe we can boil it down for soup."

Charlie descended the stairs, then paused at the street door and watched the raindrops hit and bounce off the pavement. He thought how his curiosity had just cost him fifteen dollars and that he still had no better idea what the parrot was doing in his office. Why should his mother send him a stuffed parrot? Didn't he have enough to worry about already? It seemed to be raining a little harder. Charlie's umbrella was in the milk truck about a hundred yards away. Liquid winter—Charlie flung open the door and rushed down the hill. He was drenched before he had gone twenty feet.

The engine of the truck refused to start. Charlie flooded it, then had to wait. He felt undecided about Leakey, and made up his mind to see Jespersen first. He was almost sorry that he was on such bad terms with Peterson, because he wished he had someone to talk to. He needed to attach all the facts to little pieces of wood and see if they built anything. The starter on the truck made a growling, whirring noise. Just as Charlie thought the battery was about to die, the engine turned over and caught. He shoved it into first and it lurched forward.

It was clear to Charlie that if Victor had not come rushing up Doris's back stairs, then he, Charlie, would have spent the night in Doris's bed. That single fact shoved into the forefront of his brain was enough to leave him shortwinded. A door had been opened. There had been a vision of bright light. The door had been slammed shut, leaving Charlie in the dark.

Even if the head had been in the refrigerator, its discovery would not have been worth Victor's interruption. Charlie would have delivered the head to Peterson. There would have been a certain amount of hoopla. Doris would have slept alone. Peterson, presumably, would have arrested Leakey, who was either guilty or being framed. If he was being framed, then it implied that some unknown party was keeping a fairly close eye on their activities. It meant Victor had been followed.

Who had followed him? Charlie tried to concentrate but nibbling away at his ability to think rationally were his accumulated frustrations. When would Wanamaker return from Santa Fe? Why had his mother sent him a stuffed parrot? He again thought of Butch Cassidy and the Sundance Kid searching for peace and quiet in Argentina. What did it get them? In one version, they had been surprised by soldiers while attempting to rob a bank in Mercedes, Uruguay. An American salesman named Steele had seen the bodies of Cassidy, the Sundance Kid and Etta Place half-covered with a tarpaulin in the dirt of the town square.

"The woman was outside with the horses and was shot down first," Steele had said. "The two men rushed out and were killed in the street." It was December 1911. Butch Cassidy was forty-four.

Charlie drove the milk truck along the edge of Congress Park. The windshield wipers made a violent whap-whap noise. Had any bandits managed to die of old age? The most famous was probably Frank James, but his thirty-three years of life after the murder of Jesse was a lonely and frustrated time. He had sold shoes and men's clothing. He had tended horses. He had even appeared in Saratoga in the summer of 1894 to work as a bookie.

Jesse too must have known Saratoga. Twenty years earlier he and Frank had hid out in a hotel in Chatfield's Corners, just north of Saratoga, where they had distant cousins. At that time the neighboring town of Middle Grove was named Jamesville, while the local bank, the James Bank, had been founded by an industrial tycoon, also named Jesse James, who lived on a mountain.

Charlie tried to imagine the outlaw Jesse James in Saratoga in the 1870s. Jesse had raced horses in Memphis and was said to know more about horses than any other man in Missouri. He too had been a kind of tycoon: a tycoon of disorder. Certainly he had gone to the track. Charlie was only sorry that he hadn't robbed the Adirondack Trust.

But Frank hadn't done well in Saratoga. At the end of the 1894 season, he packed up and moved to St. Louis, where he had taken a job as a "greeter" in a burlesque house. It amazed Charlie that Frank and Jesse James had probably ridden their horses along these very streets that he was now driving to Jespersen's office.

This time Jespersen's waiting room was empty except for a boy with a Great Dane whose right front paw was wrapped with about a mile of white adhesive. The Great Dane took no interest in his surroundings but stared at the bandage with his head tilted first to one side, then the other as if he were on the very brink of having his first thought.

"Put his foot in a rat trap," said the boy. "I told him not to."

After another minute, an elderly woman with a parakeet came out of a consultation room and the receptionist told Charlie to go in. From someplace in back, a dog was whimpering. Jespersen stood reading a piece of paper attached to a clipboard. He glanced up and nodded to Charlie. He was a tall man, probably six feet two or three. As before, he wore a white laboratory coat. He took off his glasses and put them in his breast pocket. Without them, his blue eyes looked watery and insubstantial.

"What's on your mind, Mr. Bradshaw?"

"Just a couple of questions. Stitt was also a breeder, wasn't he?"

"In a small way, yes."

"Did you give him a hand with that?"

Jespersen leaned back against a white Formica counter, picked up a small rubber mallet and tapped it against his palm. "About a dozen times or so. I believe there's also a vet in Bennington who he called upon, Dr. Herman Schmidt."

"What about the mare, Indian Maid? Do you remember that horse?"

"I remember her, yes. What about her?"

"She was bred with Buckdancer and the result was the colt, Sweet Dreams. Did you assist in that?"

"No, I didn't. In fact, I had very little to do with Sweet Dreams. When he injured his leg last year, I happened to see him. Maybe two or three other times as well. Actually, I've been thinking about that horse since our talk earlier this week. It struck me that the fact that I had little to do with him might be somewhat suspicious—that Willis was trying to keep me away from him. As I say, I was involved with all of his horses, but that one probably the least."

"Did you and Stitt ever breed horses by artificial insemination?"

Jespersen looked at Charlie uncertainly. "I don't know whether you are aware of this, Mr. Bradshaw, but it's illegal to breed Thoroughbreds by artificial insemination. Sometimes artificial insemination may be used as a little extra insurance, but only after the mare has already been covered by the stallion."

"So you think this Schmidt from Bennington took care of Sweet Dreams?"

"Possibly, but I don't really know."

"Was anyone else involved with that horse?" Charlie stood by a pair of tall cabinets. Nearly everything in the room was white. Suspended from a wire above him like sheets from a clothesline were five X-rays of hips.

"Not that I know of." Jespersen paused and put the rubber mallet back on the counter. "As a matter of fact, there was a local lawyer who had an interest in Sweet Dreams. He was afraid that the horse might have to be put down after his accident."

"Was his name Leakey, by any chance?"

"That's right. Roy or Ray Leakey, I'm not sure which."

"Have you ever wanted to own a racehorse?"

Jespersen laughed and again Charlie was reminded of paper being crinkled, perhaps wax paper. "Too much trouble. I advise my girlfriend sometimes. She's got a couple of horses. But that's as close as I want to get."

A few minutes later, Charlie left Jespersen's clinic. As he drove back across Saratoga toward Leakey's office, he tried to think about what Jespersen had told him. The veterinarian's calm self-assurance made it difficult to get past his words, to see what propped them up. But instead of thinking about Jespersen, Charlie again began worrying about his mother and her question as to whether he could raise any money. The answer was definitely no. If she wanted to lose a fortune in Atlantic City, that was her business, but Charlie didn't want to put a mortgage on his house just so she could lose even more. Again he imagined her sleeping on his couch. No, thought Charlie, I'd be the one stuck with the couch; she'd get the bed.

Cole Younger had been another bandit who survived to old age. Arrested with eleven bullet wounds after the Northfield

Raid in 1876, he had remained in prison for twenty-five years and then joined Frank James in the James-Younger Wild West Show. Both men were about sixty. The conditions of Younger's parole kept him from actually performing, but he sat in a special section of the theater and chatted with the audience. Later he would say a few words at a reception. These were so well received that he decided to go on the lecture circuit. His topic was "What Life Has Taught Me." Since he still had seventeen bullets lodged in his body, it could be guessed that life had taught him a great deal.

Before seeing Leakey, Charlie telephoned the veterinarian Herman Schmidt in Bennington to see if he had helped Stitt take care of Sweet Dreams. Schmidt was friendly but denied having heard of the horse. He said that in the past five years he had only visited Stitt's stable five or six times.

Charlie drove on to Leakey's office, then parked in the lot behind the Adirondack Trust. It was still pouring. Running to the lawyer's front door, he paused in the hall to wipe his face with a handkerchief before going upstairs. Leakey was in the reception room talking to his secretary. When he saw Charlie, he half turned away.

"I don't have any time for you, Bradshaw."

Charlie ignored him and busied himself with taking off his jacket and shaking it. Then he hung it on the coatrack.

"Maybe we should talk in your office," said Charlie, "unless you don't mind your secretary listening."

Leakey was about Charlie's height but at least twenty-five pounds lighter. Charlie saw a muscle in his jaw moving up and down, up and down. Like a flashing light, he thought.

"Are you deaf, Bradshaw?" he asked. "I want you out of here."

"You told me you had never heard of the horse Sweet Dreams," said Charlie. "This morning I learned you bought two of his foals. The Jockey Club has asked the Protective Bureau to investigate that horse. It seems he's a ringer."

Leakey stared at Charlie, then went to the door of his office, opened it and motioned Charlie to enter. Taking his time, Charlie brushed past him into the adjoining room. The office had a shiny leather chesterfield and two windows looking out on Church Street. Charlie could see people running through the rain to the post office.

"How much did you pay for those foals?" he asked. "Hell, they'll be good saddle horses. You like riding? Or maybe you could find a state fair someplace that won't mind seeing them run."

"Who says that Sweet Dreams is a ringer?" asked Leakey.

"The Protective Bureau. He was supposed to have been sired by Buckdancer but the blood doesn't match. Apparently the mare was artificially inseminated. The trouble is you knew there was something wrong. That's why you told me you'd never heard of Sweet Dreams. What else have you been lying about? Did McClatchy call you when he came up here?"

Leakey didn't say anything, but looked angrily at Charlie. The muscle in his jaw continued to pulsate. Charlie thought it seemed to be counting out the seconds, like a stopwatch or a kitchen timer.

"Maybe you were Stitt's silent partner after all," said Charlie. "What kind of case could be made against you? You were friends with Stitt and knew about Sweet Dreams. You bought two of his foals. Also you were a demolitions expert in Vietnam, so you'd know how to blow up a car, right?"

"You don't have a case, Bradshaw." Leakey stood by the door. Although the lawyer was clearly tense, Charlie had no feeling of personal threat.

"Last night my friend Victor broke into your cabin," said Charlie.

The muscle in Leakey's jaw grew stiff. "Say that again?"

"Victor was searching for some letters that a client of his wants to get from you. I guess you know about those letters."

Leakey unfolded his arms. He seemed hesitant, as if he couldn't understand why Charlie was telling him about the cabin. "Are you serious? He could go to jail for that."

"You have no evidence and I'll deny it if I'm asked. It's pretty much of a mess but nothing's been broken except a back window.

The main thing is that inside the refrigerator Victor found McClatchy's head."

If Charlie had expected Leakey to be surprised, he was mistaken. Mostly he looked suspicious. He stared at Charlie as if trying to make up his mind about something. "Did you see the head?" he asked.

"No, someone had taken it away by the time I got there."

"Then your friend's lying."

"No again. Victor has his faults but he wouldn't lie to me. If he says the head was there, it was there. We can draw two possible conclusions from this. Either you put it there or someone else put it there. If it was someone else, then that someone is trying to frame you for murder. You know that somebody's been sending around pictures of McClatchy's head?"

"Bradshaw, if you think you've got a case, then go to the cops. There's no reason I should talk to you. I get nothing from it and you just make me angry."

Charlie stood his ground. "I asked if you knew about the pictures?"

"Pictures? Yeah, I got a whole bunch of them." Leakey walked to his desk, opened a drawer and took out a large white envelope. He handed it to Charlie.

Opening it, Charlie found a dozen Polaroid snapshots of McClatchy's head. The eyes were half-closed and looked sleepy. In the middle of the forehead was a bullet hole, just as Victor had described. The head stood up on its severed neck on a table. Holding the head in place was a pair of bookends in the shape of rearing silver horses.

"Where'd you get these?" asked Charlie.

"They'd been slipped under my door. I found them when I came in."

"When was this?"

"This morning."

"You know what it looks like, don't you?"

"What?" The muscle in Leakey's jaw had begun to pulsate again.

"That you're the guy taking the pictures. I bet those are even your bookends, am I right?"

"Yes, they're out at the cabin."

"Why haven't you given these pictures to Peterson?"

"I haven't made up my mind yet."

It occurred to Charlie that Leakey knew something else he wasn't telling about. "You know, both Stitt and Pease were killed because they had some information that they had decided not to tell Peterson. As I say, there are two possibilities. Either you killed these people or somebody else is trying to set you up for it. Where were you last night? Where'd you go after the movie?"

"Forget it, Bradshaw, no more questions."

"What about late Saturday afternoon when Stitt was killed? Do you have an alibi for that time?"

"Get out."

"Does that mean you don't?"

"Get out!"

Chapter
Fifteen

Charlie took a swizzle stick and jabbed at the bubbles in his beer. Then he glanced across the bar at an eight-by-ten glossy of Jersey Joe Wolcott crouched down in a fighting stance ready to do somebody damage. To be a boxer, a man had to accept the possibility of getting punched in the head. Maybe the same was true of being a private detective, thought Charlie. Maybe that was why he kept going to see Roy Leakey: simply in the hope that Leakey might punch him.

Charlie was waiting for a phone call from Lenny Ravitz at the Protective Bureau, whom he had unsuccessfully tried to telephone right after seeing Leakey. It was six o'clock Friday evening. Doris was at the other end of the bar serving beers to two off-duty policemen. All three were laughing. Although the bar was crowded, Charlie had a vacant stool on either side of him. He had almost stopped noticing such details of his unpopularity.

Doris wore a blue denim dress and a string of yellow beads. Her profile was to Charlie and he kept staring at the small of her back. She was a strong woman and one time during a softball game, Charlie had watched her hit the first pitch over the center-field fence. He sometimes wondered if that was why he loved her. Charlie also played for the Backstretch team but was lucky if he managed a single during the entire day, which was why he'd been nicknamed Grounded-Out-To-Short Bradshaw.

The phone rang and Berney McQuilkin picked up the receiver. He glanced around the bar and when he saw Charlie he nodded. Charlie walked to the pay phone at the back of the room. It was Lenny Ravitz.

"I wanted to ask you," said Charlie, "who bought those other foals." There was a lot of noise in the bar and Charlie had to cover one ear.

"Three people bought them. I got their names right here on my desk. Bob Wilks, Michael Forbes and Kathy Marshall. That make any sense to you?"

"Only the last name. She's got a store in Saratoga. Do you know the others?"

"Just Wilks. He's a trainer on Long Island. By the way, the Jockey Club's pretty grateful for your help with Sweet Dreams. I guess there'd been some suspicion about his two wins. They're contacting the FBI. Interfering with the outcome of a sporting event, that's a federal crime. Anyway, if I can ever do you a favor, you got it."

"Thanks," said Charlie, "maybe you can give me a recommendation to the Pinkertons."

Ravitz assumed he was joking and laughed.

When Charlie finished his beer, he decided to drive home. It was still raining and the windshield wipers on the milk truck were ponderously slow. Gusts of wind pushed at the truck. In the morning, many trees would be bare.

The first thing he did when he got home was to call Wanamaker in Santa Fe. There was no answer. Then he made himself a ham and Swiss cheese on rye and opened a Labatts. He felt jumpy and kept his .38 tucked in his belt. Twice he drew it when he heard branches rattle against the side of the house. Then he locked the windows and pulled all the shades. As he was cleaning up, a washer broke on the cold-water tap so that no matter how tightly he turned the handle there was still a gush of water. There were no extra washers in his toolbox. He settled the problem by turning off the main shut-off valve.

Charlie went to bed early, then lay awake listening to the sound of rain splashing through the remaining leaves and hitting the roof. He kept thinking about the old age of Frank James. When faced with a bank robbery, Frank James had been bold, resolute and acted without hesitation. But when faced with living out his life, he had seemed ineffectual and clumsy. His role in the James-Younger Wild West Show had been even smaller than Cole Younger's. He rode his horse in the grand finale and, in one of the dramatic pieces, he was a passenger on a stage coach held up by desperadoes. These successes later led him to take a job with a traveling stock company. He had bit parts in two plays: *Across the Desert* and *The Fatal Scar*.

For years Frank James had hoped to be named doorkeeper for the Missouri Legislature. Some Democrats had lobbied for him but in the end it was considered politically dangerous. There had always been the suggestion that his acquittal twenty years before had less to do with evidence and more to do with the fact that the Republicans wanted him in jail and the Democrats didn't.

This rejection soured Frank James and led him to support Teddy Roosevelt and the Bull Moose Party in the 1904 election. He saw Teddy as a man of action like himself. Unfortunately, he announced his support at a reunion of Quantrill's guerrillas in Independence. The aging ex-guerrillas were fierce Democrats to a man and nearly shot Frank James. Having thrown over his old friends, James left Missouri and took up farming in Oklahoma. At the time of his death in 1915, he was so certain that unscrupulous showmen would steal his body that he had his wife deposit his ashes in a savings bank where they remained for thirty years.

It had always amazed Charlie that Frank James, who, with his brother Jesse, had led the very first bank robbery in the United States committed by an organized gang (Clay County Savings Bank, February 13, 1866—a date engraved on Charlie's heart), should have spent so much of his death in a safe-deposit vault. When Frank James's wife died in 1944, she and her husband were buried in a Kansas City cemetery. This too amazed Charlie:

that he had been a pudgy fourth-grader when Frank James was at last put in the ground.

Saturday morning, after he had finished delivering milk, Charlie drove into Saratoga to see Kathy Marshall. It was a cool morning and absolutely clear. Most of the leaves had blown down in the rain and those that were left were pale yellow. The distant line of the Adirondacks was as sharp as if drawn with a pen. Charlie kept sneezing. The side door of the milk truck didn't close completely and a cold wind tugged at his pants leg.

Charlie parked the truck by the office, then walked up Broadway to Kathy Marshall's store, the Blue Lion. When he passed the store belonging to his ex-wife he sort of crept sideways, keeping his back to the glass and his head ducked down. A young mother wheeling her child in a stroller steered a wide path around him. When he reached the Blue Lion, he straightened up and sighed. It was a large store with two large windows displaying women's clothes, cookware and expensive children's toys from Sweden. Charlie hurried inside.

Kathy Marshall was a trim woman in her mid-twenties. She had the perfect features of a movie star and when she stood, she seemed to push her face slightly forward as if for inspection. She wore a tan dress with a blue border, and a thin gold chain around her neck with a single pearl.

"Yes, I bought the foal," she said. "I like horses. Willis told me it was particularly promising, so I thought why not?" She was only a few inches over five feet and looked up at Charlie with her head to one side.

"Did Jespersen give you any advice about it?" asked Charlie. They stood at the front of the shop near the cash register. Behind Charlie was a rack of white Mexican blouses.

"Not really, although he's helped me with other horses. He just looked at the foal and said it was perfectly healthy. What do you mean, that it's no good?"

"Sweet Dreams is a ringer. His blood doesn't match up with the stallion that was supposed to have sired him. It means that none of his foals can run on a Thoroughbred track."

Although Kathy Marshall must have been disappointed, she gave no sign of it. Charlie wondered if she already knew. He found it impossible to get past her beauty and guess intelligently about her thoughts. Her blond hair was short and cut close to her head. On her left wrist, she wore a large digital watch with a gold band. She held a yellow pencil and tapped it against her front teeth as she looked back at Charlie.

"Did you come here just to tell me that my foal was no good?" she asked.

"No, I wanted to know how well you knew Willis Stitt."

"Not very well. I bought a horse from him, that's all."

"What about Roy Leakey?"

"I know him better, but I haven't seen him to talk to for about a year."

"And Jespersen, how well do you know him?"

Kathy Marshall squinted her eyes at Charlie, then shook her head. "Mr. Bradshaw, who are you?"

"I gave you my card."

"Yes, but what right do you have to ask these questions, any questions? Why should I talk to you? You see these people waiting? They want my assistance. My lawyer is Toby Brown. Why don't you see him."

"Has Chief Peterson asked you about any of these murders?" asked Charlie.

"No, he hasn't and I can't imagine why he would."

Kathy Marshall turned to a woman customer waiting nearby and smiled with what appeared to be affection and good cheer. It was like seeing a light being flicked on and the charm of it made Charlie feel doubly excluded. He hated being a sucker for pretty girls.

After leaving the Blue Lion, Charlie drove across Saratoga to visit Jespersen's ex-wife, who had an address on Diamond Street. The truck rattled terribly and the empty milk racks banged against one another. Occasionally the truck backfired, making people on the street jump and stare after him.

Mrs. Jespersen lived in a white Colonial house with two big

maples in the front yard. A teenage boy was raking leaves and stuffing them into green garbage bags. Charlie parked the truck several houses away, then walked back.

Mrs Jespersen answered the door and, when Charlie gave her his card, she invited him in. She was about forty-five, slender and very attractive. She looked like a kind of racehorse: muscular and athletic and she even had a chestnut coloring with long chestnut-colored hair that reached past her shoulders. She wore jeans and a white blouse.

Charlie followed her through the front hall. Although he assumed he was interrupting her, she seemed perfectly content to talk. She offered him coffee, then went off to make it.

"You're Doris's friend," she said from the kitchen. "She speaks very highly of you." There was the sound of cupboards being opened and closed. "All I have is instant but there's cream if you want it."

"Black's fine," said Charlie. He sat on a sunporch at the back of the house. In the backyard were flowers and a small vegetable garden in which there were still some tomatoes and one large, yellow pumpkin. After several minutes, Mrs. Jespersen came out carrying two mugs.

She sat down on a chaise longue next to Charlie. A strand of hair fell across her face and she brushed it back. "Just what did you want to talk about?" she asked.

"I was curious about how well you knew Willis Stitt," said Charlie. He sipped the coffee, then set the mug down on a glass-topped table.

"When I was still married, he was over here to dinner several times. And once after that he asked me out, but I refused. I didn't dislike him but neither was I attracted to him. He was involved in various business deals with my husband but they didn't seem to be close friends."

"Do you think your husband could have owned horses with Stitt?"

"Possibly. My husband confided in me very little."

"Doris told me you'd been thinking of hiring a private detective and that she had recommended me. Do you mind telling me why you wanted a private detective?"

Mrs. Jespersen hesitated. She had long, thin fingers with long, narrow nails. She touched one hand to her throat. "I'm not sure I want to talk about that," she said. "The reason I wanted a private detective had to do with my settlement with my husband. We finally came to a compromise. Is it important?"

"I think it is," said Charlie. "At this point, anything I can learn is important."

Mrs. Jespersen sipped her coffee. "My husband's the sort of man who reveals very little about himself. I used to think he was just modest but really I think he hates to let anything go or to have anything known about him. He offered very little in the settlement and I felt he had more. David is very fond of Kruger-rands—you know, those South African gold coins. He buys them, then tucks them away. He grew up very poor and part of him expects to be poor again. I once found twenty of them in a jar, way at the back of the closet. He also owns a fair amount of property in the country. I told him I thought he was being unfair about the settlement and that unless he offered more I would hire a private detective. When we married, I had a little money and David used it to pay for veterinarian school. I didn't feel I was robbing him."

"And he agreed to give you more money?"

"Yes. He hated the idea of a private detective. Three years ago he ran for city commissioner and I'm sure he'll run again. He was afraid that a private detective would attract bad publicity."

The sunporch was furnished with white metal furniture with green cushions. A variety of green plants hung from the ceiling. Charlie recognized a begonia but that was the only plant he knew. "Did you ever happen to meet the jockey Jimmy McClatchy or hear your husband speak of him?"

"No. I never heard of him until I read he'd been killed at your house."

"What about Rodger Pease?"

"I don't recognize the name."

"What about Roy Leakey?"

"Isn't he a lawyer? I've never met him but I remember hearing that he was once involved with Kathy Marshall. If that's true, then David must dislike him. He can be very jealous."

"What kinds of things is Jespersen interested in?" asked Charlie. "You think he likes horses?"

"I suppose he must but I don't really know. You'd think after twenty-five years of marriage I'd know him like the back of my hand, but that's not true. After the first few years we didn't spend much time together. We had a child who died." Mrs. Jespersen drank a little coffee. She held the blue mug with both hands as if to warm them. "We were never close after that. This is a big house and we each had our own life."

"But there must be things he really likes."

"He likes women. He likes to be thought of as important. He likes money. He's also quite keen on karate. It frightened me sometimes how he could just smash things with his hands."

"Could he commit murder?"

Mrs. Jespersen looked out at the backyard. The leaves had been raked into several piles and a gray squirrel ran back and forth from one pile to another. "I don't know," she said.

Charlie left Mrs. Jespersen around three, and went to his cousin's hardware store where he bought washers to fix his broken faucet. As always the clerk gave him a ten percent discount but treated him like a poor relation, which is true enough, thought Charlie.

Then, for the remainder of the day, Charlie learned what he could about Jespersen. He had been a veterinarian in Saratoga for ten years. Before that he had a practice in White Plains, where he also looked after horses at Belmont and Aqueduct. He'd spent three years in the Army and six years at Cornell. Jespersen had always been involved with horses but never seemed to own any. He played golf, was a member of the Rotary Club and also the Lions.

Early in the evening Charlie spent some time trying to locate Bob Wilks, the trainer on Long Island who had bought one of

Sweet Dreams's foals. He finally reached him having dinner at a Deer Park country club.

Wilks said he bought the foal because Stitt had assured him it was a hot prospect. He and Stitt had trained horses together on Long Island in the early 1970s. No, he had never heard of Leakey or Jespersen. Yes, it was a shame about Stitt's death. Wilks said he had meant to fly into Saratoga for the funeral but at the last moment something big had come up.

Charlie left his office around eight and drove home. He took the stuffed parrot with him, then stopped at the first trash can and tossed the parrot inside. So much for bad jokes, he thought. He had the sense that he was beginning to cope with the chaos around him. When he got home, he made himself a bowl of tomato soup and a couple of toasted cheese sandwiches. During the evening he called John Wanamaker three times without success. A man at Wanamaker's rooming house said he hadn't seen him all week. Charlie fixed the washer in the cold-water tap, worked a little at adjusting the lift wires in the bathroom toilet, then went to bed early but had trouble sleeping. His .38 was under his pillow and each time he touched it he woke up frightened.

The next morning Charlie opened his eyes at six with the knowledge that he had to see Flo Abernathy. It was as if the idea itself had waked him. Having registered the idea, he tried to go back to sleep but couldn't. Outside it was still dark. The water was loud against the shore. He could hear the wind blowing through the trees and the branches seemed to be whipping and lashing each other. At last Charlie got up. As he made breakfast, he put on a Benny Goodman record just to drown out the noise of the weather.

At eight thirty, he drove into Saratoga by way of Route 29 so he could stop at a greenhouse and buy some flowers. He got a dozen long-stemmed roses wrapped in green paper. It seemed like a good idea at the time, but when he arrived at Flo Abernathy's door with a dozen roses under his good arm, he began to feel foolish.

He hadn't seen Miss Abernathy since Tuesday at Rodger Pease's funeral. When she opened the door, she smiled, then stepped back to let Charlie enter. She wore a long, blue silk dressing gown with cloth-covered buttons. Her white hair hung loose down her back. She seemed paler somehow, more transparent. At first Charlie thought she was sick, then he realized it was grief.

"I brought you some flowers," he said.

She took the roses as if uncertain what to do with them. In contrast to the red of the flowers, her skin was the color of a cloud. "I'll put them in water," she said. "Have you come to give me a progress report? At least you seem to have no more bruises. How's your arm?"

"Still stiff, but I hope to go swimming with it next week."

The air in the room smelled stale and there seemed to be more general clutter. Charlie guessed there were at least twenty chairs. He picked up an ivory carving of a mountain with a little hut near the top and two men outside the door smoking their pipes. A zigzagging trail led up to the hut. He put the carving back on top of a bookcase filled with leatherbound books.

"Would you like some coffee?" asked Flo. "I'm afraid I have no chocolate-chip cookies but I could make some cinnamon toast."

"Just coffee would be fine." Charlie threaded his way between the furniture to the turret, which was half-filled with plants. Each of the four narrow windows looking out on Ludlow had a window seat with a red leather cushion. Down on the street three boys on bikes attempted synchronized wheelies as a beagle puppy ran around them barking.

Flo Abernathy found a tall blue vase for the roses but there seemed to be no unoccupied surface on which to put it. She removed several photograph albums from a table and set them on the floor. The teakettle began to whistle.

Shortly, she joined Charlie in the turret with the coffee and a plate of cinnamon toast. Each piece of toast was cut into three long sections. She offered the plate to Charlie. "When I was a child," she said, "we called these Trotwoods, I'm not sure why. It had something to do with *David Copperfield*."

Across the room, Charlie saw the brass horse that he had dug out of the ruins of Rodger Pease's house, all polished and standing on a white doily in the middle of a small round table. It reminded him of the two silver horses that had been used to prop up McClatchy's head. "You grew up in Glens Falls?" he said.

"That's right." Flo Abernathy sat down on a window seat across from Charlie.

"Do you still have family there?"

"A brother. I haven't seen him since my mother's funeral in 1950." She gestured vaguely toward the rest of the room. "It was my mother who left me this furniture. Sometimes I read about my brother in the paper. He and the rest of my family, they all disapproved of my quitting college and remaining in Saratoga, and disapproved of Rodger too, of course."

"Why don't you get in touch with your brother?" asked Charlie.

"It's been too long."

"It's only a telephone call, or I could even drive you up there." He had a momentary picture of Flo Abernathy in the milk truck.

"He wouldn't care to see me."

"Why don't you find out? Aren't you curious about him?"

Miss Abernathy looked at Charlie, then smiled. "I'll consider it," she said. "You know, after I last saw you, I realized I had known your father. He was one of the first people I met after I decided to remain in Saratoga and become a singer."

"Did he borrow money from you?" asked Charlie.

"No, nothing like that. I had been auditioning at the Chicago Club. It was in the middle of the afternoon. A rainy September day. I was waiting for Rodger to pick me up but he thought I'd be longer. I didn't get the job. Your father was the only other person in the lounge. The whole town seemed empty. He came over and sat down and began to talk. He had heard me singing and told me how much he liked it. He wasn't being fresh or trying to flirt. I remember I liked his face. It was bright and energetic. His shiny black hair was slicked back and not a strand was out of place. It turned out that he knew Rodger. I'm not sure how it happened but soon we were betting pennies on the raindrops that were rolling down the big window. We did this for at least an hour. I remember I won fifteen cents. Then Rodger arrived and your father took us both out to dinner. I expect I saw him another half dozen times before I heard he had committed suicide."

Charlie didn't say anything. He had hardly any memory of his father: a vague recollection of being tossed in the air, of falling and being caught at the last moment. He remembered the suicide only because the house had been full of policemen who were kind to him.

"By the way," said Charlie, "I wanted to ask you if you know what happened to Rodger's dog. I'd forgotten about it."

"I have no idea. I assume it was buried."

"Did Rodger ever have to take it to a vet?"

"Certainly, it was quite old and had all sorts of complicated problems."

"What vet did he go to?"

Miss Abernathy smiled as if remembering a joke. "Rodger used to boast that he got free service from the best vet in Saratoga."

"Who was that?"

"I don't recall his name but he once ran for city commissioner."

Not long afterward, Charlie left Miss Abernathy and drove over to see Victor, who turned out to be sleeping. Charlie had to hammer on his door for several minutes. From the other side he heard various grumbles and groans and at last the door was opened. Victor was naked but held a dirty sweat shirt to his waist.

"Don't you realize this is Sunday?" he asked.

Charlie pushed past him. Moshe, the one-eyed cat, stared at Charlie, then ran into the kitchen.

"Where were you last night?" asked Charlie.

Victor scratched the gray hairs on his chest and began pulling on some tattered underwear. "Storming the heights of sexual transport. Have you ever known a woman who could walk on her hands?"

Victor's clothes were scattered around the room. Charlie removed a pair of pants from a rocking chair and sat down. On the wall above him was a poster of the Three Stooges.

"I wanted to ask you," said Charlie, "about the woman who hired you to get back those letters."

"Ruth MacDermott, what about her?" Victor continued to get dressed, putting on blue jeans and a black sweat shirt. He looked in the mirror over the mantel, bared his teeth, picked at the front ones with one fingernail, then grinned at himself.

"Why did she think the letters were at Leakey's cabin?"

"Beats me. I figured she'd been out there."

"Where does she live?"

Victor gave him an address on Seward. "You going to bother her?"

"Just a couple of questions. What's she like?"

"Helluva bosom. Nice big eyes. You might do worse." Victor began picking his clothes off the floor. When he had an armful, he went to the closet and threw them in.

"One other thing," said Charlie, standing up, "I want you to keep a close watch on Roy Leakey. Forget everything else but that."

Victor paused in the middle of the room. "Why? You want him to beat my head with a stick, maybe kick me in the balls?"

"I think he's in danger."

"Couldn't happen to a nicer guy."

"I want you to stay near him. If you see Jespersen hanging around, then call me right away."

"Why Jespersen?"

"I think he killed McClatchy."

"You going to tell Peterson?"

"Not yet."

Ruth MacDermott's bosom gave the appearance of having been made from a feather bolster. It was large, cream colored and dotted with freckles. She wore a dark red dressing gown, which exposed a sizable V of flesh. Charlie looked away to the wallpaper, which was red with paisley designs in black velvet. It was like the wallpaper in a whorehouse, thought Charlie, who had never been in a whorehouse. Some fellow soldiers had attempted to take him to one in Germany but at the last moment he had got cold feet.

It seemed to Charlie that the whole room was like a room in a whorehouse, a Western whorehouse like Fanny Porter's Sporting House in San Antonio: overstuffed furniture covered with red velvet, thick red drapery, a Persian carpet, dark mahogany tables and sideboards, oval portraits of big-bosomed women with dreamy eyes. On one of the overstuffed chairs, a white Persian cat lay washing itself.

"I hadn't thought of the cabin until I talked to Kathy Marshall at a cocktail party. She used to be intimate with Roy. She told me that he kept all his letters up there. That's why I told Vic. Isn't he sweet?"

"Who?" asked Charlie.

"Why, Victor. He's so eager."

Charlie glanced at Ruth MacDermott, who sat perched on the edge of a chair with her hands in her lap. She was a large woman, almost heavy. Charlie had never thought of Victor as sweet. "He's a good friend," said Charlie, not knowing what else to say.

"I adore roguish men," said Mrs. MacDermott.

"Just when did Kathy Marshall tell you about the cabin?" asked Charlie.

"Last Tuesday evening at the Warnkes'. There was a small party."

"Was she with Jespersen?"

"No, he was busy "

"Do Jespersen and Leakey know each other?"

"Slightly, but Jespersen dislikes Roy for having been involved with Kathy Marshall. He prefers his women unused."

Mrs. MacDermott had masses of dark red hair piled on top of her head. She took a purple cigarette from a box on the table and lit it with a small silver lighter. Charlie glanced at her again, then looked back at the wallpaper. "Were you ever involved with Jespersen?" he asked.

"Good heavens, no. He's too fond of the tomboy type."

"And when did you tell Victor about the letters?"

"Wednesday, the very next day. I'm sorry he didn't find them. Sometimes a woman in love can be indiscreet. I would hate to think of someone reading those letters and misunderstanding." She kept the purple cigarette in one corner of her mouth and it waggled up and down as she spoke.

Charlie wished he could take a look at those letters. "I expect to see Leakey in a day or so," he said. "I'll tell him again that you want them back."

Mrs. MacDermott turned the force of her brown eyes in Charlie's direction. "Then I would be completely in your power," she said.

Sunday evening Charlie spent several hours typing up what he knew about the three murders and his reasons for suspecting Jespersen. He had continued to be on mildly agreeable terms with a lawyer in the prosecutor's office, and on Monday he meant to pay him a visit and present his charges. Presumably the lawyer would call in Peterson. Although Charlie had no real proof of Jespersen's guilt, he knew Peterson well enough to believe that the police chief would open an investigation. If once the police actually questioned Jespersen, then kept plaguing him in an official sort of way, it might be too much for him to stand. After all, Jespersen had political ambitions. Even the slightest legal attention would be damaging.

But Charlie felt dissatisfied. He wanted to arrest Jespersen himself, to confront Peterson and Caldwell with the established fact of Jespersen's guilt. That, however, seemed impossible and Charlie tried to dismiss his desire as no more than vanity. Still, he hated to hand all his work over to Peterson, then scurry back to his cottage on the lake.

Twice that evening Charlie tried calling John Wanamaker. The manager of the rooming house told him that although Wanamaker's belongings were still in his room, Wanamaker himself had apparently disappeared. Charlie imagined him hit by a car and lying unconscious in some hospital.

Apart from Wanamaker, Charlie also worried that he hadn't

heard from his mother. He expected her to call and beg him to get her out of trouble. Maybe he would have to rush down to Atlantic City. As a result, Charlie felt jumpy and alert. All day he had carried his revolver and was constantly aware of its pressure against his stomach where he kept it tucked beneath his waistband. He knew Jespersen must be desperate. Again he sought out Victor to make sure he was watching Roy Leakey. He had even gone so far as to ask Victor to hire Eddie Gillespie if he needed help.

Charlie went to bed around ten. The wind was still roaring in the trees and he thought how the noise would keep him from hearing anyone sneaking up on the cottage. Just as he began to get scared, he fell asleep. At midnight he was awakened by the ringing of the phone. It was Victor.

"Hey, Charlie, I know this is a bad time to call but I just saw someone slipping out of the back of Leakey's house and if I was a betting man I'd give you even odds it was Jespersen. Is that worth waking you up for?"

"I'll be right over."

Charlie dressed, grabbed his revolver and hurried out to the milk truck. All the way into town, he kept the pedal flat to the floor. The empty milk crates banged and rattled against each other over the roar of the motor. There was no other traffic.

Charlie turned down Leakey's street and saw Victor leaning against the red Renault. All the houses were dark. As Charlie drew to a stop, the brakes of the milk truck made a screeching noise.

"Madcap Bradshaw and his Milkmobile," said Victor.

Charlie was tired of jokes about the milk truck. "What makes you think it was Jespersen?" he asked. He looked over at Leakey's house, a white split-level. It too was dark.

Victor stood scratching his elbows. "It was a tall, thin guy sneaking away from the back of the house. Maybe it wasn't Jespersen. Maybe it was only a sneak thief."

"How long have you been here?"

"I followed Leakey home around eleven. He went in. All the drapes were shut so I couldn't see anything. After about forty-five minutes the lights went out and about five minutes later I see this guy in the backyard."

"Did you follow him?"

"Heck no, I get paid for watchin', not tacklin'."

Charlie and Victor stood whispering between the Renault and the truck. The air was cold and Charlie wished he had brought a heavier coat. There would be frost tonight for sure. In the air was the lingering smell of burning leaves.

"Hand me the flashlight in the glove compartment and let's go," said Charlie.

"Where we going?"

"We're going to poke around."

Victor looked unhappy. "Charlie, I don't want to get shot and I don't want to spend the night in jail. Tell me those things won't happen."

"Come on," said Charlie.

Charlie cut across Leakey's lawn to the front steps and rang the bell. It chimed like Big Ben—eight long notes. Charlie waited a minute, then rang again. The porch had a black metal railing. Victor waited on the grass, flapping his arms to keep warm.

"Let's go around back," said Charlie.

Without waiting for Victor, he hurried around the side of the house and immediately stumbled over a barbecue grill, which clanged noisily as it collapsed on the stone patio.

Victor helped Charlie to his feet. "I should have called the local drum and bugle corps," he said.

Reaching the back door, Charlie tried the knob but it was locked. Between the house and grass was a border of stones and small shrubs. Charlie picked up a stone, hit it against a pane of glass, then hit it harder. The glass shattered.

"When I think of the grief you gave me about breaking that tiny window at the cabin," said Victor.

"Don't you ever stop joking?"

"You think I'd be joking if I wasn't terrified? Leakey's probably listening to rock-and-roll music through the stereo headphones. Won't he be surprised when we come rushing into his bedroom holding a .38 and a chunk of granite. That's how people get strokes."

Charlie opened the back door, felt around for a light switch, then flicked it on. The presence of light was comforting. They were in a back hall leading to the kitchen. The house was silent except for the hum of the refrigerator.

"I'll check upstairs," said Charlie. "You look around down here."

"What're we looking for?" They stood in the kitchen next to a large butcher block with a place for knives and meat cleavers. Victor removed a meat cleaver and ran his thumb along the blade.

"We're looking for Leakey," said Charlie.

"Wouldn't it be better to stick together?"

"No, it wouldn't. You want the gun? Take it."

Victor replaced the meat cleaver. "I'd only hurt myself," he said.

The stairs were by the front door. Whenever Charlie came to a light switch, he turned it on. At the top of the stairs was a long hall hung with reproductions of Impressionist paintings. All the floors were carpeted. Charlie looked through one bedroom, then another. He could hear Victor banging around downstairs and whistling. At the end of the hall was the master bedroom. On the door was a large white plaque that said CAPTAIN. Charlie found Roy Leakey lying on his back across the double bed. He wore a dark brown suit. His tie was undone and his shoes lay on the carpet. Next to him on the white bedspread was a small syringe.

Bending down, Charlie put his fingers against Leakey's throat to feel a pulse. It was very slow. Leakey's skin looked gray, like dust or cardboard. He dragged Leakey into a sitting position and shook him. The lawyer had been so carefully groomed when Charlie saw him before that to see him all rumpled made him look like another person. Leakey made a faint groaning noise. Charlie slapped his cheek and shook him again but couldn't bring him around. Standing up, he slipped his arm out of its sling, then grabbed Leakey's wrist and pulled him off the bed and onto his shoulder. Briefly, in the mirror, he saw his reflection with Leakey on his back. It looked as if they were wrestling. Charlie put the syringe in his pocket and headed for the door.

Victor met him at the bottom of the stairs. He was holding a sheet of paper. "Is he dead?"

"Not yet. I'm taking him to the hospital."

"Guess what I found," said Victor, holding up the paper. "Leakey confessed to all three murders."

"Is it signed?"

"No, but it was in his typewriter."

"Go look in the refrigerator, then meet me at the car."

"You think it's there?"

"Just check."

"I don't want to see it again."

"Check!"

Chapter
Sixteen

The red plastic carrying case between Charlie's feet was designed to look like a barn. A pair of brass hooks held together the two halves of the green gambrel roof. It was nine thirty Monday morning and Charlie was sitting on a hard wooden chair in the waiting room of Jespersen's clinic. The carrying case belonged to Victor's cat, Moshe. Charlie wore his khaki milkman's uniform and the starched collar chafed his neck.

Across from Charlie sat an old woman with a white German shepherd that lay on its stomach sniffing and whining. Charlie's .38 was in his back pocket and gouged him uncomfortably. He would have shifted it but the old woman kept staring at him.

"What's wrong with your poor cat?" she asked. She wore a trench coat and had bright circles of pink makeup on her cheeks.

"He won't eat."

"Ralphie usually likes cats," said the woman.

Charlie smiled. He hoped he wouldn't have to discuss the complexities of pets. He half-regretted coming to Jespersen's office and again told himself he was only being motivated by vanity. Better to leave the whole business to Peterson. Well, Peterson was supposed to arrive soon enough.

The door to the examination room opened and Jespersen began

to pass through it. When he saw Charlie, he stopped.

Charlie took hold of the case and stood up. "Victor's cat is sick," he said. "He wasn't able to come so I brought him."

Jespersen gave Charlie a long look. He held a clipboard in his arm as if to shield himself. "What seems to be the matter?" he asked.

"He won't eat."

Jespersen glanced out the window. The Wholesome Dairy milk truck was parked behind his white Buick in the U-shaped drive-way. "Come on in," he said, reaching for the case.

Charlie handed it to him. The case slipped from his fingers and would have fallen if Jespersen hadn't grabbed for it.

"This cat usually makes a lot of noise," Jespersen said.

"He's very sick."

Charlie followed Jespersen into the examination room, then went over and leaned against the far door. He found himself remembering how Victor had described his method as a detective: the clown over the barrel of water at the carnival, as if Charlie proceeded solely by means of aggravation. Perhaps that was true, thought Charlie.

Jespersen put the case on the stainless-steel table. He wore his white laboratory coat with the row of pens in the breast pocket. Charlie couldn't imagine why anybody needed a dozen pens. All of Jespersen's movements were cautious and deliberate. From the kennel in the back it seemed that about fifty dogs were barking.

Jespersen undid the hook securing the top of the case. On the wall behind him was a poster showing the canine family tree. "For how long hasn't he eaten?" he asked.

Charlie didn't answer.

Jespersen folded back the lid. Inside was McClatchy's head. All of Jespersen's muscles seemed to become rigid at the same moment. He took a quick breath, then glanced at Charlie. "What's this supposed to mean?"

"You left it in Roy Leakey's refrigerator and I'm returning it."

Jespersen stared at the head, which lay facing upward. From

where Charlie stood, he could see the tip of McClatchy's nose sticking above the sides of the case: a small, white stub of a nose like a stub of chalk.

"You have any proof?" asked Jespersen.

Charlie nodded toward the door of the waiting room. Jespersen turned to look. For a moment nothing happened except that sweat broke out on Charlie's forehead. Jespersen looked back at Charlie, questioningly, and as he turned again the door opened to reveal Roy Leakey leaning against the doorframe. He appeared ill and very weak.

Leakey pushed himself up straight. "I'm still here, Jespersen," he said. "It didn't work."

Jespersen remained by the table, his hands resting on the edges of the cat-carrying case. Then he removed his glasses and put them in a pocket under his laboratory coat. Taking out a cigarette, he lit it and blew a stream of smoke through his nose. Near him was a tray of scalpels. He no longer appeared tense. Indeed, Charlie thought, his long, angular face seemed almost peaceful. Jespersen stared down at his cigarette, then tapped some ashes onto McClatchy's forehead. The case looked like a miniature barn in the middle of the stainless-steel table.

Charlie and Roy Leakey stood blocking the two doors. Charlie removed his left arm from its sling and felt for his revolver in his hip pocket. Then he paused to look at his watch. Peterson was late.

"You killed Jimmy McClatchy," said Charlie. He glanced past Leakey for any sign of the police. "You want to say anything about that?"

Jespersen dropped the cigarette on the floor and stepped on it. Then he reached into the cat-carrying case. Slowly he lifted out McClatchy's head, raising it until it was level with his own. It was a fat, doughy face with fat cheeks and a fat little chin. The mouth had fallen open and Charlie could see a glitter of gold teeth. The eyes looked unfocused and stupid. The brown hair looked as if it had never been combed. The face was the color of snow. Jespersen held it, Charlie thought, as one might hold the face of a lover.

"He tried to blackmail me." Jespersen had long fingers and he clasped the head by the jawbone, pressing his thumbs over the corners of McClatchy's mouth. "He called me from your house. He said he was going to tell the grand jury about Sweet Dreams. I couldn't let that happen."

"Put down the head," said Charlie. He again began to reach for his revolver. As Charlie moved, Jespersen wheeled and tossed the head at him so that it spun over and over through the air. Then he snatched up a scalpel and ran toward Leakey. Charlie started to duck but at the last moment he caught the head with both hands.

Leakey attempted to block Jespersen, who knocked him aside and slashed at him with the scalpel. Leakey raised an arm to protect himself, then yelped as the scalpel cut through his shirt. Jespersen shoved him out of the way and ran through the door.

Hurriedly, Charlie stuck the head back into the case. There was shouting from the waiting room, as well as the barking of a dog. Charlie's hands felt filthy. Roy Leakey knelt on the floor holding his arm. Running to him, Charlie crouched down and saw blood soaking through his shirt over his left shoulder.

"Go after him," Leakey said. "I'll be okay."

Charlie jumped to his feet just as Victor came barreling through the door and bumped into him, knocking him back toward the table.

"He cut my coat," said Victor. He pointed indignantly to a rip in the front of his tan raincoat. "First the back, now the front— my whole coat is a wreck."

Charlie pushed past him and ran into the waiting room. The receptionist and the old woman stood by the door looking frightened. The white German shepherd began barking and lunging at Charlie as the old woman tried to hold the leash. Jespersen's white laboratory coat lay on the rug. Charlie kicked the coat toward the dog as he tried to dodge around it toward the door.

Just at that moment, he bumped into someone's arms. He turned to see Peterson's face about six inches above him. Charlie looked out at the street but there was no sign of Jespersen. Peterson lightly shook Charlie's shoulder as one might shake the shoulder of a troublesome schoolboy.

"Now Charlie," he said, "what's all the fuss?"

"Where's Jespersen?" Charlie felt so frustrated that he could have wept.

"He just hurried by me. You been bothering him?"

"Where the hell have you been?" Charlie asked. The German shepherd again began barking and whining.

"I had an important long-distance call."

"If you had got here when I said, you could have arrested Jespersen for the murders of McClatchy, Pease and Stitt."

Peterson stood in the middle of the waiting room with his hands in his back pockets. "Those are pretty serious charges, Charlie. I hope you got proof."

"I'll get you some," said Charlie, and walked past Leakey into the examination room. Victor stood by the table poking one finger through the tear in his raincoat. Fastening the lid of the cat-carrying case, Charlie returned with it to Peterson.

"Here," said Charlie. "Anything else you want to know, you can ask Leakey. Let's go, Victor." Charlie gave the case to the police chief who looked at it curiously.

"What's this?" he asked.

Charlie went outside. Leakey had parked his BMW in front of Jespersen's white Buick, boxing it in. Wherever Jespersen had gone, he had gone on foot. As Charlie walked toward the milk truck, he heard Peterson make a peculiar strangulated cry. It reminded Charlie of the sound of a bagpipe played by a beginner with no musical talent. He climbed into the truck, turned the key and began pumping the gas.

Victor jumped in the other side. "You think that was necessary?" he asked.

Charlie backed out the driveway onto Clark Street. "There are moments that are destined to happen," he said.

"You gotta watch out, Charlie, it's no fun being known as a practical joker. What are we gonna do now, wait for our reward?"

"No, everything's been messed up. If we don't find Jespersen after all that foolishness, we'll look pretty stupid. Since Peterson passed him, then maybe he was going downtown. We'll try Kathy Marshall's store." It was a warm, Indian-summer day, even though the trees were mostly bare. Charlie shifted into third and gunned the motor.

"I don't mind looking stupid," said Victor. "Why don't we just let Peterson get him?"

"Because I want to do it myself. I don't like heads being thrown at me."

"Why'd you catch it?"

"Because I couldn't stand the idea of watching it bounce."

"What'd it feel like?"

"Sort of hard and cold and soft all at the same time."

Victor braced himself between the front window and a stack of milk racks. "I don't see why you brought it in the first place."

"I thought it would create an effect."

"It did," said Victor.

With only a partial load of milk in the back, the truck was at its noisiest. Charlie held onto the wheel with both hands, ignoring his bad arm as he tried to coax more speed out of the engine. Glancing at Victor, he saw that his friend was again investigating the cut in his raincoat. Charlie found himself worrying about the housewives who were beginning to look down the street, waiting for their eggs, milk and cream. He had only done a third of his route that morning before coming into Saratoga.

"What do you think Jespersen's up to?" shouted Victor over the noise.

"I expect he'll try to get out of town."

Charlie pumped the brakes, downshifted, turned right onto Broadway, then accelerated. The light at Circular Street turned yellow. Charlie leaned on the horn and kept going, yanking the wheel to the left to pass a car that had stopped. There was a crash from the back as some milk racks tipped over. As Charlie again hit the brakes, a white wave of milk spilled into the cab.

"His wife told me that he likes to hide money," continued Charlie. "Maybe he'll try to retrieve some." Charlie saw three of his fellow swimmers talking together in front of the Y. They turned and stared as he roared past.

"You ever been to the milk-truck races in Oneonta?" asked Victor.

Charlie didn't answer. He roared down Broadway, riding the middle line and swerving around slower cars. There seemed to be a lot of traffic. The truck's horn sounded old and feeble, more like a joke than a horn. Milk from the broken bottles spilled out of the truck from the back and side doors, leaving a white trail down the center of the street.

Charlie pulled up to the fire hydrant in front of his ex-wife's boutique. Drawing the .38 from his back pocket, he jumped down from the truck. About a dozen people on the sidewalk stopped to stare at him. In his khaki milkman's uniform, he felt almost official, almost like a policeman. He ran into Kathy Marshall's store. An attractive brunette in a tight red T-shirt glanced up from behind the cash register. There was no sign of Jespersen or Kathy Marshall.

"Was Jespersen here?" asked Charlie.

"He left just a minute ago," said the girl.

"Did Kathy go with him?"

"No, she's in Albany. He wanted her car."

"What did he do?" asked Charlie.

The girl shut the drawer of the cash register. "I don't know," she said. "He went into Kathy's office." She kept looking at the gun in Charlie's hand.

"Do you know why?" he asked.

The girl hesitated.

"He's wanted for murder," said Charlie.

"Kathy kept a pistol in her desk," said the girl. "David took it. I saw it in his hand when he ran out of the store."

"Which way did he go?"

"He turned left."

Charlie ran back to the truck. Victor stood beside it. Little waterfalls of milk flowed from beneath the doors. As Charlie climbed back into the cab, he heard his name being called. Even four years after his divorce, his ex-wife's voice made him jump. He decided not to turn around. Pressing down on the horn, Charlie swerved out onto Broadway, cutting off a blue pickup and making a U-turn. Victor barely managed to jump back inside. Glancing over his shoulder, Charlie saw his ex-wife and his cousin Jack standing on the sidewalk.

"He picked up a gun," said Charlie.

"Great," said Victor, "just what we need."

"You want to get out?"

"Hey, what's a coupla bullets between friends?"

Two blocks up Broadway in front of the newsstand, Charlie noticed a retired bookie that he used to arrest each August. Charlie slowed down and called to him across the street. "Louie, have you seen the vet, David Jespersen?"

"He ran into Congress Park a few minutes ago."

"Thanks."

Charlie again leaned on the horn and pulled into traffic. The horn made a noise like *tootle-tootle*. He turned left on Spring Street adjoining the park. Jespersen was nowhere to be seen. Driving all the way around the park, Charlie passed the YMCA for a second time. His fellow swimmers were still talking out in front. Again they stopped and stared after him.

Charlie turned into the park, drove past the red brick Canfield Casino, then turned around at the duck pond and drove back to Broadway. Pausing at the light, he turned right, then turned right again at the library. Two police cars with lights flashing and sirens wide open shot past him down Broadway toward Jespersen's office. After another minute, Charlie drew to a stop at the corner of Circular and Union Avenues. There was no sign of Jespersen. He felt stumped.

"Why should he come in this direction?" asked Charlie. "His house, office, girlfriend and even his ex-wife are all on the other side of the park."

"Maybe he wanted to visit the site of past glories," suggested Victor.

"What's that?"

"The track." The Saratoga racetrack lay four blocks up Union Avenue.

"We'll try it. If we can't find him, we'll try the Northway. He might be trying to hitch a ride south. If he's not there, you can help me deliver the rest of my milk. It was stupid to play that game at Jespersen's office, especially if he gets away. Peterson can really make trouble for us."

He continued to drive slowly down Union Avenue. The day was becoming hot. In front of the Victorian mansions, people were raking leaves or putting up storm windows. Some students near a Skidmore dorm were throwing a Frisbee. Nearly half the big houses were closed up for the winter with shutters over the windows—homes for summer residents from New York or Boston or Montreal. Charlie coasted through the light at Nelson Avenue. To their right were the grounds of the track. The tall elms and maples were entirely stripped of their leaves. To the left were the four white columns of the National Museum of Racing.

The main gate of the racetrack stood open. Inside, a small army of carpenters, painters and maintenance men were making the track ready for the winter, covering the clocks with sheets of plastic, stacking the hundreds of wooden red chairs, taking down the red-and-white striped awnings. The trees around the outside buildings and jockeys' quarters were evergreens and looked as they did in August. All that was missing were the thousands of people.

Charlie drove around to the left of the grandstand on a gravel path that led the short distance to the track. The old white grandstand with its red trim and gray slate roof was empty except for some men painting and piling up chairs. A yellow grater was plowing the dirt in front of the tote board.

"There's someone running on the track," said Victor.

Charlie looked. A thin figure was running along the far turn of the track by the three-eighths pole. "It's Jespersen," he said.

He was running along the rail past one of the several towers used for filming the races. They looked like guard towers in a prison or concentration camp.

Charlie drove the milk truck onto the track through the gate by the chute. The surface was soft and spongy.

"But what's he doing?" asked Victor.

"He's heading for the shed rows along the backstretch. That's where Sweet Dreams was stabled."

"Yeah, but why now?"

Charlie pushed his foot down on the accelerator. "I'm not sure, maybe he hid something there."

"Like what, Sherlock?"

"Like maybe some money."

As Charlie accelerated through the soft dirt, the rear end of the truck began to slew back and forth. The remaining milk bottles rattled together and the metal milk racks banged against the sides of the truck. The floor was swamped with milk, and Charlie's shoes were soaked with it. He could feel his socks squishing between his toes. In order to keep the truck roaring ahead in a reasonably forward direction, Charlie had to hunch over the steering wheel and hold it with both arms. Crossing the track every fifteen feet was a ridge of dirt like an oversized mole's tunnel and whenever the truck bounced over one, all the milk racks rose up a foot, then crashed back down. This is what cacophony means, thought Charlie. The truck screamed along at the very top of third gear but Charlie was afraid to take his hands from the wheel in order to shift into fourth.

Victor tried to brace himself against the door. "What're you going to do?" he shouted.

"Arrest him."

"But you're not a cop."

"So what?"

The truck zigzagged forward. Jespersen glanced over his shoulder, then stumbled, scrambled to his feet and tried to run faster. A metal fence kept him from crossing over the far side of the track, but about twenty yards ahead, the horse ambulance gate out of the backstretch stood open. He stumbled again. Then, by the three-and-a-half furlong pole, he stopped and turned to face the truck. Charlie could see a gun in his hand.

"Oh-oh," said Victor.

There was the faint crack of a pistol shot and a hole appeared in the middle of the windshield. The bullet ricocheted through the metal milk racks as the truck swerved from left to right.

"Get down," shouted Charlie.

"That much I can figure out for myself. Where the hell's your gun?"

"In my back pocket."

"Why don't you shoot him, for cryin' out loud?"

"I can't let go of the wheel."

Victor began to tug at the .38 in Charlie's back pocket. The spur of the hammer caught on the fabric and Victor pulled harder. Charlie imagined the gun accidentally discharging.

"Leave it alone!"

There was another gunshot and the glass on Victor's side of the truck disintegrated. Victor crouched back down on the floor. His pants were soaked with milk and bits of glass were caught in his hair.

To his right, Charlie saw the small lake in the middle of the track, a few naked elms and the last of the red flowers. There was a third gunshot and Charlie's half of the windshield blew apart, covering him with pellets of glass. Without the windshield, everything was noisier and the wind blew in their faces, making Charlie's eyes water.

"They're going to love you at Wholesome Dairy," shouted Victor.

Jespersen stood in the center of the track with his legs apart. He held the pistol in both hands, stretching his arms straight out in front of him. He wore a blue jacket and white shirt. His tie had blown back over his shoulder and his hair fluttered in the wind, flicking long yellow strands across his forehead.

Charlie had crouched down so that he was just barely peering over the edge of the windshield. His arms half-surrounded the wheel and each time he let go to reach for the revolver, the truck swerved toward the rail.

Jespersen kept firing, aiming into the truck. The bullets ricocheted and crashed into the milk crates. Steam began pouring through a hole in the radiator. Charlie was no more than twenty feet from Jespersen. He could see his face, furious and concentrated. Jespersen lowered the pistol and shot at the front tire. There was an explosion as the tire blew up, making the truck veer sharply to the right.

Charlie spun the wheel but without effect. The truck began to skid in a circle, throwing Charlie against the door. He had no idea where Jespersen was. Through the empty windshield he saw a swirl of clouds, trees, blue sky and trees again as the truck spun around. Crash followed crash as the remaining milk crates tipped over. There was a thump against the side of the truck. Attempting to stand, Charlie stumbled against Victor and splashed to the floor. The truck smashed sideways against the rail. There was a long tearing sound, then the truck came to a halt. All the noises stopped except for the dripping and splashing of milk.

Charlie yanked the .38 from his back pocket, jumped from the side door and fell forward onto his stomach in the soft dirt. Five feet away Jespersen lay face down. The truck had slid into him, knocking him into the rail. His gun was still in his hand. Charlie scrambled to his feet, hurried over and kicked the gun into the grass. Then he bent down beside him.

"Is he dead?" asked Victor.

"No, just unconscious."

"We going to wait for the cops?" asked Victor. "I think some of these horse people are going to be pretty pissed." A group of men were hurrying toward them across the center of the track.

"We're going to deliver him," said Charlie.

Charlie retrieved Jespersen's pistol. It was some sort of foreign make that he didn't recognize. Then Charlie tied Jespersen's hands with his necktie.

"Help me carry him," he asked.

Victor lifted Jespersen's feet and Charlie lifted his shoulders. Together they put him on the floor of the truck, lying on his back in the milk. Then Charlie took his place behind the wheel and pushed the starter, listened to it grind and grind until the engine turned over. The truck backfired. It seemed that only four cylinders were working. Revving the engine, Charlie made a U-turn and accelerated down the track toward the stands. A zigzagging trail of milk showed the way they had come. The men in the center of the track began shouting at them. Charlie drove faster. He had to press his whole weight down on the wheel to keep from veering to the right. The truck was spattered with mud and its windshield was gone. Its front was pockmarked with bullet holes and it was still spewing steam. Along the right side was a deep crease and tear in the metal where it had hit the rail. Loose milk crates jangled together and there was the sound of broken glass sliding back and forth on the metal floor. The right front tire went flappety-flap, flappety-flap.

Charlie drove out of the chute and onto the gravel path leading to the front gate. A group of about fifteen workmen watched silently. Continuing out of the grounds onto Union Avenue, Charlie turned left toward town, lurching forward at no more than 10 miles per hour. The floor of the milk truck was an inch deep with milk, which swirled and lapped around Jespersen as if around a large island. He made a groaning noise, tried to sit up, then fell back with a splash. Three police cars roared past on the way to the track. Charlie felt tremendously pleased. He glanced at Victor, who stood leaning forward with his head half through the empty windshield. His fluffy gray hair blew in the wind and he was grinning.

Charlie turned onto Circular, drove past Doris's apartment, then turned left onto Lake Avenue. All along the street, people stared at the truck. Victor waved to them. When they reached the police station, Charlie drew to a stop and leaned on the horn. He no longer cared that it went tootle-tootle. He kept leaning on it until a policeman hurried out. It was Emmett Van Brunt.

"Get that truck outta here, Charlie. Are you fuckin' off your rocker?"

"I want Peterson," said Charlie.

"He's organizing a statewide search."

"Tell him not to bother," said Charlie.

Chapter
Seventeen

What upset Charlie most was the long-distance call that had delayed Peterson's arrival at Jespersen's office. The call had come from the police chief of Santa Fe, New Mexico. John Wanamaker had been arrested in the middle of a burglary. The police had found him hiding in a closet. Neither closet nor house belonged to him. When the police went back to Wanamaker's room, they found odds and ends from about fifteen earlier burglaries. There had been a rash of break-ins in Santa Fe during the past month by an unknown person whom the newspaper had labeled The Cat. Now The Cat had been captured.

"He never even *had* a mother," said Charlie. "The whole thing was a lie."

Victor wiped up a last piece of French toast from his plate. "I never trust those religious types," he said.

They were having a late breakfast at the Spa City Diner and waiting for the bus from New York. Charlie's mother had called at seven o'clock that Tuesday morning asking him to pick her up. Although he thought of himself as happy to see her, he was also uneasy and even suspicious. He had made a date that evening with Doris and he wanted nothing, but nothing to get in the way.

"Not only didn't he have a mother," said Charlie, "but the only reason he went to Santa Fe was to rob houses. Jesus, when you think how I worried."

"You're too soft," said Victor.

But Charlie wasn't listening. Someone was waving to him across the restaurant and he gave a brief nod in reply. In the half hour in which they had been eating, about a dozen people had spoken to Charlie and more had simply stared. This was owing to the publicity.

The offices of the *Daily Saratogian* lay catty-corner across the street from the police station and while Charlie had been honking the horn of the milk truck for Peterson, an enterprising photographer had hurried over to record these moments on film. As a result, Charlie had been all over the front page of the afternoon edition, plus being featured on the six o'clock news of the Albany television stations. This had had various consequences.

For instance, when Charlie returned to the Wholesome Dairy late Monday afternoon, he had been immediately fired. The truck was a wreck, the milk was ruined and angry customers had been calling all day. But after the paper and TV stations began showing pictures of Charlie standing next to the Wholesome Dairy truck wearing his Wholesome Dairy uniform as Jespersen was being handcuffed, the owner of the dairy had personally telephoned Charlie to offer him a permanent position.

Charlie had refused. He refused despite the fact that the Pinkertons had turned him down for a job, saying that he appeared to lack the stable personality required of a first-class Pinkerton operative. He refused even though it appeared he would have to support his mother, as well as pay for the damage to the milk truck.

Another result of the publicity was that people who had been treating Charlie like a piece of gum stuck to the sole of a shoe now half fell over themselves to be friendly. Five people had offered him jobs: drugstore clerk, used-car salesman, assistant realtor, insurance salesman, bartender. Charlie again refused, suspecting their motivations and even their purity of heart.

"Think of it this way," Victor had said, "they'll always lend you money."

"I don't want their money," said Charlie.

David Jespersen had been charged with the three murders but refused to talk. From Kathy Marshall, however, the police learned that Jespersen had indeed been Willis Stitt's silent partner. She had agreed to testify in return for not being charged with anything herself. In any case, in Jespersen's home police found the revolver used in two of the murders, as well as a Polaroid camera of the kind that had taken the pictures of McClatchy's head. Throughout Charlie's interviews with the police, the press and the district attorney's office, Chief Peterson had played the role of Charlie's dearest friend. Charlie had been polite but not warm. During these proceedings, he had expected to see Hank Caldwell, but the FBI man had apparently disappeared.

Victor signaled to the waitress for more coffee, then turned back to Charlie. "Let's say that when I found McClatchy's head at the cabin, I'd taken it to the police. What would Jespersen have done then?"

"He would have had to fake Leakey's suicide a lot sooner."

"How did he know I'd find the head?"

"He had Kathy Marshall tell Ruth MacDermott that was where Leakey kept his love letters, then he followed you. I expect he should have left the head in the cabin and killed Leakey right then, but Leakey had gone off with the woman in the red pants and Jespersen had to delay. That was probably a mistake. When he finally acted on Sunday, it was too late."

Victor poured several tablespoons of sugar into his coffee. "Was that his biggest mistake?"

"Maybe. But it was also a mistake not to tell me he knew Pease. When Flo Abernathy said that Pease took his dog to Jespersen, then it was clear he was lying."

"And what's going to happen to the head?" asked Victor.

"Peterson wanted to give it to the Racing Museum but McClatchy's family objected. He was buried in Philadelphia. They plan to dig him up and put the head back in place."

"It's better that way," said Victor, "otherwise I'd always worry that I might run into it."

Mabel Bradshaw's bus arrived at the Spa City Diner shortly after eleven. Charlie and Victor were waiting outside to meet it. It was a cool morning and the sky was clear with the sort of deep blue that made Charlie think of forgetfulness or loss. On the roof of the Spa City Diner stood a statue of a small chestnut filly.

The first person off the bus was a miniature old lady in a black dress and a blue straw hat.

"Is that her?" asked Victor. For the occasion he had exchanged his gray sweat shirt for a bright red turtleneck.

"Wait," said Charlie.

The second person off the bus was a large, rather blowzy woman with blond hair, a tight purple dress and purple gloves that reached her elbows. Draped over one shoulder was a silver fox, while around her neck were several strands of pearls. She hesitated on the bottom step, glanced around and when she saw Charlie, she waved.

"You're kidding," said Victor.

Mabel Bradshaw tottered toward them on spindly high heels. Although sixty-six, she looked fifty. She half fell into Charlie's arms and began to weep. Since Charlie had last seen her, she had dyed her hair and put on thirty pounds. He patted her back. Then, just as abruptly, she stopped weeping, pulled away and said, "Help me with my boxes. There's a dear."

Charlie introduced his mother to Victor.

Mabel held out a hand. Several large rings twinkled from her gloved fingers. "You're cute," she said.

From under the bus, the driver was stacking box after box of Mabel's possessions.

"Is all that stuff yours?" asked Charlie.

"Just a few odds and ends. Where's your car?"

Charlie pointed to the Renault. He was greatly relieved that it wasn't the milk truck. "Did you lose very much in Atlantic City?" he asked.

"Lose? Are you pulling my leg? I won. I won over fifty

thousand dollars. Play big, win big—that's my motto. Tomorrow I'm going to see about buying a hotel: a big hotel with lots of red satin and soft things to sit on."

"Fifty thousand dollars?" said Charlie.

"That's right," said his mother. "Didn't you get my lucky parrot? That's how I did it. I never made a bet without that parrot right beside me and when I had my bundle, I sent it to you for safekeeping. That parrot saved my life."

"Aha," said Charlie, not knowing what else to say. He wondered if Doris would mind spending the evening searching through the Saratoga city dump.

Mabel took their arms and led them toward the Renault. "How would you boys like to work for me?" she said. "Charlie, you can be night manager. And you, cutie..." She paused to give Victor an affectionate poke, "I'll keep you for room service."

Victor waggled his hips. "Room service is my middle name," he said.

FOR THE BEST IN PAPERBACKS, LOOK FOR THE

In every corner of the world, on every subject under the sun, Penguin represents quality and variety—the very best in publishing today.

For complete information about books available from Penguin—including Pelicans, Puffins, Peregrines, and Penguin Classics—and how to order them, write to us at the appropriate address below. Please note that for copyright reasons the selection of books varies from country to country.

In the United Kingdom: For a complete list of books available from Penguin in the U.K., please write to *Dept E.P., Penguin Books Ltd, Harmondsworth, Middlesex, UB7 0DA.*

In the United States: For a complete list of books available from Penguin in the U.S., please write to *Dept BA, Penguin*, Box 120, Bergenfield, New Jersey 07621-0120.

In Canada: For a complete list of books available from Penguin in Canada, please write to *Penguin Books Ltd, 2801 John Street, Markham, Ontario L3R 1B4.*

In Australia: For a complete list of books available from Penguin in Australia, please write to the *Marketing Department, Penguin Books Ltd, P.O. Box 257, Ringwood, Victoria 3134.*

In New Zealand: For a complete list of books available from Penguin in New Zealand, please write to the *Marketing Department, Penguin Books (NZ) Ltd, Private Bag, Takapuna, Auckland 9.*

In India: For a complete list of books available from Penguin, please write to *Penguin Overseas Ltd, 706 Eros Apartments, 56 Nehru Place, New Delhi, 110019.*

In Holland: For a complete list of books available from Penguin in Holland, please write to *Penguin Books Nederland B.V., Postbus 195, NL-1380AD Weesp, Netherlands.*

In Germany: For a complete list of books available from Penguin, please write to *Penguin Books Ltd, Friedrichstrasse 10-12, D-6000 Frankfurt Main 1, Federal Republic of Germany.*

In Spain: For a complete list of books available from Penguin in Spain, please write to *Longman, Penguin España, Calle San Nicolas 15, E-28013 Madrid, Spain.*

In Japan: For a complete list of books available from Penguin in Japan, please write to *Longman Penguin Japan Co Ltd, Yamaguchi Building, 2-12-9 Kanda Jimbocho, Chiyoda-Ku, Tokyo 101, Japan.*

FOR THE BEST IN MYSTERY, LOOK FOR THE

☐ **A CRIMINAL COMEDY**
Julian Symons

From Julian Symons, the master of crime fiction, this is "the best of his best" (*The New Yorker*). What starts as a nasty little scandal centering on two partners in a British travel agency escalates into smuggling and murder in Italy.

220 pages   *ISBN: 0-14-009621-3*   **$3.50**

☐ **GOOD AND DEAD**
Jane Langton

Something sinister is emptying the pews at the Old West Church, and parishioner Homer Kelly knows it isn't a loss of faith. When he investigates, Homer discovers that the ways of a small New England town can be just as mysterious as the ways of God.   *256 pages*   *ISBN: 0-14-778217-1*   **$3.95**

☐ **THE SHORTEST WAY TO HADES**
Sarah Caudwell

Five young barristers and a wealthy family with a five-million-pound estate find the stakes are raised when one member of the family meets a suspicious death.

208 pages   *ISBN: 0-14-008488-6*   **$3.50**

☐ **RUMPOLE OF THE BAILEY**
John Mortimer

The hero of John Mortimer's mysteries is Horace Rumpole, barrister at law, sixty-eight next birthday, with an unsurpassed knowledge of blood and typewriters, a penchant for quoting poetry, and a habit of referring to his judge as "the old darling."   *208 pages*   *ISBN: 0-14-004670-4*   **$3.95**

FOR THE BEST IN MYSTERY, LOOK FOR THE

☐ **MURDOCK FOR HIRE**
Robert Ray

When he is hired to find a dead man's missing antique coin collection, private detective Matt Murdock discovers an international crime ring that is much more than a nickle-and-dime operation.

        256 pages   *ISBN: 0-14-010679-0*   **$3.95**

☐ **BRIARPATCH**
Ross Thomas

This Edgar Award-winning thriller is the story of Benjamin Dill, who returns to the Sunbelt city of his youth to attend his sister's funeral—and find her killer.

        384 pages   *ISBN: 0-14-010581-6*   **$3.95**

☐ **DEATH'S SAVAGE PASSION**
Orania Papazoglou

Suspense is killing Romance, and the Romance Writers of America are outraged. When a fresh, enthusiastic creator of the loathed hybrid, Romantic Suspense, arrives on the scene, someone shows her just how murderous competition can be.   *180 pages*   *ISBN: 0-14-009967-0*   **$3.50**

☐ **GOLD BY GEMINI**
Jonathan Gash

Lovejoy, the antiques dealer whom the *Chicago Sun-Times* calls "one of the most likable rogues in mystery history," searches for Roman gold coins and greedy bird-killers on the Isle of Man.

        224 pages   *ISBN: 0-451-82185-8*   **$3.95**

☐ **REILLY: ACE OF SPIES**
Robin Bruce Lockhart

This is the incredible true story of superspy Sidney Reilly, said to be the inspiration for James Bond. Robin Bruce Lockhart's book tells the thrilling story of the British Secret Service agent's shadowy Russian past and near-legendary exploits in espionage and in love.

        192 pages   *ISBN: 0-14-006895-3*   **$4.95**

☐ **STRANGERS ON A TRAIN**
Patricia Highsmith

Almost against his will, Guy Haines is trapped in a nightmare of shared guilt when he agrees to kill the father of the man who will kill Guy's wife. The basis for the unforgettable Hitchcock thriller.

        256 pages   *ISBN: 0-14-003796-9*   **$4.95**

☐ **THE THIN WOMAN**
Dorothy Cannell

An interior designer who is also a passionate eater, her rented companion who writes trashy novels, and a rich dead uncle with a conditional will are the principals in this delicious thriller.   *242 pages*   *ISBN: 0-14-007947-5*   **$3.95**